HAUNTED HOTELS

HAUNTED HOTELS

Eerie Inns, Ghoulish Guests, and
Creepy Caretakers

Retold by Tom Ogden

Guilford, Connecticut

Designed by Sheryl P. Kober
Layout: Kevin Mak
Project manager: Kristen Mellitt

Library of Congress Cataloging-in-Publication Data is available on file.

ISBN 978-0-7627-5659-9

Printed in the United States of America

For Dylan, Jordyn, and Peyton,
the newest members of the clan

CONTENTS

ACKNOWLEDGMENTS

It would have been impossible for me to complete *Haunted Hotels* without the assistance and support of many people. My thanks go to Betty Jean Morris (for providing background on the Hotel del Coronado and the *Queen Mary*), Roxana Brusso (for the Marina Hotel), Gary Fitzgerald (for the Black Hawk Hotel), Bonnie Gordon and Nancy Tassin (for the Myrtles Plantation), Barrett Ravenhurst (for the Inn at Jim Thorpe and the Emporium of Curious Goods), Fay Presto (the house magician at Langham's), Greg Lyczkowski (who first pointed me toward the Knickerbocker Hotel), Kathy Haggerty (for information on the St. James Hotel), Kyle Carter (for an update on the renovation of the Black Hawk Hotel), Jay Matz (for information on railway aficionados), Chris Donovan (the staff historian at the Hotel del Coronado), and the Lake George Chamber of Commerce (for information on Millionaires Row).

Other friends shared their first-person ghost encounters, but for one reason or another the tales did not make the final cut. Thank you Chuck and Bambi Burnes, Shawn McMaster, S. Earl Statler, Kate Ward and Marty Rosenstock, Ian Varella, and Mark Willoughby.

As always, my gratitude goes out to David Shine, Michael Kurland and Linda Robertson, Dustin Stinett, Joan Lawton, and Max Maven for their advice, feedback, and patience.

Finally, continued thanks to my editors Meredith Rufino and Mary Norris, project editor Kristen Mellitt, copy editor Justine Rathbun, and my agent, Jack Scovil, for their guidance and support.

INTRODUCTION

As I sit here finishing up work on *Haunted Hotels,* it's hard for me to believe that this is my fifth title for the Globe Pequot Haunted series. What a journey it's been! Although I'd authored other books about ghosts, the selection and writing of these tales have led me in satisfying and fascinating directions I never anticipated. During my research I realized that just about every ghost story can be told in a hundred words or less by answering a few basic questions: Whose spirit is it said to be, where does it haunt, and what kind of spectral activity occurs?

As I examined many of the folk tales, I was surprised by the disparity in the amount of detail associated with the various sightings. Many ghost legends are nothing more than a few vague reports. Other tales, however, give a precise record of the manifestation, including the name of the person who saw the apparition (or experienced the spirit activity), the identity of the spirit, and the date and time that the encounter took place.

In most cases, after putting together all of the information I collected, I added a fictional layer of invented characters and circumstances to retell the tale. Hopefully I've wound up with something that differs significantly from ghost stories found in most other collections. If I succeeded, these yarns will not only be fun to read but will also have such a sense of verisimilitude that you'll believe the hauntings are real.

And maybe they are.

Among my other discoveries was the sheer number of haunted places out there. And not just the stereotypical "haunted houses." No, examples can be found of every imaginable type of venue—highways, cars, trucks, buses, trains, planes, ships, schools, playgrounds, churches, graveyards, castles, battlefields, stores, theaters, restaurants—you name it.

But for this particular book, my assignment was to seek out haunted hotels. There are hundreds, perhaps thousands, of hotels said to have resident spirits. In some cases, owners have embraced the rumors and included them in their promotional materials. Others have been more circumspect and ignore the legends, afraid that the stories might scare off potential visitors. A few places deny them outright. From a business standpoint, there are arguments to be made on all sides. But while the wisdom of acknowledging reports of paranormal activity is debated, guests at the facilities continue to run into the apparitions nonetheless.

Have *you* ever walked into a place and thought, "If only these walls could talk?" Hotel rooms have been witness to passion, hate, misery, joy, life, sickness, and death. It's easy to believe that some sort of residual energy from all those emotions has permeated the aether and lingers.

(There are proponents of the theory that apparitions aren't really ghosts at all but are some sort of psychic force that the deceased unknowingly imprinted on their surroundings while they were alive. In one way or another, the space soaked up and stored the impressions of events that had happened there. What people see today is a "residual haunting," like a film replaying itself over and over in an endless loop.)

For more than a century, paranormal societies have sought to document ghostly occurrences and ascertain their authenticity, beginning with the granddaddy of them all,

London's Society for Psychical Research, founded in 1882. Contemporary readers might be more familiar with groups such as TAPS, the Atlantic Paranormal Society, whose team members lead investigations on television's *Ghost Hunters*.

All of these groups agree there are certain factors that can precipitate a haunting. They include

- A violent death
- A sudden death, in which a spirit might not know he or she has died
- An unfulfilled life or mission
- A strong emotional attachment to a particular place
- A need to impart a message or warning
- A desire to guard over a venue
- A wish to be remembered

And the list goes on and on.

It would be impossible to profile all of the hotels that are purported to house spirits from the Beyond. But I've carefully picked ones for this volume to include all different types of lodging and ghosts. The phantoms range from a bride who died from a tragic fall on her wedding day to a cardsharp gunned down after winning an Old Westr boardinghouse in a poker game. More than half of the spectre-filled hostelries I've profiled can be found in the United States. The rest are located in Canada, Ireland, England, and faraway Singapore. So pack those bags. It's time to visit some of the most haunted hotels in the world—where the ghosts check in, but they don't check out.

Chapter 1

The Bride Who
Was Not To Be

Golden North Hotel
Skagway, Alaska

In 1898, a young woman checked into the Golden North Hotel in Skagway, Alaska. There, she anxiously awaited her fiancé, who was out seeking his fortune in the Klondike gold fields. But he never returned. Mary, as legend has named the lonely bride-to-be, fell ill and died at the small hotel, and it's thought to be her spirit that greeted overnight guests—especially those who stayed in her old room, number 24.

Ashley couldn't wait to settle in and explore the town.

The first time she visited Skagway she'd come by cruise ship. She had taken the Alaskan voyage to see ice-filled Glacier Bay. But the first stop on the itinerary, the day after the ship left Juneau, was Skagway, which served as a starting point for thousands of prospectors who, beginning in 1897, streamed northward during the Klondike gold rush.

The moment Ashley set eyes on Skagway, she fell in love.

Most of the storefronts along Broadway, the main drag through town, had been restored (or maintained) to reflect the pioneer hamlet's glory days. And even though almost a million tourists visited annually, somehow the tiny municipality with less than a thousand full-time residents managed to remain, well, quaint.

This time, Ashley wouldn't be a cruise line day-tripper. She'd be staying almost a week to give herself a chance to hike the trails, take a sightseeing flight over the surrounding glacier fields, visit the old graveyard at the edge of town, and ride the White Pass & Yukon Route narrow-gauge railroad up the mountainside into Canada. Most of all, Ashley wanted to soak up the atmosphere, to try to relive the memories of an almost forgotten time in America's history. To make the experience complete, rather than stay in one of the more modern accommodations, she chose to room at a renovated lodge that dated to the 1890s: the Golden North Hotel.

To get to Skagway, Ashley first flew into Juneau. She then followed the same water route to the north end of the Tayai Inlet of the Lynn Canal that the stampeders had taken more than century before. The five-hour ferry ride gave her plenty of time to ponder the town's storied past.

The flat expanse at the mouth of the Skagway River in the Alaska Panhandle had been occupied by the Chilkoots and Chilkats of the Tlinget tribe since ancient times. They named the spot Skagua, which means "a windy area." About two miles from the water's edge, steep mountains rose to a high plateau, which led into the Yukon Territory.

As the nineteenth century drew to a close, rumors circulated that gold could be found along the tributaries of the Yukon River. In October 1887, a sea captain–surveyor named William Moore and his son Ben, who had heard the stories, homesteaded 160 acres at what is today Skagway, believing that it would be the logical place for any prospectors to begin their journey into the hills. To stake his claim, Moore built a cabin, founded a sawmill, and constructed a pier. Within a year, a city of ten thousand had risen out of his settlement.

Lightning struck in August 1896. A Native American called Skookum Jim Mason, his sister Kate Carmack, and her husband, George, discovered gold on Rabbit Creek (later christened Bonanza Creek). Other prospectors already panning in the area flocked to the stream, and before long, a shantytown, Dawson City, grew up nearby. Two years later, the town would have thirty thousand inhabitants.

No one in the Lower 48 knew anything about the find until the following July when the first Alaska steamboat of the season arrived in San Francisco and, two days later, Seattle. Newspapers reported that suitcases filled with gold were being carried down the gangway, and overnight the charge to the Klondike had begun.

Few of those taking the journey had any idea of what was in store for them. The California gold rush of 1849 had been a cakewalk in comparison. After the prospectors got as far as Skagway, they would still have to follow a treacherous route up the mountains through the dizzying White Pass to Bennett Lake, from which they could float to the head of the Yukon River. Then, they had to raft another five hundred miles down the Yukon to Dawson City. The passage was so difficult that Canada's North West Mounted Police required that anyone making the punishing expedition had to carry a full year of supplies.

(An alternate path into the Yukon left from Dyea, which is also located on the Lynn Canal about ten miles from Skagway. That route, following an old Tlinget trail through the Chilkoot Pass, wasn't quite as difficult as the climb up White Pass but was much longer.)

On July 29, 1897, the first of hundreds of boats landed at the wharf in Skagway. About forty thousand diehards did make it into the Yukon, but many prospectors and camp followers died in the attempt. Some found the hurdles insurmountable and turned back. Others, having gotten as far as Skagway, never made the final assault. They decided it was safer—and more profitable—to stay put, opening businesses in the frontier town to cater to the needs of those passing through.

As Ashley's ferry passed the town of Haines, she could see Skagway far ahead down the canal. Whitecaps peaked on the waves as the strong wind whipped down the narrow cove. Ashley stepped out onto the deck and closed up her parka against the blast of unexpectedly cool summer air. As if on cue, a gray humpback breached and flipped its giant tail as it slid back beneath the surface.

Ashley had never felt so alive.

The ferry nestled up to the dock, and within minutes Ashley had passed down Broadway, checked in at the front desk of the hotel, and made her way up to her room, number 24 up on the third floor.

The Golden North Hotel dated to 1898. But, interestingly, it had started life not as a boardinghouse but as the Klondike Trading Company. The building, which originally stood at Third and State Streets, was a two-story wood structure with a large, gold-painted onion-shaped dome, similar to those found on Russian Orthodox churches, towering over one corner of the roof.

For a time the supply depot did big business. But by the end of 1898, the gold rush was over. The larger gold flakes and nuggets had been panned out of the streams very quickly, and dredges were brought in to sluice out the rest. There was some ore in the ground, but it was buried under permafrost.

The boom went bust. Almost overnight, the economy in Skagway collapsed, and the population dwindled. With no more demand for its services, the Klondike Trading Company leased its building to the army to act as a barracks. Sometime in 1908 or 1909, George Dedman and Edward Foreman bought the structure, raised it off its foundation, and moved it to the southwest corner of Third Street and Broadway. They added a third story and remodeled the store into a hotel.

Ashley's first two nights passed comfortably. Each afternoon, as the last cruise ships left for the day, a peaceful calm settled over the community. Around midevening, the restaurants and bars began to empty out, and by midnight, the noise from the street had completely disappeared.

It was on Ashley's third night in the hotel that it happened. She had just settled into bed and was finishing up a chapter in *The Call of the Wild,* the Jack London novel partially set in Skagway, when she heard faint footsteps shuffling across the carpet in the hallway outside her door. At first she dismissed them, figuring they belonged to one of the other half dozen people who were staying at the hotel. But when the sound continued, pacing back and forth, on and on, Ashley became curious.

She slid out of bed, cracked the doorway, and peeked out. The footsteps instantly stopped. And the corridor was empty.

Puzzled, Ashley gently closed the door and turned back into the room. To her surprise, just ten feet in front of her, hovering over the bed, was a small circle of light. She thought she must be seeing the glow of a streetlamp on the other side of the window, but she soon realized that, no, she was on the third floor, and there was no way that something so far below could be reflecting up into the room. As Ashley stared, rooted to the spot, the shimmering, translucent haze began to pulsate. Then, as if a light switch had been suddenly snapped off, the unnatural luminescence went out.

It wasn't until the next morning, after a fitful night of sleep, that Ashley found out she had been visited by a ghost.

Back in 1898, a fearless eighteen-year-old woman, whom legend has named Mary, supposedly traveled to Skagway to meet her finacé, who had sent for her. She stayed in Room 24 at the Golden North Hotel while he went to the Klondike to pan for gold. Days turned into weeks, but the young man never came back. Then, sadly, the lass, who was already frail when she arrived, fell sick with tuberculosis (or possibly pneumonia). Several mornings later, when the hotel manager looked in on her, he found Mary dead, lying on her bed wearing a lace-trimmed bridal gown.

Over the years, Mary has made herself known to a number of guests. In addition to hearing the footsteps and seeing light orbs, visitors have felt an unseen presence sit on the bed next to them. Some guests have become overcome with nausea or felt faint without explanation. A very few have seen a female figure in a long, white nightgown, presumed to be Mary, walking the hall outside Room 24. Similar phenomena have been experienced in rooms 9, 13, and 14 as well.

Rather than become frightened when she heard Mary's story, Ashley felt exhilarated. She had come to Skagway to immerse herself in a time long ago. Instead, she found herself part of an intimate, spectral dance between the present and the past.

The careful reader may have noticed a discrepancy in Mary's story. How could the stranded bride have died at the Golden

North in 1898 if the Klondike Trading Company wasn't turned into a hotel until a full decade later?

Fortunately, the incongruity can be explained thanks to research by Shirley Jonas, author of *Ghosts of the Klondike*. With the assistance of Frank Norris, a historian for the National Park Service, she was able to locate another Golden North Hotel that predated the current structure. According to a 1910 map, it stood at Fourth Street between State and Main and was also owned by Dedman and Foreman. That hotel would have been standing at the time of the stampede to the Klondike and would have been the one in which Mary stayed. Unfortunately, no guest records of the older inn have been preserved. Indeed, the building itself was torn down after the gold rush ended.

But why has Mary's ghost turned up at a hotel that she never visited? It's rare for a spirit to hop from one venue to another, but it's not unprecedented. With both hotels having the same name and owners, apparently there was enough of a connection for Mary's spirit to make the transition.

Regrettably, it's impossible to check whether the ghosts are still active at the Golden North Hotel because it was closed to overnight guests in 2002. Other haunted structures dating to that period can still be visited, however.

One, Red Onion Hall, was opened in 1897. It was a typical frontier saloon, but its second floor was a bordello—a hotel of sorts. The dark form of a female figure can be spied standing at the window in the former madam's office, disembodied footsteps are heard walking the floorboards, and the intense odor of perfume wafts through what were once the working girls' rooms.

Eagles Hall, built in 1899, is the local Aerie #25 for the Fraternal Order of Eagles. With a front facade covered by short logs shaped into decorative patterns, the place is unmistakable. Unexplainable cold spots (which are thought by paranormal investigators to be an indication of a spectral presence) have been felt in the clubhouse's corridors, and people have been known to flee the building after spotting ghostly activity on the second floor. According to some sources, the hall was originally two separate hotels that were joined together to form a single structure. No one knows if the spirits are former lodgers or whether they're from more modern times.

Skagway's Golden North Hotel is not the only hotel in the region to have a resident ghost. Just eighty-six miles to the southeast lies Juneau, Alaska's state capital. The Alaskan Hotel, built in 1913, is centrally located on the city's main street near the downtown wharf. Among its early residents was a young woman named Alice who was left behind when her husband departed for the Yukon. After three weeks, she was destitute and was forced to enter the world's oldest profession in order to survive. Her husband finally did return, a full month later, but when he discovered how his wife was making ends meet, he killed her in her hotel room. Many believe that it's her troubled spirit that haunts the hallways.

The old hotel is filled with cold spots, and guests have reported feeling an invisible spirit stroke their faces or sit by them on the bed. Her reflection has also been spotted in several of the hotel's mirrors. For some reason the rooms on the south side of the hotel seem to have the most paranormal activity. The room that most often figures in ghost legends is 219, but 218 and 308 are also frequently mentioned.

The Yukon gold rush is one of the most colorful parts of our nation's history. But for poor Mary and the other spectral residents from the period like her, the past is very much alive.

Chapter 2

The Heathman
Hauntings

Heathman Hotel
Portland, Oregon

For some reason all of the rooms in Portland, Oregon's, Heathman Hotel that end in the numbers 03 seem to be home to supernatural phenomena. But the most active of all is the dreaded Room 703. Does it really house the returning spirit of a long-forgotten suicide?

It felt good to be home. Portland, Oregon. Max hadn't been there in years.

After high school, he'd gone east for college and then moved to New York to work for a small travel agency right after graduation. When his parents died he returned briefly, packed up what few mementoes he thought might fit into his East Village apartment, discarded the rest, and sold the old homestead. This was his first time back.

A wan smile crossed his lips. Now he lived in Manhattan. But when he was growing up, Portland was the Big City. He had actually been raised seven miles west in Beaverton, itself a fair-size metropolis—the sixth-largest city in the state. But if he and his friends wanted to have real fun come weekends, they headed into Portland.

Max realized that most of the country probably thought the place was a hick town, without much to offer. Sure, there were great views of Mount Hood and a lot of city parks and flowerbeds. (Not for nothing is Portland known as the City of Roses.) But excitement? To find anything really interesting to do, wouldn't you have to go to Seattle, at the very least?

Well, people who felt that way had obviously never been to Portland. Its youth embraced punk early on, making Portland a center for hip, underground music. Counterculture chic led to Portland establishing the world's only H. P. Lovecraft Film Festival. And how many cities take part in the annual World Naked Bike Ride?

For the jocks Portland has an NBA team, the Trail Blazers. And the city has more strip clubs per capita than anywhere else in the United States—some say even more than in Vegas. (Max always politely demurred when his friends back in New York asked if the saying "If you don't know any strippers, you can't be from Portland" was true.)

And then there's the beer. Portland has not one, not two, but *five* annual beer festivals—which shouldn't be all that surprising since there are twenty-eight microbreweries in town, earning the city the nicknames Beervana and Beertown. Party animals can visit any number of "theater pubs" where movies are free as long as the customers keep buying brewskies. The drinking age is twenty-one, just like everywhere else in the country, but Max and his high school buds had, shall we say, lots of friends who could help them out on a Saturday night. Ah, memories.

It was really the economy that had Max returning, if only for a few days, to his roots. With Expedia, Travelocity, and similar online sites increasingly eating into his company's revenues, he was let go. But thanks to contacts he had established in the Big Apple over more than a decade in the industry, he was able to start a new career: writing freelance travel articles.

Most recently, he had talked to both Southwest and Alaska Airlines, proposing a series of stories highlighting the secret joys to be found in often-overlooked destinations on their regional maps. To his amazement, both airlines were interested and wanted him to submit a sample piece for their editors.

Write what you know. That's what they always told you in class, Max thought. He decided he might as well go back to the beginning: Portland.

As he flew west, childhood capers had flooded back to mind. Before long, the plane had made its final approach to the airport following the Columbia River. Max picked up his rental car and headed south on I-205 and I-84 toward the city. Within forty-five minutes of touching down, he had pulled up in front of the Heathman Hotel.

Max knew it well, or at least its public areas. He had attended functions in several of their eight meeting rooms, and now and then, when the family had something special to celebrate, his parents would treat him to dinner in its main restaurant, which was renowned for its collection of fine wines—not that Max was ever allowed to partake. (He was a bit upset that on this trip he had just missed the hotel's annual Beaujolais Nouveau Festival celebrating the season's new harvest.)

Other than a clumsy attempt to book a room at the Heathman on prom night—an embarrassing faux pas that was probably best forgotten—this would be Max's first time staying overnight in one of the grand hotel's 150 guest rooms and suites. It was also his first time there since a $16 million renovation had been completed in 1984 as part of a major redevelopment of downtown Portland.

He had forgotten how central the place was to everything Portland had to offer: It was in the heart of the business and entertainment districts, literally next door to the Portland Center for the Performing Arts and the Arlene Schnitzer Concert Hall (the former Paramount Theatre). Even when the hotel was brand new, the street on which it's located—Broadway—was nicknamed Portland's Great White Way.

The hotel had been a local landmark since its opening on December 17, 1927, and was added to the National Register of Historic Places in 1984. At the beginning of the twentieth century, as American timber interests moved westward to take advantage of the land's plentiful natural resources, George E. Heathman Jr., a real estate developer, saw the need for upscale residential lodging in the city.

Mind you, there were already several fine hotels downtown at the time: the Imperial Hotel (built in 1894), the Seward Hotel (constructed in 1909 and later renamed the Governor Hotel), the Benson Hotel (dating to 1912), and the more recent Commodore Hotel, which was completed in 1925. Heathman himself owned two other hotels in the city: the Roosevelt and another Heathman Hotel, both built between 1925 and 1927.

But George Heathman had given up control over those two properties almost as soon as they were finished. By 1927 he had envisioned a "New Heathman Hotel" that would cater to a more discriminating clientele. In addition to its deluxe accommodations, it would boast a restaurant with the finest cuisine in town.

The ten-story Italian Renaissance–style structure, designed by local architects DeYong and Roald, was built in record time—just seven months. The facade was faced with brick, and windows were set off by ornamental stone. Inside, the lobby was paneled with dark, expensive woods. On the mezzanine level, freestanding plaster columns and mock half columns set into the walls were decorated with painted acanthus leaves.

Heathman insisted that his new hotel also be accessible to the public at large. From 1927 until 1953 when the television era began, KOIN radio aired its popular broadcasts from the mezzanine of the Heathman. The ground floor of the building housed one of the largest coffee shops in the entire Pacific Northwest.

Heathman invited all twelve hundred laborers who worked on the hotel to a huge party to celebrate its completion. A formal opening and dedication followed, attended by the state governor, the city mayor and commissioners, and heads of the business community.

In the 1950s and '60s, people throughout America deserted its city centers and moved into the suburbs. It was no different in Portland, and for three decades the Heathman Hotel, along with the rest of downtown, suffered the consequences. George Heathman died in 1930 at the age of forty-nine, but his wife, Katherine, and two of his four children retained an interest in the hotel until the 1960s. One son, Harry, managed the property until two years before his death in 1962.

Finally in the 1980s, far-sighted civic leaders in an alliance with citizens, investors, and the art community began to turn around the city's fortunes. The hotel's refurbishment was critical to the revitalization plan. Although it had been luxurious by 1930s standards, the Heathman was completely remodeled into an upper-end boutique destination hotel. A sense of the original decor was maintained throughout. The elegant Tea Court was reopened, with eighteenth-century French landscapes by Claude Lorrain on the walls and an antique Czechoslovakian chandelier overhead. Throughout the hotel, original artworks, including several lithographs from Andy Warhol's Endangered Species series, were put on display in the hallways. Guest accommodations were redecorated in a variety of nineteenth-century styles, including Empire, Regency, and Biedermeier. The Heathman also expanded its library, adding several first editions signed by contemporary writers who had stayed at the hotel, and it instituted a Books by Your Bedside program for overnight guests.

Indeed, upon check-in that first night, Max was both surprised and delighted to find that the concierge had had a travel book by a local author placed on his nightstand. Surprised because Max didn't remember telling anyone what he did for a living; delighted because, well, it was a really nice, personal touch,

Unless the book was put there by a ghost, Max laughed to himself as he settled beneath the covers.

His first morning walking the streets of downtown reawakened memory after memory. Sure, the skyscape had changed, but each block recalled faces and events that he hadn't thought about in years. And, for the most part, all of them were happy. None of the remembrances of things past made him want to pack up and move back to Oregon, but it was very satisfying to let the warm glow of reminiscences wash over him.

Making his way back to the hotel, Max hoped he could capture what he was feeling with pen and paper. He crossed the lobby, made his way to the elevator, and headed up to 703. As he dipped his keycard into the slot on the door, an odd sensation suddenly hit him, a premonition. He wasn't sure *how* he knew, but there would be something out of place, something *wrong,* on the other side of the door.

He snapped on the light switch as he entered and immediately turned to look into the bathroom. No one there. It was empty. As was the rest of the room. Housekeeping hadn't been in that day, so everything seemed to be right where he left it. And yet . . .

Max closed the door warily behind him. *What is wrong with this picture?* he thought. That old cartoon puzzle came to mind where you had to compare two drawings: One showed what the scene is supposed to look like. The other had been slightly altered. The challenge was to figure out what was different.

His eyes scanned the room, moving first from the bed to the dresser. His suitcase lay open on the stand, his clothes and toiletries undisturbed. The TV was off, the remote sitting to one side.

Then it hit him: the table. He hadn't sat down at the table the night before, but the chair, which he hadn't moved, was pulled out, turned to one side. And resting on the table were the two water glasses from the bathroom. He didn't remember putting either of them there.

He walked into the bathroom and reached down to pick up the towel he had dropped on the floor after showering. Now he was *sure* something odd was going on. There were not one but *two* towels at his feet. He might have stumbled into the bathroom half asleep and carried out a couple of glasses the night before, but he knew for certain that he had only used *one* towel to dry himself that morning. Where had the other one come from?

Someone had been in his room!

Max raced over to the phone and punched at the keypad. "Hello, front desk. How may I help you?"

"Yes," said Max, trying to keep his voice calm. "This is 703. Has housekeeping been in my room today?"

"Just a minute, sir. Let me check." The receptionist put him on hold briefly, then came back to report, "No, sir. I just spoke with the head of housekeeping. We're very sorry, but they're running a little behind today. She'll come over immediately."

"No, no, that won't be necessary. I mean, that's not the problem. It seems that someone's been in my room."

There was a long pause at the other end of the line. Then, "We'll send someone right up."

Max set the phone back into the cradle and immediately began to wonder whether he had done the right thing. Had he forgotten moving the chair and the glasses and using an extra towel? If anyone had been there, it certainly wasn't a robbery. No one had rummaged through his suitcase. In fact, it seemed that none of his stuff had been touched.

The hotel manager showed up at his door within seconds, accompanied by security, who thoroughly checked out the room. They assured Max that electronic records showed no one else had been in the room that morning—at least not by using a key. Then they dropped the bombshell.

It may have been the ghost. It seemed the Heathman was haunted.

Ever since the renovations back in the early 1980s, all of the rooms in the hotel ending in 03 have experienced paranormal activity. Some spectre must have been disturbed, and it has now attached itself to all of the rooms in a vertical column from the top floor down to the lobby. And the phantom was most active in 703.

The most frequently reported ghostly phenomena were objects moving on their own or a mussed-up towel here and there. But some guests have felt sudden chills and cold spots in their rooms; others have heard tapping noises or disembodied heavy breathing. One man swore he was temporarily trapped beneath the sheets of his bed when they pulled themselves taut around him. And a few people have seen dark shadows moving around the room or on the walls, though there's never been a complete manifestation of an apparition.

The hauntings are attributed to a woman who, years earlier, committed suicide by throwing herself down the emergency stairwell adjoining Room 703. Of course, there's no record of such a death ever having occurred, but details like that don't usually matter when it comes to ghost stories, do they?

The manager offered Max his sincere apologies and suggested he change rooms immediately. But Max decided to stay put, partly in the hopes that his spectral visitor would return. Wouldn't that be something to write about: meeting the Heathman haunter face-to-face?

Unfortunately, the rest of Max's stay was uneventful—as least as far as the playful spirit was concerned. Still, Max was able to come away with a tale that was much better than anything he could have hoped for. The only problem was, he wasn't sure whether anyone would believe him.

Chapter 3
The Marilyn Mirror

Hollywood Roosevelt Hotel
Hollywood, California

At least three hotels in Hollywood, California, can claim resident ghosts, including two haunted by screen siren Marilyn Monroe. In one, the Hollywood Roosevelt, she shows up in an unlikely way: as a reflection in a giant mirror. And she's not the only celebrity to return to the hotel from the Next World.

"Mirror, mirror, on the wall. Who's the fairest one of all?"

Kristen couldn't resist. *Snow White and the Seven Dwarfs* was her favorite Disney film, and here she was in Hollywood! Could there be a more perfect place to find a magic mirror? Of course, she knew the narrow, six-foot-tall glass wasn't magical at all. But it *was* located on hallowed ground. It was mounted on a landing overlooking the grand lobby of the fabled Hollywood Roosevelt Hotel, which opened its doors back in 1927.

The grande dame had been built by a consortium of business folk and film royalty, including Douglas Fairbanks, Mary Pickford, and Louis G. Mayer. The twelve-story hotel, with more than three hundred rooms, was intended to complement Grauman's Chinese Theatre, the movie palace catty-cornered across Hollywood Boulevard that opened only three days after the hotel. Given the landmark's proximity to where so many red-carpet movie premieres would take place, it was only right that the first Academy Awards ceremony was held in its banquet hall, the Blossom Room.

As much as Kristen appreciated the historic significance of the Hollywood Roosevelt, she really wasn't there to bathe in the ambience. She was waiting to hook up with a friend of hers, Tamara, who was working as a Marilyn Monroe look-alike in front of the Chinese.

On any given day there would be at least a half dozen look-alikes on that block-long stretch of Hollywood Boulevard, offering to pose with tourists in exchange for a small gratuity. There were perennials like Batman and Superman, and there were usually a few imitators dressed as screen icons in their most famous roles, like Charlie Chaplin as the Little Tramp or Johnny Depp looking all the world like Jack Sparrow. And always a Marilyn.

Kristen's friend Tamara had been portraying Monroe for about three years, primarily at special events, private parties, and industry functions. And in between, she tried to spend a few hours each week on Hollywood Boulevard.

Tamara actually had fun with all the out-of-towners. She realized that they knew she wasn't actually Marilyn, but for a few minutes, all of them were able to forget about reality and enter the world of fantasy that is Hollywood. She knew exactly how to pose with the tourists, how to pucker her lips and bend slightly forward in her pleated white skirt. She'd coo, purr, pout, talking the breathy, husky Marilyn voice she had practiced for years—whatever it would take to bring Marilyn back to life for a moment or two. Tamara would do almost anything not to break the spell for sightseers, which is why she was meeting Kristen over in the hotel lobby rather than out there on the street.

While waiting, Kristen wandered from the lobby up to the gift shop on the mezzanine. She grabbed some juice and a PowerBar—it might be an hour or more till she and Tamara got some solid food. On the way, she encountered the mirror.

As Kristen stared into the glass and recited the wicked queen's incantation, she became aware of her friend standing behind her. Tamara was smiling, staring straight into the mirror, not acknowledging Kristen or making eye contact. "Marilyn" fluffed her hair, dabbed a fingertip against her beauty mark, and licked her reddened lips to moisten them, all without making the slightest sound.

Kristen, surprised at Tamara's sudden appearance and a bit annoyed that she was toying with her, spun on her heels. "What's the deal, girl? I'm hungry!"

No one was there.

Kristen was stunned. She had seen her friend over her shoulder only seconds before. Where had she gone? And how could get away so quickly?

Kristen scanned the mezzanine. It was empty. There wasn't a soul in sight. She peered over the railing and caught sight of a girl all in white rushing into the lobby from the street door to Hollywood Boulevard. It was Tamara. Kristen ran down the stairs and hurried up to her friend.

"How did you do that? How did you get all the way down here?"

"What are you talking about?" Tamara asked, truly baffled. "I just walked in the door." Then she added: "Is everything okay? You look like you've seen a ghost."

Maybe Kristen had.

✛

According to legend, that very mirror in the Hollywood Roosevelt Hotel, is indeed haunted by Marilyn Monroe. Supposedly she was first seen by one of the housekeeping staff, who noticed the reflection of the blonde bombshell standing behind her as she polished the glass. (Some versions of the story have the discovery being made in a suite where Marilyn used to stay; others place the mirror in a manager's office.)

The tale soon became common knowledge among employees, and pretty soon it was leaked to the public. Before long, everyone wanted a peek at the shiny surface. For many years the Roosevelt hung the mirror by the downstairs elevators, located near the valet stand at the rear of the hotel. Tongue-in-cheek, the hotel placed two large posters of the sex symbol on the walls opposite the lifts so that, either by accident or with a bit of deliberate finagling, people could catch a glimpse of Monroe in the glass. Around 2000, the mirror was moved to a spot near the gift shop, where it hung for about a decade. The glass, as of this writing, is in storage while the mezzanine and gift shop undergo restoration, and no decision has been reached when or even whether the mirror will be put back on public display.

Interestingly, when Marilyn's ghost shows up at the Hollywood Roosevelt, it doesn't always stay confined to the mirror. She also allegedly appears in Room 229 and Suite 1200, two of her favorites at the hotel, as well as in Cabana 246 and on deck chairs in the pool area, where she did her first modeling shoots.

Marilyn Monroe is not the only celebrity spectre in the Hollywood Roosevelt Hotel. Upstairs, Room 928 is haunted by Montgomery Clift, who stayed there for four months while shooting the movie *From Here to Eternity*. In fact, the actor walks the entire ninth floor. Guests hear the disembodied sound of a bugle coming from his former room (even when no one's staying there) and in the hallway where Clift used to pace while practicing.

Some sort of strong residual essences, thought to belong to Clark Gable and Carole Lombard, can be detected in the twelfth-floor penthouse where the couple honeymooned. A thirty-inch-diameter column of icy air, a typical paranormal "cold spot," can be felt in the Blossom Room, the hotel's ballroom. The ghost of an unidentified man has also been spied there. Usually he's described as being dressed all in black, although a few sources have him in white instead.

People staying at the hotel have found themselves dead-bolted out of their own suites. Invisible children can sometimes be heard playing in the hallways. Now and then, apparitions appear in the rooms, often as reflections in the mirrors. (Shades of Marilyn!) And then there are the phone calls to the switchboard that come from unoccupied guest rooms.

You know, the usual stuff.

Marilyn Monroe, it should be noted, has a few other ethereal hangouts in Greater Hollywood. People have claimed that they've seen her standing on the sidewalk outside the Brentwood house where she died. Her spirit also manifests by her crypt in Pierce Brothers Westwood Village Memorial Park in Westwood.

For several years she also used to return to the Knickerbocker Hotel on Ivar Avenue until renovations at the hotel around 2000 forced the lobby nightclub to close. The building first saw the light of day in 1925 when it opened as an apartment building. Within a few years it had been converted into a hotel for overnight and long-term occupancy.

Among the celebrities who stayed there were Milton Berle, Bette Davis, Cary Grant, Laurel and Hardy, Jerry Lee Lewis, Elvis Presley, Frank Sinatra, Red Skelton, Barbara Stanwyck, Lana Turner, and Mae West, among many others.

The hotel has seen its share of tragedy and notoriety. In 1943, police dragged actress Frances Farmer, half naked, kicking and screaming from the hotel on assault and DUI charges. Director D. W. Griffith, who kept an apartment at the Knickerbocker, died of a cerebral hemorrhage under the grand chandelier in the lobby in 1948. The MGM costume designer who went by the single name Irene, despondent after her marriage broke up, committed suicide in 1962 by jumping from a fourteenth-story window. William Frawley, best known for his role as Fred Mertz on TV's *I Love Lucy*, was also a longtime resident. He was walking back to his small studio apartment in 1966 when he suffered a heart attack and died. (Reports vary. Some have him collapsing on the sidewalk in front of the hotel; others place him on the outside staircase or on Hollywood Boulevard.)

During the height of the Jazz Age, Los Angeles police often looked the other way as a notorious speakeasy operated in the hotel just off the lobby. In time, the art deco, dark-wood-paneled Lido Room became a popular Hollywood watering hole for the famous and well connected.

Marilyn Monroe's association with the Knickerbocker started when she began seeing baseball great Joe DiMaggio. She used to enter the hotel through the service entrance to avoid the press and then meet up with the slugger in the nitery. After the two got married, part of their honeymoon was spent in the Knickerbocker. In the last few years of the nightclub's operation, women visiting the ladies' room were sometimes surprised to see a golden-haired phantom powdering her nose in front of the mirror. It was Marilyn! Once spotted, Monroe would quickly disappear.

The nightspot is also of particular interest because it was the longtime postmortem haunt of one of Hollywood's greatest stars of the silent screen, Rudolph Valentino. The Sheik's ghost has returned to a number of spots, including his Beverly Hills house known as Falcon Lair and the attached stables, as well as two spots up the coast—an Oxnard beach house and the Santa Maria Inn. His presence has also been felt, and occasionally his spectre's been seen, lingering near his crypt in the Hollywood Forever Cemetery. But for many years his apparition most often appeared in the Knickerbocker Hotel bar. While he was alive, the Latin Lover would often tango the night away on its tiled dance floor, and he apparently enjoyed doing so long after his demise.

By the 1960s, the Lido Room had ceased operation. The nightclub was reopened in 1993 by entrepreneur David Fisher as the All-Star Cafe and Speakeasy. It was mostly during Fisher's tenure there, up until the venue lost its lease in 2001, that Monroe's and Valentino's spectres were spotted.

The hotel has been transformed once again, this time into the Hollywood Knickerbocker Apartments, serving adult and senior residents. With the nightclub out of business and access to the building limited to tenants, there's no telling if either of the legendary spirits is secretly cutting a rug behind closed doors.

Before leaving the Knickerbocker completely, it's worth noting that the hotel has at least one more connection with the Spirit World. Magician Harry Houdini lived during the heyday of Spiritualism, and during the last third of his career he actively debunked fraudulent mediums. It's unclear why. Perhaps Houdini was incensed that such con artists were preying upon those who had lost loved ones. Or, it may have been a personal crusade: He was very close to his mother, and it's believed that he desperately wanted to find a true medium who could contact her after her death. Then again, maybe the showman simply realized that it would be good business to include something so topical in his act.

Regardless, Houdini made a pact with his wife, Bess, that whoever died first would try to get in touch with the other from the Beyond. Any message had to contain a specific, secret word (*believe*) to be proof of actual spirit communication. For ten years after the master illusionist's death, from 1926 to 1936, Bess held a séance on the roof of the Knickerbocker Hotel on Halloween, the anniversary of Houdini's death. No word ever came through. The only possible sign that the world-famous escapologist was, indeed, watching from overhead came on the night of the last séance. At the instant Bess wished Harry a final farewell, an unexpected rain began to pour. Was he giving a sign after all?

Another haunted hotel in Tinseltown deserves mention: the Oban Hotel. Now known as the Hotel Hollywood, the small, three-story peak-roofed structure was built beginning in 1922 and had its grand opening in 1927. It stands on Yucca Street, one block north of Hollywood Boulevard and around the corner from the Knickerbocker.

For many years Hollywood wannabes came to its door during their struggle to the top. Among the Oban Hotel's many guests were James Dean, Clark Gable, Fred MacMurray, Glenn Miller, Paul Newman, Orson Welles, and, yes, Marilyn Monroe. (That lady did get around!) The rooms were simple, with a bed, desk lamp, dresser, ceiling fan, desk and chair, and private bath with a toilet, sink, and stand-up shower. But it was enough for those just starting out.

Times have changed. The former Oban Hotel was completely remodeled in 2002 with up-to-date amenities including flat-screen televisions, DSL, and Wi-Fi.

And at least two ghosts. Possibly more.

One of the spirits belongs to an early resident of the hotel, a Hollywood hopeful named Charles Love. For whatever reason he never "made it." Instead, Love settled for the life of a props manager. It's an essential job on any movie set, but still . . . Love did manage to be seen on-screen, but only as a double for silent film comedian Harry Langdon.

On February 15, 1933, after a fight at the studio followed by a long drinking spree, the thirty-three-year-old Love returned to his tiny flat. According to the *Los Angeles Times*, he composed a "note of farewell" to Langdon, then shot himself to death with a single bullet to the head.

Suicides are particularly prone to becoming earthbound entities, and Love was no exception. The unusual part, though, is that his spectre has not been trapped in the room where he died. Rather, he seems to have retired to the basement, the stairs leading down into it, and the landing immediately above. Most often, his presence is indicated by an intense cold spot hovering outside the door leading down to the cellar. According to Laurie Jacobson and Marc Wanamaker in their classic book *Hollywood Haunted*, Love also makes himself known by emitting an incredibly foul, pungent stench that reeks of methane gas.

Love's spectre has become visible from time to time, but only in the form of a shadow. The foggy apparition turns from black to dark brown and finally rust colored. Some believe that his spirit is sometimes joined at the top of the stairwell by the phantom of a former owner. And at least one psychic has suggested that the second floor is haunted by a resident female ghost who stays near the room she used to occupy at the front of the hotel.

About ten miles outside of Hollywood is the seaside city of Santa Monica. In 1933, a Mrs. Rosamond Borde opened the Lady Windermere Hotel, and it soon became a getaway for folks from the film industry. The place was perfect to escape from the glare of the spotlights and the press, and movie stars mingled with mobsters in the downstairs Prohibition-era speakeasy. Regulars included Gable and Lombard, Stanwyck, Humphrey Bogart, Frank Capra, and, it's said, Bugsy Siegel.

The inn was remodeled and renamed the Georgian Hotel in the 1950s, and it was refurbished and modernized again in 2000. Today, a mix of Old and New Hollywood can be seen in the hotel's restaurant and lounges along with tourists visiting the West Coast. There also appears to be a goodly number of spectral guests staying on from the days gone by.

Most of the reports of hauntings come from the hotel staff. Disembodied voices have been heard in the lobby, the bar, on the main staircase, and back in the kitchen. The sounds are usually unintelligible murmuring, but every so often a recognizable phrase will pop out. More than one waiter cleaning up after hours or setting the tables for breakfast has come into the restaurant to see the room filled with phantoms dressed in 1930s-style clothing. After a beat or two and the blink of an eye, the apparitions vanish. Individual spirits have also been spotted by housekeepers and service personnel. And wraithlike music will float through the air long after any bands have ceased playing for the evening.

The ghosts don't limit themselves to the ground level. Unexplained footsteps on hardwood floors, including the sound of women wearing high heels, are sometimes heard upstairs—even in hallways and rooms that are carpeted. The third and fourth floors seem to be especially active. The Georgian Hotel, née the Lady Windermere, has always been a relaxed, comfortable place for friends to meet and greet. Perhaps that's why more than one phantom hasn't wanted to let the good times go.

Chapter 4

The Riddle of
the Black Dahlia

Millennium Biltmore Hotel
Los Angeles, California

The mystery surrounding the unsolved murder of Elizabeth Short, nicknamed the Black Dahlia, has been the subject of dozens of books, magazine articles, films, and television documentaries. The ill-fated twenty-two-year-old's naked and mutilated corpse was found dumped in a vacant lot in Los Angeles, but her ghost walks the halls of the luxury hotel where she was last seen alive.

It was good to get back to the hotel. It had been a grueling day on the floor—Ryan hated attending trade shows—and he was ready to collapse. As head of his sales force at the L.A. Convention Center, he not only had to be the public face of his company, the glad-hander, but he was also the final arbiter of any deals that might be closed that week. And if that weren't stressful enough, it was the first sales meeting for most of his team, and they had to be trained on the spot.

The Biltmore was Ryan's oasis.

Built in 1923 by John McEntee Bowman, the Millennium Biltmore Hotel, as it's now known, takes up the better part of a city block in downtown Los Angeles. At the time of its construction, the residential palace was the largest hotel

west of Chicago. (Even today it has 683 guest rooms, including seventy-six suites.)

The renowned architectural firm of Schultze and
Weaver—they had previously designed the Breakers Hotel
in Palm Beach as well as the Waldorf Astoria in New York—
used Italian-Spanish Renaissance and Beaux-Arts influences to create their West Coast masterpiece. Its three-story
Renaissance Court off the Pershing Square entrance, where
the lobby originally stood, was modeled after the court of
Queen Isabella of Spain, and it boasted marble floors and
a replica of the elaborate Escalera Dorado (or Golden Staircase) in Spain's Burghos Cathedral. Italian artist Giovanni
Smeraldi, whose work also appeared in the White House,
the old Grand Central Station, and the Vatican, painted the
fresco ceilings throughout the lobby.

Perhaps the hotel's pièce de résistance—for which it
became justly famous—is its thirty-foot-high, 11,500-square-
foot Crystal Ballroom on the Galleria level. Gold leaf and
giant backlight panes of stained glass adorn the ceiling,
accented by enormous Austrian crystal chandeliers.

Ryan was first drawn to the Biltmore by its beauty and
lavish accommodations. What always brought him back was
the palpable sense of history that pervaded the premises.
Film buffs recognized parts of the hotel from scenes in *A
Star Is Born, Chinatown, The Fabulous Baker Boys, Vertigo,
Ghostbusters,* and *The Sting* among many other movies that
were shot there. And they knew that eight Academy Awards
ceremonies were held there in the 1930s and '40s. JFK made
the Biltmore his L.A. headquarters during the 1960 presidential campaign. When the Beatles stayed there in 1964,
the streets around the hotel became so crowded that the
band had to arrive by rooftop helicopter. And in 1984, the

International Olympic Committee worked out of the Biltmore when the games were in town.

But, unknown to Ryan as he crossed the lobby that fateful night, there was also a sinister footnote in the hotel's legendary past. Back in 1947, it was the last place anyone remembered seeing Elizabeth Short before she died.

The notorious tale of the young lady known as the Black Dahlia is heartbreaking. The gruesome manner of her death, luridly described in detail by the *Los Angeles Examiner* and other newspapers, as well as the inability of police to solve the crime, made the case a national sensation.

Elizabeth Short was born in the Hyde Park section of Boston in 1924 and was raised in nearby Medford, one of five daughters. When she was six years old, her father, Cleo, who had been wiped out in the stock market crash, deserted the family. Her mother, Phoebe, managed to keep the family together by working a variety of odd jobs. Elizabeth was prone to asthma and bronchitis, so starting when the girl was sixteen, her mother began to send her to Florida for the winter to stay with family friends.

About that time, Cleo surfaced in Vallejo, California, and wrote his wife, asking to be allowed to return. She refused. But when Elizabeth was nineteen, the young woman traveled alone by train to stay with her father. Before long, they moved to Los Angeles.

Elizabeth's relationship with her father was tumultuous from the start. He expected her to play the docile and obedient daughter, but she was having none of it. She got a job at Camp Cooke (today's Vandenberg Air Force Base), and, surrounded by soldiers, the attractive teenager blossomed. She was flirtatious and soon spent evenings out on the town. That came to a stop in 1943 when Elizabeth was arrested for underage drinking in Santa Barbara, and police sent her back to Medford.

From there she moved to Florida, where she met an airman, Maj. Matthew Michael Gordon Jr. He was deployed to Southeast Asia, but they remained in touch, and he proposed marriage by letter from a hospital bed in India. Elizabeth accepted, but before he could get back to the States, Gordon died in an airplane crash.

In 1946, Elizabeth returned to Los Angeles to visit an ex-boyfriend, Lt. Gordon Fickling, who was stationed in Long Beach. Her attempt to get back together with him didn't work out, but she decided to remain in Southern California. According to most sources, it was during this period that friends nicknamed her the Black Dahlia—a play on the title of a then-current movie, *The Blue Dahlia*—because of Elizabeth's penchant for dressing all in black. (Other reports say that, instead, an unknown newspaperman covering her murder created the sobriquet.)

Elizabeth never seemed to have a job or a permanent residence. With little money, she was forced to move from one fleabag hotel or boardinghouse to another, basically surviving on the goodwill of others. Her longest period in one place in 1946 seems to have been one month, from mid-November to mid-December, when she stayed in a two-room apartment with eight other young women. Even at a dollar a day for her share of the room, she found it too expensive.

Despite reports to the contrary, Elizabeth never resorted to prostitution, nor did it appear from later investigation that she was particularly sexually active. But she was quite aware of her physical allure, and she knew that by frequenting bars and clubs she could meet people—men—who would provide her with a meal or two and perhaps a night's lodging in return for a few hours of friendly, though usually platonic, companionship.

Sometime in late December 1946, Elizabeth began living with a family in San Diego. A concessions girl at a twenty-four-hour movie arcade found her sleeping in the theater, took pity on her, and invited Elizabeth to stay with her at her mother's house. Elizabeth accepted, but she was far from an ideal guest. What was supposed to be a brief stay stretched into weeks. She didn't find work, laid about the house all day, and stayed out all night.

Whether Elizabeth left on her own or was eventually asked to leave is unclear. She had been seeing a twenty-five-year-old married salesman named Robert "Red" Manley whenever he was in town for business, and she begged him to take her back to Los Angeles, where he also lived. On January 8, 1947, he picked her up around noon, but rather than head north immediately, he rented a local hotel room for the night—although, according to his later testimony, they slept separately.

They set out for L.A. the next morning. They stopped at the downtown Los Angeles bus station so that Elizabeth could check her luggage, then continued to the Biltmore Hotel. Elizabeth claimed she was going to meet her sister, who would be taking her to live with her in Berkeley. Manley walked Elizabeth into the hotel through the Olive Street entrance; the two said good-bye and parted company around 6:30 p.m. Hotel staff later reported seeing Elizabeth in the lobby for a time, but for all intents and purposes, that was the last that anyone remembered seeing the Black Dahlia alive.

That was more than fifty years ago. Ryan stepped into the elevator, pressed the button for his floor, and breathed a sigh of relief as the doors closed in front of him. In less than five minutes he would be back in his room, with his shoes and tie off and a drink from the minibar in hand. What did he want to do tonight? He *should* spend an hour at the gym, and he could check to see if anything was going on at the Staples Center just a few blocks down the street. But he was so exhausted he would probably just call room service and crash.

The elevator was passing the second floor when Ryan realized that the button to another floor was also glowing on the panel. He hadn't noticed that before. He looked quizzically over his shoulder and there, standing silently in the corner, staring straight ahead, was a woman—a stunning woman, in her early twenties, dressed head to toe in black, with piercing blue eyes and dark, wavy hair swept back high over her head.

She's beautiful enough to be a movie star, Ryan thought. He wondered if a motion picture was being shot in the hotel because the stranger's hairstyle and wardrobe made her look like a femme fatale straight out of a 1940s film noir.

The elevator slowed to a stop, and the doors quietly opened. Ryan instinctively stepped to one side to let the woman by, and as she passed, he was enveloped by a sudden chill. The woman had gotten no more than a few steps out into the landing when she turned and stared straight at Ryan. What was he seeing in her eyes? Panic? An unspoken cry for help? Was she in some kind of trouble?

But before either could say a word, the doors slid shut. Ryan frantically punched the OPEN DOOR button. It seemed like it took an eternity, but after just the slightest hesitation, the elevator reacted, and the doors slowly began to slide apart.

The girl was gone!

Ryan rushed out of the lift and peered down the long hallway in both directions. The corridor was empty. There was no way that anyone could have gotten into a room in that amount of time. The woman had been out of sight for mere seconds. It was as if she had evaporated.

Ryan stood there, hoping she would show herself. Anything to prove that he hadn't been hallucinating. But when no one turned up in the hall after ten minutes, Ryan resigned himself to the fact that the woman's identity and how she had disappeared so quickly would remain a mystery.

And so it was, for several days. While nosing in a bookstore on his last night in town, however, Ryan ambled into a section for works about Los Angeles and the Southland. As his eyes scanned the titles, he was suddenly riveted in place. There, staring out at him from the cover of one of the books, was the smiling face of the bewitching siren he had seen in the elevator. It was the Black Dahlia!

What little Ryan recalled of the murder flooded back to mind, and the book, which he hurriedly bought, told him the rest. Elizabeth's body was discovered in a scruffy lot in Leimert Park in the Crenshaw district of Los Angeles on January 15, 1947. The corpse was so pale that, at first, the woman who found it thought that she was looking at a discarded department store mannequin. The victim's torso was naked and had been sliced cleanly in half at the waist. The lower part of the cadaver lay with its legs spread wide. The upper half was posed with the arms bent at ninety-degree angles and raised above the head. Cords attached to the wrists and ankles suggested that the woman had been held in bondage, and there were cigarette burns all over her body. Her mouth had been slashed from the corners up toward the ears, and most of her fingertips had been sliced off. Partial prints positively identified her as Elizabeth Short.

Despite the macabre way in which she was disfigured, she had died from internal bleeding caused by repeated blows to the head. It was also *not* a sex crime: There was no evidence that she had been violated, nor were any bodily fluids from the killer found.

A couple of days after Elizabeth's body was discovered, a note arrived at the *Examiner* offices, its message written in letters that had been cut and pasted together. Enclosed with the letter were Elizabeth's Social Security card and birth certificate, various photographs, the claim check for her baggage, and her address book with a page torn out.

Over the days, weeks, and months that followed, the police interviewed thousands of people. There were about two dozen serious suspects, but after a thorough investigation they were all eliminated. Manley, initially the prime suspect, passed repeated interrogations and two lie detector tests. Incredibly, almost sixty people, men and women, confessed to committing the crime. But all of the leads eventually led to a dead end.

To this day, the murder remains unsolved.

Elizabeth Short, the infamous Black Dahlia, is buried in Mountain View Cemetery in Oakland, California. But her spirit obviously prefers the Biltmore Hotel. Over the years, her ghost has been spotted in the main lobby, the hotel's ground floor public areas, the elevators, and some of the residential hallways. As is the case with so many ghost legends, there is no definitive proof of any of the sightings.

In many versions of the Black Dahlia haunting, including the one popularized by Troy Taylor (author of *Beyond the Grave* and *Field Guide to Haunted Graveyards*), Elizabeth

Short's apparition leaves the elevator on the sixth floor. The man who reported seeing the spirit and later recognized it from a photograph in a book was named James Moore.

There are many reasons the ghosts of murder victims are said to return from the Other Side. Some may not be aware they are dead; others are trapped in the venue where they met their violent end. It's thought that some spectres come back to search for their killers.

But Elizabeth Short left the hotel alive: There was no sign of struggle or blood from her vicious vivisection found in any of the rooms. So why has the Black Dahlia reappeared in the building where she was last seen? And why in the elevator? If, as legend suggests, her ghost gets off the lift at a particular floor, is it because that was where she met her killer?

More than a half century after Elizabeth Short's death, the murder may have to be solved before the many questions surrounding her haunting can be answered. In the meantime, look around you the next time you visit or stay at the historic Biltmore Hotel. That silent stranger dressed all in black standing next to you in the lobby just may be the Black Dahlia herself.

The Biltmore is not the only haunted hotel in downtown Los Angeles. Only four blocks away, a ghost walks the corridors of the Alexandria Hotel. When it was built in 1906, the eight-story structure was the most elegant lodging house in the city. It became *the* place to hold social events, especially after the addition of its magnificent Palm Court ballroom in 1911. Receptions were held there to honor President Woodrow

Wilson and Gen. John J. Pershing, and Rudolph Valentino regularly danced to its orchestra under the baton of Paul Whiteman. Charlie Chaplin, Mary Pickford, and D. W. Griffith met at the Alexandria in 1919 to found United Artists, and other celebrity guests of the hotel included Sarah Bernhardt, Humphrey Bogart, Enrico Caruso, Winston Churchill, Jack Dempsey, Clark Gable, Greta Garbo, Mae West, and Presidents Theodore Roosevelt and William Howard Taft.

When the luxurious Biltmore opened its doors in 1923, the Alexandria Hotel lost its appeal. By 1932, it was bankrupt. The hotel closed two years later, and its furnishings were auctioned off. In the 1950s, it reopened as a transient hotel, and for about two decades the former Palm Court was used as a training ring for boxers.

The Alexandria was refurbished in the 1980s, though it was never restored to its original splendor. In 2007, its rooms were converted into studio apartments as affordable urban housing, and Company of Angels, the city's oldest repertory theater company, relocated to the third floor of the hotel.

It was during the 1980s renovations that a spectral Lady in Black began to appear at the Alexandria Hotel. In their book *Hollywood Haunted*, Laurie Jacobson and Marc Wanamaker describe the unidentified apparition as dressing completely in black and wearing a large black hat. The spirit's clothing suggests she lived in the early part of the twentieth century, when the hotel was in its heyday. The Alexandria may not be the splendid palace it once was, but it must hold enough memories for at least one of its former residents to still call it home.

Chapter 5
The Gray
Ghost

The Queen Mary
Long Beach, California

A transatlantic liner gained its spectral nickname because its war-time camouflage allowed it to elude its enemies' sight. But now, out of service and permanently docked as a tourist hotel, the Queen Mary's *name has become associated with a different type of ghost—the all-too-human kind.*

Nick wasn't sure what to expect. He knew that the *Queen Mary* was supposed to have ghosts onboard—he and Jody *were* taking its Haunted Encounters tour—but he didn't know whether people were still seeing things around the ship. He was sure that the chances a phantom would show up while he and his girlfriend were there were slim to none.

It didn't matter to them. They weren't really there to try to see spirits. They were interested in getting down into the bowels of the ship, and guests were only admitted there if they took one of the daily guided tours.

Nick had learned all sorts of new things about the *Queen Mary* in the brief introductory film that started out the tour. In 1930, Cunard Line began construction of the ship to provide weekly express service between Great Britain and New York City. After a delay caused by Depression-related financial difficulties, work was resumed on the vessel in 1934.

Cunard intended to christen the ship the HMS *Queen Victoria*, but there was a misunderstanding when they asked King George V for royal permission to name the ocean liner for England's "greatest queen." He enthused that his consort, Queen Mary, would be pleased to accept the honor. Needless to say, *Queen Mary* it was.

The ship's maiden voyage was on May 27, 1936. Traditional in many ways, but with modern art deco interior design, the vessel soon became the most popular transatlantic cruiser afloat. She was also one of the fastest. In August 1936, the *Queen Mary* won the prized Blue Riband by capturing the record for the quickest Atlantic Ocean crossing to date—just three minutes short of four days. (The honor would go to the *Normandie* the following year, but the *Queen Mary* recaptured it in 1938 and held on to the prize until 1952.)

Its speed came from four giant propellers turned by enormous steam turbines. Nick and Jody marveled as they walked the metal catwalk through the engine room. The long, narrow stretch was known as Shaft Alley, no doubt because it was located directly above the propellers. The young couple couldn't imagine how horrendous the heat and noise must have been when everything was going full blast.

Back in 1940, the *Queen Mary* was en route to New York when England and France declared war on Germany. After dropping off its passengers, the ship diverted to Australia, where it was painted battleship gray and remodeled into a transport ship to carry troops. During the last two weeks of July 1943, it would set a record for carrying the most people ever aboard a single ship—16,683—15,740 of whom were in the armed services.

The ocean liner was so fast it could outrun any German U-boat. That capability, along with its camouflage color, allowed it to appear almost invisible as it floated by, earning it the nickname the Gray Ghost.

Despite its speed, the *Queen Mary* was a big target, so she was always surrounded by protective escorts. On October 2, 1942, one of them, the HMS *Curacoa*, cut in front of the *Queen Mary*'s bow. The megaliner cut the smaller vessel in half, instantly flooding the *Curacoa*'s lower decks. The *Queen Mary*, under orders not to stop for any reason whatsoever, helplessly watched as 338 of the 400 men onboard sank to their deaths.

Some of those guys are probably haunting this baby, thought Nick. *I wonder if anyone's ever seen them?*

"C'mon, Nick," called Jody. "Everyone's heading up to the pool."

Indeed, he was lagging behind. The tour had started at the stern of the ship on G, one of the bottom decks. They were about to head up to C, the lowermost deck that would have been used by passengers.

After the war, the *Queen Mary* was completely restored. There were standard second and tourist classes, of course, but the first-class accommodations could only be described as luxurious, at least for its day. Every room was paneled with the richest woods available and was individually designed to take advantage of the unique layout of the suite. Each cabin had its own phone and toilet facilities.

The ornate first-class dining room, known as the Grand Salon, was gigantic, two stories high supported by massive columns. It was so large that all three ships from Columbus's first voyage could have been squeezed inside. For a more private evening, guests could dine on the Sun Deck in the intimate Verandah Grill, which sat eighty. At night, the cozy cafe was transformed into the Starlight Club, which acted as an alternative to the popular Observation Bar located above the bow.

First-class passengers also had access to shops and a full wraparound Promenade Deck, plus the exclusive use of a library, smoking salon, children's nursery, kennel, and on-deck tennis court. And, there was the indoor swimming pool.

Located slightly forward of midship, the pool was completely enclosed by four walls decorated with brown, tan, and beige rectangular tiles, accented with stripes of seafoam green. A staircase at one side led up to dressing rooms on a balcony that overlooked the bathing area.

For about two decades after the war, the liner was the transatlantic ship of choice for the rich and famous. But the golden era of transoceanic cruising came to an end. The first commercial jet flight took place between London and New York on October 4, 1958, and, before long, the well-to-do were choosing to fly to Europe rather than spend days at sea.

Cunard held out for seven years, but in 1966, the line was forced to sell the vessel (along with its sister ship, the *Queen Elizabeth*). A consortium of buyers brought the *Queen Mary* to Long Beach, California, in 1967 with the intent of turning her into a hotel and maritime museum. She was eventually moored permanently at Pier J, where she became completely dependent on onshore utilities and services. (The *Queen Elizabeth* was sold for scrap in Hong Kong the following year.)

To refit the *Queen Mary* for the next phase of her life, almost everything below what is now R (for *restaurant*) deck was razed. The boilers, engines, and all but a short, representative piece of the propellers were removed. Initially, the indoor pool was saved for use by hotel guests, but it was soon determined to be structurally unsound. Although the pool was never taken out, its water was drained.

Cabins on A and B decks were turned into hotel rooms. The library, music room, and several other public spaces were made into a shopping arcade, and additional retail venues were opened on Sun Deck. Most of the passenger lounges and dining rooms became banquet rental halls.

On November 2, 1972, the first 150 hotel rooms were opened to the public. While the number has varied under different owners, there are currently 307 suites onboard.

Nick and Jody caught up with the rest of the group at the side of the pool. The guide allowed people to poke around for a few minutes on their own, and while Nick shot photographs on the lower level, Jody took the opportunity to explore. She walked up the stairs behind the diving board and made her way back to the old changing rooms. As she walked into the ladies' facilities, she felt an odd presence, almost as if there were someone standing there watching her. But no, no one had followed her inside.

Confused by the sensation, she walked back out onto the upper ledge overlooking the pool and stared down. Nick and most of the group were at the far end of the pool. But then a small motion almost directly below her caught her attention. She walked halfway around the balcony to get a better look. There, on the pool level, was a girl, about nine years old, quietly laughing and playing by herself. Jody was sure she hadn't been with them on the tour. Where had she come from?

And why did no one else seem to see her?

Jody stood transfixed as the youngster walked back and forth, so close to the edge of the deep, empty pool that she was afraid the child would fall in. Then Jody saw it: Trailing behind the girl on the smooth tile was a line of wet footprints.

Jody caught Nick's eye to point out the girl, then glanced down to make sure the youth was standing in the same place.

But she was gone.

In fact, she wasn't anywhere. The girl had dissolved. Only the damp imprints of her soles were left behind.

The old first-class pool may very well be the most haunted area of the ship. In addition to the little girl, a sad-looking boy has also been seen from time to time. Several adult female phantoms have been reported in the two-tiered room, including a woman wearing a 1960s miniskirt, a petite brunette in everyday wear, an elderly swimmer in a 1930s-era one-piece bathing suit and bathing cap, and (seemingly out of place) a blonde woman in white evening gown with long sleeves. Sometimes one of the spectres would appear standing on the balcony; other times one would be seen on the diving board ready to plunge in. None of them sticks around for long, however, and they'll fade from view if anyone tries to watch them.

There are other paranormal phenomena in the area as well. It hasn't been filled for years, but the sound of splashing sometimes echoes off the walls. Many visitors to the changing room cubicles have felt some unexplainable aura within the closed quarters. (Some psychic investigators have suggested that the facilities may be a vortex or portal to the Other Side.) Small circular orbs of light often show up in both digital and regular photographs, even though the glowing circles weren't visible when the pictures were taken.

There seems to be an endless stream of entities throughout the *Queen Mary,* but interestingly none of them was reported until after the ship was docked in Long Beach.

One of the most famous spooks is John Pedder, who haunts Shaft Alley around watertight door 13. His tale is gruesome. On July 10, 1966, during one of the ship's last voyages, the *Queen Mary* entered a fog bank. The captain took the usual precaution of closing all watertight doors to prevent flooding if, heaven forbid, the ship collided with an unseen vessel in the mist.

Eighteen-year-old Pedder, from Skipton, Yorkshire, England, had joined the ship's crew the previous March. He had finished three tours as a fireman in the boiler room and was on his second sailing as a bilge pump operator in the engine room. No one knows precisely what actions Pedder took that morning when he heard the unmistakable sound signaling the closure of the several-ton steel door. But his lifeless body was discovered about 4:00 a.m., crushed between the hydraulic door and its frame.

Had the door malfunctioned? No, it was tested three hours later and was found to be in perfect working order. Had he slipped? Unlikely. He was found in a standing position, his head and shoulders thrust halfway through the opening. The massive door takes a full six seconds to travel the three feet to its closed position, so the most probable solution was that Pedder had tried to run or jump through at the last moment and was, well, just too late.

People have seen the lad's phantom at the doorway, wearing a beard and dressed in his overalls (variously reported as white or blue). Security dogs supposedly refuse to pass through the portal, and some people have reported feeling a rush of air pass by them in the "tunnel." Is it Pedder, desperately trying to make it through the door before it closes in on him?

The ghosts of two other crew members have been spotted nearby. Although unidentified, one is a man in a white boiler suit; the other has black hair and a long beard and wears bluish gray coveralls. Both tend to go about their business, oblivious to present-day staff and those on tour. In addition to seeing the men's apparitions, people also hear unexplainable banging on the metal pipes.

Also below deck, there's spectral activity all around the area of the hull that was repaired after the *Curacao* collision. People have heard loud sounds of knocking on the metal, ripping steel, and rushing water. Most disconcerting are the ghostly cries of the men who were killed in the accident.

A phantom crewmember named Senior Second Officer William Eric Stark manifests in his old living quarters and out on deck. On Sunday, September 18, 1949, the staff captain told Stark that he had a bottle of gin in his cabin and that he and two other officers were free to go there and have some after completing their shift at 10:00 p.m. Stark got there before the other two men. While waiting, he found what he believed to be the proffered gin in a closed cabinet and poured himself a drink.

Because he had a cold, Stark didn't notice the liquid's unusual odor, but he knew that something was wrong as soon as it hit his tongue. Upon closer examination, he discovered that someone had filled an empty gin bottle with the poisonous cleaning solvent carbon tetrachloride.

After his initial panic, Stark was relieved when there were no immediate consequences. He joked about the accident with his friends and the staff captain, but his flippancy was premature. He felt a bit queasy the next day, but the ship's doctor only recommended bed rest. By Tuesday, Stark's condition had deteriorated, and he was admitted to the hospital. Within hours he had sunk into a coma and died.

A little relaxation, a simple mistake, and the result was death. No wonder Stark's soul has never come to rest.

Other than the unknown ladies by the pool, the best-known female ghost on the *Queen Mary* is the Lady in White, who always appears dressed to the nines in a long, white, backless evening gown. Her spirit used to sweep into the Queens Salon, which had once been the ship's main lounge. She would make her way to the grand piano or, sometimes, stay on the dance floor and sway in time to the music. Regardless, after a few minutes, she'd startle onlookers by instantly disappearing.

When Sir Winston's restaurant was opened in the hotel, the piano was moved to the new, elegant eatery. And wouldn't you know it? The mysterious Lady in White moved right along with it. She's not seen very often these days, but that doesn't mean she's not around.

Behind crew doors, another presence has been seen, heard, and felt in the main kitchen. One old wives' tale says that it's the ghost of an unpopular cook who was thrown into an oven, either by angry staff or troops. Another suggests it's Leonard "Lobster" Horsborough, who was a chef onboard for fifteen years before dying from heat stroke or heart trouble on November 13, 1967, during the ship's final voyage. His body was buried at sea, but perhaps his spirit prefers to spend its time in his old kitchen rather than Davy Jones' Locker!

Of course, the ship's wraiths don't keep to the public and crew areas. They infest the hotel rooms as well. Dozens of guests have reported seeing spectres in their "cabins." Many have gotten up to answer knocking at their doors, only to discover that there was no one in the hallway. In some of the rooms, the showers and other fixtures have a way of working by themselves. Guests who stay in the suite that Winston Churchill occupied during his crossings on the *Queen Mary* have reported smelling and seeing cigar smoke in the room.

These hauntings are only the tip of the iceberg. The sounds of children laughing and playing ring out in the old nurseries and up on deck. The barking of an unseen dog has echoed out of the former first-class kennel. Plates, trays, and other objects move on their own in the lounges, dining rooms, and corridors. And front desk personnel have looked up to see people vanish while standing in the middle of the lobby.

For more than forty years now, hundreds of sightings have occurred on the *Queen Mary,* and the manifestations continue to this day. Few hotels embrace their reputation for being spook-ridden as wholeheartedly as the *Queen Mary*. If you want to see one of the spectres, your best bet may be to stay overnight. That stranger who greets you as you take a midnight stroll on the Promenade Deck may not be another hotel guest. He may be sailing for eternity on the Gray Ghost.

Chapter 6

The Phantom
in the Del

Hotel del Coronado
Coronado, California

Was it suicide that killed Kate Morgan at the famed Hotel del Coronado in 1892? And was that really her name? She's been gliding down the hotel's hallways for decades, and spectral phenomena still plague the room where she stayed in the days leading up to her death.

"Will there be anything else, sir?"

"No thanks. I think everything will be fine."

"I hope so, sir. Good luck."

Tim tipped the bellhop, then locked and chained the door behind him. The well wishes might have seemed odd under any other circumstance, he mused, but he *was* in Room 3327.

Tim had been trying to stay there for years, but the room had always been booked when he had vacation. Ordinarily, management at the Hotel del Coronado in Coronado, California, doesn't even rent the room unless it's specifically requested, but that hasn't diminished its popularity.

After all, it's haunted.

The sightings date back to the turn of the twentieth century. In the 1880s, a tremendous land boom sprang up on the West Coast, and as people began to flood south from

Los Angeles, railroad magnate Elisha Babcock and Hampton L. Story (of the Story & Clark Piano Company) decided the time was right to build a luxury, seaside resort in San Diego. Rather than place their hotel in the downtown Gaslamp Quarter of the city, they decided to purchase Coronado Island, which sat just offshore in San Diego Bay. They would subdivide the land and position the hotel at the island's southernmost tip along a wide sandy beach.

In 1969, a tall, modern bridge was raised to connect the island to the mainland, but up until that time the only way to reach Coronado was by boat. That automatically added a veneer of exclusivity and a certain mystique to the venue.

Work on the new hotel began on twenty-eight acres of beachfront property in March 1887. The original plans for the Del, as the Hotel del Coronado is nicknamed, called for just under four hundred rooms. The main lodge has been significantly expanded over the years, though, and today, with the addition of the Ocean Towers and California Cabanas, the total is up to 679 rooms, plus an additional seventy-nine cottages and villas.

The suites in the original structure, now known as the Victorian Building, were luxurious, and the hotel was the first on the West Coast to be wired for electricity. There were tennis courts, a tea garden—even a saltwater pool (despite the fact that the ocean was mere steps away across a broad lawn and beach). Perhaps the inn's most outstanding feature was its 23,500-square-foot main dining room, the Crown Room, with its high, arched, pine wood–paneled ceiling. The entire exterior of the Del was painted a pristine white, set off by deep maroon roofs.

Building costs far exceeded estimates. It turned out that almost all of the necessary resources had to be brought from outside the area during the hotel's construction, including the lumber and the labor force. Plus, fresh water had to be pumped over from the city. A real estate bust threatened to sink the endeavor, but at the last minute John D. Speckels, the sugar king, offered a welcome infusion of cash. By 1890 he had bought out the other partners completely.

The Hotel del Coronado, now a U.S. National Landmark, opened to great fanfare in February 1888. By the Roaring Twenties it had become a perfect getaway for Hollywood celebrities. Among the film stars who dropped in during its early days were Tallulah Bankhead, Charlie Chaplin, Tom Mix, Mary Pickford, Rudolph Valentino, and Mae West. It would also become a backdrop for many movies, most notably the 1959 Marilyn Monroe–Jack Lemmon–Tony Curtis motion picture *Some Like It Hot*.

Other major figures to visit included Sarah Bernhardt, Thomas Edison, Charles Lindbergh, Babe Ruth, and L. Frank Baum (who may have used the hotel's Queen Anne–style turrets as inspiration for his description of the Emerald City). Political figures such as Edward, Prince of Wales (later King Edward VIII) and eleven U.S. presidents, beginning with Benjamin Harrison, have also been drawn to its doors.

But perhaps the Del's most frequent guest—a five-night stay that has stretched into forever—is Kate Morgan.

On November 25, 1892, a wan woman in her midtwenties walked into the lushly furnished foyer and inquired about a room. She was later described by a coroner as being five foot six, with a fair but sallow complexion, two moles on her left cheek, medium-length black hair and brown eyes and weighing about 150 pounds.

A female traveling alone, especially one without suitcases, certainly drew suspicion and was frowned upon in

Victorian times. But the woman assured the desk clerk that she'd been traveling with her brother, a Dr. M. C. Anderson. He had gotten off the train in Orange but would be arriving shortly. She had no luggage because he was holding the claim tickets.

The sympathetic clerk took the woman at her word, registered her under the name Mrs. Lottie A. Bernard of Detroit, and showed her to Room 302 on the north side of the building. (In later years, the room's number was changed to 3312. It is currently 3327.) Over the next few days, she repeatedly asked the staff about her brother. Had he arrived? Had he sent a message? The answer was always a polite but regrettable no.

Meanwhile, her worsening health was obvious to anyone who saw her. Several people, including the pharmacist who ran the hotel's drugstore, recommended that she visit the house physician. She assured them that she had already been diagnosed. She suffered from neuralgia, and her brother would treat her as soon as he arrived. Later, when the hotel manager pressed her further, she confessed that she had stomach cancer. (At the same time, he discreetly asked as to how she was planning to pay for her stay, and she told him to wire a G. L. Allen in Hamburg, Iowa. Indeed, money arrived by wire the morning her body was discovered.)

Despite her sickly condition, on November 28 "Lottie" managed a trip into San Diego, where she purchased a gun and ammunition. That night, she was seen by guests on a hotel veranda, looking out across the bay as an impending storm approached.

The next morning, a hotel electrician found the secretive woman, dead, on a small set of stone stairs leading down to the beach on the west side of the building. There was a gunshot wound in her right temple and a forty-four-caliber pistol beside her on the steps.

According to police, there was no doubt the mysterious person had committed suicide. But why had the "Beautiful Stranger," as newspapers dubbed her, done it? Was she merely ending the pain of a fatal disease? And why had her brother abandoned her? In fact, was anyone really supposed to meet her at all?

No one was sure. Only one thing became certain: The woman was not Lottie Bernard. After almost two weeks of inquiry, it was determined that her real name was Kate Morgan.

She had been born Kate Farmer sometime around 1865 in Iowa, and on December 30, 1885, she married Thomas Morgan. At the time of her death, Kate was employed as a domestic by the L. A. Grant family of Los Angeles, working under the assumed name of Mrs. Katie Logan. She had told the Grants and her coworkers that she had fled from her husband, who was an inveterate gambler. Other than that, she never commented about her past.

On November 23, Kate had told the Grants that she was going to take a one-day trip to San Diego. When she didn't return, they contacted the police, who in turn connected her disappearance with the news reports coming out of San Diego. When Kate's trunks were opened back at the Grant residence, papers found inside confirmed that she was living a double or triple life.

But why was she heading to San Diego? And what was the true manner of her illness? An autopsy was never performed. Clues to her reason for committing suicide may have been destroyed when Kate burned a large stack of papers in the fireplace in her hotel room. And the unclaimed suitcases, purportedly left behind at the train depot, were fictitious.

An anonymous "prominent physician" suggested in the *San Diego Union* newspaper that the early symptoms of pregnancy were almost identical to stomach cancer. It was his conclusion that Kate was "enceinte" and was using the medications found in her room, including camphor and quinine pills, to induce a miscarriage.

An eyewitness reported that he had seen Kate arguing with an unidentified male on the train heading to San Diego. The man got off in Orange, just as Kate claimed her brother had, but to the observer it seemed to be more of a lover's spat than a squabble between siblings. Had Thomas Morgan unexpectedly come back into Kate's life? Or was it, perhaps, a boyfriend who had gotten her pregnant and then, after a final quarrel, deserted her?

And there was the question of the missing day. Even in 1892 it was only a few hours' journey between the two cities, but she didn't arrive in San Diego, or at least at the Coronado, until two days after she left her employer's house.

Given the notoriety of the case—indeed, it drew national press—and no family to object, Kate's body was put on display at the local mortuary, Johnson & Company, where it was being kept while officials decided what to do with the remains. Eventually Morgan was buried in Mount Hope Cemetery just east of downtown San Diego.

But it seems that her spirit wanted to return to the Del.

Which leads us to the question: Why? According to paranormal investigators, people whose lives have been cut short or who die violently sometimes find it difficult to find eternal rest. Sometimes a life is snuffed out so abruptly that the person doesn't even know that he or she is dead. Such might be the case with Kate. On the other hand, perhaps she's still waiting for her "brother" to arrive. Then, too, she was certainly pampered at the hotel during her last days. Maybe she enjoyed the service so much she never wants it to end.

Regardless, hundreds of people have reported spotting Kate's ghost in Room 3327. But Tim wanted to see her for himself. Or, if not her ghost, he at least wanted to experience some of the other strange paranormal phenomena that took place there.

It's been said that personal items left lying out would go missing, then turn up elsewhere in the room. Guests might wake up in the morning to find the place a complete mess, as if some unseen intruder had picked up stuff at random and thrown it around the room. People have heard the sound of disembodied footsteps in the dark or sensed brief whiffs of a flowery perfume in the air. There might be sudden drops in temperature. Blankets had been ripped off guests as they slept, and the television and ceiling fan had been known to turn on by themselves.

And sometimes the main attraction herself showed up: a dark-haired woman dressed in 1880's clothing. Even when she didn't appear, people often entered the room to find an impression on the bed as if someone had been lying there. No wonder maids prefer to service the room in pairs.

Kate doesn't like to stay in her room. She's been encountered floating down the third-floor hallway, and she's manifested outside in the garden, on the stairs where she breathed her last, and on the beach. When she doesn't choose to materialize, people will nonetheless occasionally get the impression that someone is watching them. "Sensitives"—as people who can discern the presence of invisible spirits are called—have reported being overwhelmed by feelings of hopelessness and despair when they walk down the stairs where Kate's body was found.

Tim, who wanted nothing more than to cross paths with a visitor from the Other Side, had been adamant about staying in 3327. Unfortunately, it turned out to be a quiet night at the hotel. No moving curtains over the windows, no shifting blankets on the bed. No filmy phantom passing by the nightstand or inanimate objects flying about the room. Not even the creak of a sagging floor board. He forced himself to stay awake until three, but finally Tim drifted off to sleep.

He woke with a start—wide-awake—at 6:00 a.m. There was just a hint of predawn light peeking through the drapes. What had disturbed him? He looked around the room cautiously, but, no, he was alone. Yet something was telling him, *compelling* him, to get dressed and head down to the beach. Within minutes he was walking through the lower lobby toward the steps leading to the sand.

Then, as he passed the classic boutique Established in 1888, something caught his eye. The shop, which specialized in gifts tied to the history of the Del, was shut up tight, but a shadowy figure seemed to moving among the displays. Tim leaned forward and placed one hand up against the glass to shield his face from the light of the hallway lamp. There! The form of a woman had moved again and was back behind the checkout counter. It was too dim for Tim to make out her face, but she was average height, wearing an old-fashioned, high-collared, long black dress. She seemed to be hurriedly though methodically searching for something. Tim saw her focus her attention beneath the counter. She knelt down, out of sight.

Although it was none of Tim's business, he was curious. Who was the woman? She didn't seem to be a burglar. In that garb, she was probably an early arriving member of the shop staff. But he wondered what she was so eager to find. When she stood up, she'd no doubt be holding it her hands. Tim figured if he just waited a few more seconds . . .

Okay, maybe a little longer. Five minutes went by, then ten. But the ghostly figure he had seen duck behind the table never stood up. Where had she gone? Had he actually seen her? He hadn't gotten much sleep. Maybe his mind was playing tricks.

Then it dawned on him: Whatever spirit had told him to go to the beach had done so because it knew he would walk in this direction, right past the shop. It knew he would run into . . . Kate Morgan!

Tim stood there, stunned, unsure whether he could believe what had just transpired. Soon, as it approached seven, he became aware of the opening of windows overhead and the rattling of service trays down nearby hallways. The hotel was coming back to life.

As Tim continued walking toward the beach, lost in thought, he purposely took the infamous set of stairs where Morgan's lifeless corpse had been found more that a hundred years before. He paused midway down the steps, spun around, and looked back in the general direction of the room where she had stayed—and where he had just spent the past evening.

"Thank you for coming through, Kate," he mumbled. "It was worth the wait."

Skeptics say that all of the spooky goings-on at the Hotel del Coronado can be attributed to the natural creaks and groans of any century-old seaside hotel. But after his experience, Tim knew better. So, too, does the staff. Every year when they celebrate their employee Christmas party, they make sure there's an extra name on the guest list: Kate Morgan. Their resident ghost is always welcome.

But it turns out, Kate's not the only spook haunting the Del.

Burning, iridescent eyes, thought to be those of a woman, have startled guests in Room 3312 as they glowed in the darkened chamber. Other visitors have had to endure flickering lights, had the windows open and shut by themselves, seen the curtains sway even when the windows were closed, heard unnatural sounds emanating from the plumbing, or had the bed shake. Many just felt a general restlessness and anxiety.

Sometimes, passersby in the hall have seen unusual lights radiating out from under the door. In the summer months, the maintenance crew finds it almost impossible to keep the room's window screens from falling off. And what causes the light bulb at the bottom of the nearest stairwell to burn out after only one or two days?

It's said that 3312, which was once numbered 502, was where Elisha Babcock clandestinely met his mistress. She supposedly committed suicide in the room after finding out she was pregnant. The gossip was impossible to verify: By the time police arrived, her body had somehow disappeared.

Then there's Room 3502. During a visit to the Hotel del Coronado by Vice President George H. W. Bush, one of the men from his Secret Service detail was assigned to the room.

In a single evening, the agent suffered shifting drapes, cold gusts, and a strange luminescence filling the room. At one point he called down to the front desk complaining about the loud talking and footsteps from the guests overhead. The receptionist, puzzled, assured him there wasn't anyone in the room directly above him. Then the spectral form showed up. The agent asked to be transferred to another room before morning.

Even more phantoms infest the Hotel del Coronado. The ghost of the Crown Room's first maintenance supervisor appears, testing the dining room's floor with his cane. An ethereal woman in period dress gaily dances across the hotel ballroom. The spirit of a terminally ill young girl who was rushed to a hospital in 1950 has returned to roam the corridors looking for the doll she left behind. There are other phantom children as well: The spectres of a little boy and girl are seen throughout the property, either racing in the halls or running up and down the stairs.

As memorable as Tim's morning was at Established in 1888, the event was far from unique. Several people have spied a dark form moving behind its locked door after hours. One shop manager arrived to discover that all of the books on a lower shelf near the register had been disturbed. Some were on their sides; others were scattered on the floor and lying open.

But the strangest thing that took place in the shop had to do with the Marilyn Monroe memorabilia concerning the filming of *Some Like It Hot*. Staff members would see the souvenirs not just fall but literally fly off the shelves. Was there a jealous spirit in the house? Or had Marilyn herself returned to move the items simply to let people know she was there? (She's already getting plenty of attention haunt-ing several spots back in Hollywood!)

Eventually the shopkeepers moved the Monroe collect-ibles behind the counter where they weren't so prominently displayed. The tchotchkes never moved another inch.

Chapter 7

The Marina
Manifestation

MGM Grand Hotel and Casino
Las Vegas, Nevada

Even before it became part of the MGM Grand Hotel and Casino, the old Marina Hotel in Las Vegas had a reputation for being haunted—at least according to eight-year-old Roxana, who clearly saw the apparition of a man in golf attire standing at the foot of her bed.

I woke up—dead awake—something I don't remember ever having happened before. I knew immediately that something was going on.

I must have been seven or eight at the time; I'm not sure. My parents had taken my grandmother and me on vacation with them to Las Vegas, and we were staying at the old Marina Hotel located right on the Strip. My folks were in one bed; my grandmother and I were in the other.

It must have been the second or third night there. I remember being sound asleep; then the next thing I knew I was sitting upright in my bed. It was around three in the morning, certainly well after midnight. It took me a couple of seconds to figure out where I was, since I didn't get to stay in hotels all that often. But then it all came back to me.

The room was dark, but there was a soft glow of light coming in from underneath and around the edges of the heavy curtain. (Even with the drapes, there was no stopping the giant neon signs from shining through the window.) I looked down to the end of the bed, and standing there—I'll never forget it—was a man. A stranger.

And though I was just a kid, I somehow knew he was a ghost. I mean, he didn't look like ghosts in the movies or cartoons. I couldn't see through him or anything. He looked real. Or real enough. But there was just *something* about him that didn't add up.

I'd never seen him before. He was an older man, I would guess in his sixties, very tall and very thin. I don't recall what he was wearing other than the fact that he had on a small hat. The type that newsboys or, I guess, golfers wear.

I must have been afraid. My heart was racing. But I didn't scream. He was standing sideways to the bed, but his head was turned toward me. I don't know how long we stayed like that, staring at each other. Then, for no reason, his eyes squinted up and he started laughing. His mouth opened wide, but no sound came out of him. There was complete silence.

I couldn't understand what he found so funny. I hadn't done anything. I hadn't moved an inch from the moment I spied him. After what seemed like hours—though I'm sure it was only a couple of minutes at most—he started to fade away. At first, his entire body, then everything but the head gradually turned translucent and disappeared. The last thing to vanish was his face, his eyes locked on mine to the very last second.

With the spell broken, I pulled the covers up over my head and pressed myself down into the bed. I didn't know what to do. Should I wake my grandmother? My parents?

But I was afraid to peek out from under the blankets in case he was still there. I started crying, careful not to make any noise. I told myself that it would soon be morning. It would be over. Once it got light out, everything would be all right.

I don't think I dozed off the rest of the night. I just lay there, waiting. Eventually I heard my parents moving around, so I knew it would be safe to look out. Sure enough, they had opened the curtains, and the room was flooded with light. Grandma had gotten up, too, and they were beginning to go over their plans for the day.

I jumped out of bed and ran over to my mom. I grabbed ahold of her, and the words started tumbling out, one over the other. I doubt if I made any sense. I knew my parents wouldn't believe me. Why should they? A ghost? In *our room?*

"Now, Roxana," my mother cautioned. (I knew she was being serious, because she only called me "Roxana" when I was in trouble. Otherwise I was "Rox" or "Roxy.") "It must have been your imagination."

And so it went. I pleaded with them to move to another room. I didn't want to stay there another night. What if the man came back? But they were having none of it.

I'm not sure how I got through that last night. I suppose I just willed myself to sleep. And, fortunately, the ghost *didn't* come back, or I slept soundly and missed him. Anyway, the next day none of us said another word about my encounter, and over the years I put it out of my mind.

Until one day in November 1990, when I was around eighteen. My mom and I were watching the news on television, and a reporter announced that the Marina Hotel would be closing its doors at the end of month. The year before, Kirk Kerkorian had bought it and changed its name to the MGM Marina. But now he was planning to tear it down to build a new MGM Grand on the property.

"And you know," the guy on TV told the anchor, "they say the place is haunted. I wonder where all of the spooks are going to go."

In an instant, all of my memories from that night in the hotel came back to mind.

"See, Mom. Did you hear that?" I called triumphantly. "I told you I wasn't making it up. That's where I saw the ghost."

"Of course you did," she said in that dismissive tone of hers I'd come to recognize. I never spoke to her about it again.

But the broadcast made me curious. If a news program said the hotel was haunted, even in passing, then other people must have run into the ghost, too. What were *their* stories?

This was years before the Internet, so the only thing I could think of was to call the chamber of commerce in Las Vegas. The lady who answered the phone was very sympathetic (and very patient) and gave me the number of a man who owned a souvenir shop who was "really into that sort of thing." I don't remember his name. I talked to him for about ten minutes, then he had to go because of some customers. We played phone tag back and forth a few times, but we never connected and I finally lost interest.

It's funny you should ask me about all this now. It was all happened—what?—thirty years ago? Still, sometimes I wonder. How many other little girls in that hotel woke up in the middle of the night to find a ghost standing at the foot of their bed?

The Marina Hotel and Casino opened in Las Vegas in 1975 on Las Vegas Boulevard (aka the Strip) just north of Tropicana Avenue. It was a tiny hotel by today's standards, a mere 714 rooms. In addition to the ubiquitous slots, the casino held a sports and racing book and four poker tables. Its main restaurant, decked out in a nautical theme, was aptly called Port of Call.

Two years before the Marina was built, Kerkorian had opened the doors to his MGM Grand Hotel and Casino less than a mile down the Strip at Flamingo Road. When it first greeted guests on December 5, 1973, the hotel, set on forty-three acres with 2,084 rooms on twenty-six floors, was one of the largest and certainly one of the most luxurious in the world. It contained two showrooms, the Ziegfeld Stage for spectacular revue shows and the Celebrity Room for head-liner acts.

On November 21, 1980, around seven in the morning, with approximately five thousand people in the MGM Grand, a fire broke out in the Deli, a restaurant adjacent to the casino on the second floor. The flames were mostly contained to that level and the lobby, but toxic fumes and smoke billowed up the elevator shafts and stairwells, all the way to the roof. Eighty-five people were killed in the disaster, most of them from smoke inhalation and carbon monoxide poisoning, and another 650 were injured. Only seven people died in the casino itself. Most of the victims were found in the stairwells on the upper floors.

Despite the severity of the damage, the hotel was renovated and reopened in just eight months. A second residential tower was added in 1981. Five years later, the casino hotel was sold to Bally Entertainment Corporation, and it became Bally's Las Vegas.

In 1989, Kerkorian bought the Marina Hotel and renamed it the MGM Marina. He next acquired the hundred-acre Tropicana Country Club, which was next to the Marina. His original plan was to raze them both, then build a brand new MGM Grand Hotel and Casino on the site. But after consideration he decided to incorporate the old Marina tower into his design for the new megaresort.

When it was finished in 1993, the sprawling MGM Grand was the biggest hotel in the world, with just over five thousand rooms. (With the addition of several guest residential areas in recent years, the hotel's room total now tops 6,800.) Kerkorian, a former owner of Metro-Goldwyn-Mayer, took advantage of his association with the studio to work many of MGM's most famous images into the decor, including the MGM lion and characters from *The Wizard of Oz*.

The Marina rooms, though smaller than the new rooms, were completely remodeled to blend in with the rest of the hotel. Once the outside of the former Marina was painted emerald green to match the other sections, it was hard to tell where one structure ended and the other began. The Marina tower has since been revamped once again and is now promoted as the MGM Grand's exclusive West Wing.

Rumors have circulated for years that both Bally's and the current MGM Grand Hotel are haunted. The former comes as no surprise to paranormal specialists. It just makes sense that there are unsettled spirits among the dozens who perished in the catastrophic fire.

Why phantoms turn up in the West Wing of the new MGM Grand is more of a quandry. The spooks definitely date back before the Marina rooms became part of the present resort, but there doesn't seem to be enough information about the apparitions for anyone to identify them or figure out why they're hanging around.

There have been numerous reports that at least two other Las Vegas casino hotels, the Flamingo and the Hilton, are also haunted. The Flamingo's ghosts date back to the earliest days of the city, when it first became a desert getaway.

In the latter months of 1945, organized crime figures including Benjamin "Bugsy" Siegel traveled west to check out the fledgling Nevada town where gambling and off-track betting were legal. Siegel's first investment was the purchase of the El Cortez Hotel on Fremont Street, in what is now downtown Las Vegas.

Seven miles away on what would one day become the Strip, William R. "Billy" Wilkerson, the owner of the *Hollywood Reporter* as well as Ciro's and the Cafe Trocadero nightclubs on the Sunset Strip, had started work on a hotel of his own. He quickly became strapped for cash, however, and he had to turn to Siegel and his partners for financing. In the end, Wilkerson wound up with only a one-third interest in the property.

Siegel knew nothing about hotel construction, but he muscled his way into the day-to-day operations. Soon there were delays and enormous cost overruns, neither of which enamored him to "the boys" back East. Finally, the 105-room Pink Flamingo Hotel and Casino opened the day after Christmas, 1946. Folklore has it that Siegel named the place for his girlfriend, Virginia Hill, whom he had nicknamed Flamingo because of her long legs.

The hotel had cost $6 million, an astronomical sum at the time. That would have been acceptable if gamblers had flocked to its doors as promised. But they didn't. Then, from

January to March 1947, the hotel had to be closed while construction was completed.

To say that Siegel's "investors" were not pleased would be an understatement, and there was talk that Siegel was skimming money. By spring, the casino was starting to turn a profit, but it was too little too late. In a mob hit that continues to be shrouded in mystery, Bugsy Siegel was gunned down on June 20, 1947, while sitting alone in the living room of Hill's Beverly Hills mansion.

Siegel is buried in the Hollywood Forever Cemetery in California, but that's not where his spectre has chosen to reappear. His apparition, sometimes accompanied by that of Hill, has been spotted back at the Flamingo, walking through the rose garden in the central outdoor courtyard or upstairs in one of the presidential suites. Perhaps the hotel is where Bugsy's heart and soul really lie, but his materialization is a bit puzzling. The Flamingo Hotel and Casino that's standing today is an entirely different structure (or, more precisely, collection of structures) than the hotel built by Siegel.

In 1967, Kirk Kerkorian purchased the property. Six years later, he sold it to the Hilton Corporation, which rechristened it the Flamingo Hilton in 1974. Over the next twenty years, additional hotel towers were built on the property. In December 1993, the last remaining section of the original Pink Flamingo was torn down to make way for the hotel's famed garden oasis. After another change of ownership in 1998, the Hilton name was dropped, and the following year the hotel adopted its current moniker, the Flamingo Las Vegas.

As for Siegel's ghost holding court at the current incarnation of the Flamingo, it's not unheard of for spirits to show up in new buildings that occupy the same space as those they formerly haunted.

The Las Vegas Hilton, a mile or two east of the Strip on Paradise Road, opened in 1969. It has just shy of 3,200 rooms, a casino, and its own convention center. (The separate Las Vegas Convention Center is right next door.) The hotel, originally called the International Hotel, was built by Kirk Kerkorian. (Is that name starting to ring a bell?)

From its inception the place was known for its star showroom, which was inaugurated by Barbra Streisand. The shows by the lounge's next headliner, Elvis Presley, are mythic: fifty-eight sold-out performances, followed by equally exciting appearances in 1970 and 1972. For most of the rest of the 1970s, the Hilton's resident superstar was Liberace.

On February 10, 1981, just three months after the devastating fire at the MGM Grand, an arsonist set flames to the Las Vegas Hilton. Because of safety procedures introduced after the MGM misfortune, only eight lives were lost at the Hilton.

The Hilton *is* haunted, but not by any of the people who died there. Instead, one of the spectres belongs to the very recognizable Elvis. No less than Wayne Newton, himself, synonymous with the Vegas Strip, claimed that he saw the King of Rock and Roll's apparition backstage at the hotel.

Liberace turns up, too, and he's quite a prankster. Stagehands say that they sometimes hear him singing or his very distinct laughter, and they blame him when their tools disappear from one place and turn up in another.

Mister Showmanship, as the flamboyant pianist/entertainer was known, gets around. His phantom also visits his namesake museum in Las Vegas as well as the Tivoli Gardens

Restaurant next door. Liberace owned the shopping center in which both are located. He opened the Italian-American restaurant in 1983, personally supervised its decoration, and was known to cook there for friends.

Lee—as his friends called him—died just four years later in 1987. The restaurant closed for a little over a year until Carluccio's, a popular eatery on East Tropicana, bought it and relocated there in 1988. Patrons began to notice unusual activity in the bistro almost immediately: shadowy movements, things falling off shelves, unexplained sounds. According to John Hosier, who purchased the restaurant in 1999, anomalies persist. Toilets flush themselves, there are unexplainable cold spots, and electricity and kitchen appliances go on the fritz. The phenomena seem to occur most often on Liberace's birthday and the anniversary of his death.

They say that what happens in Vegas stays in Vegas. That might help explain why so many spirits have chosen to remain there.

Chapter 8

The Ben Lomond
Banshees

Ben Lomond Suites
Ogden, Utah

Some hotels can claim one or two resident ghosts. The Ben Lomond
Suites Hotel has at least six. Most of the spectres seem to date from
the 1940s to the 1970s, but some may have been around for even
longer. The hotel's been there in one form or another for more than
a hundred years. .

Jay loved trains. All trains. Even the modern if impersonal
Amtrak cars and the Bullet Train in Japan. But his real passion was the old steam engines, the smoke-bellowing work-
horses that built America—so much so he only allowed
trains led by steam engines to run on the tracks of the
model railroad that had overtaken his garage.

Yes, Jay was a "railfan" (that one-word nickname given
to real devotees), but he was no foamer (as excessive enthusiasts are sometimes known) and certainly not an FRN (a
comically derisive and unprintable acronym—delicately, an
"effen rail nut"—reserved for the most over-the-top rail
zealots).

As he grew up, Jay had plenty of opportunity to visit
the many railroad museums scattered throughout the Northeast. But his great ambition in life, his dream, had always
been to one day travel west to Utah to stand on Promontory

Summit, where back in 1869 a ceremonial golden spike was driven to link the United Pacific and Central Pacific rail lines, creating the first transcontinental railroad.

(Jay scoffed at those who erroneously called the site Promontory Point, which is actually thirty-five miles south of the Summit. Intellectually, he understood the mistake: Newspapermen had reported the wrong location, and the error has stuck all these years. What he couldn't comprehend was why people cared so little about such an important event in American history. Maybe, Jay mused, he *was* a closet FRN.)

When, after thirty years of working in the same office, Jay's company was downsized and he was offered early retirement and a generous severance package, he jumped at the chance. He would now be free to take his fantasy vacation: a nationwide road trip by rail. He'd head west on the California Zephyr, which passed through a spectacular cut in the Rockies between Denver and Grand Junction, and then return on the Southwest Chief.

He'd have to travel down to Los Angeles to make the loop, but he really didn't care whether he made it all the way to the coast. The only essential stop was the visit to Promontory. And so, that following spring, Jay set out. His plan was to be at the Golden Spike National Historic Site on May 10, the anniversary of the date on which the fabled spike had been driven, when there would be a reenactment of the ceremony, including two steam engines meeting nose-to-nose on the same track.

The national park wasn't the easiest place to get to, as least not by train. Rail service over the summit had been discontinued in 1904 when a trestle was built across the Great Salt Lake to allow locomotives to cut out a steep grade and forty-three miles of curves. The nearest city of any size is Ogden, Utah, but in order to get there, Jay first had to travel into Salt Lake City, then take a commuter rail, the FrontRunner, for the last forty miles into Ogden. After that, Jay would have to rent a car to travel the fifty-six miles west to Promontory Summit.

But for Jay, it would all be worth it.

By the time he made it to Ogden, after so much time in sleeper cars on the train, Jay welcomed a couple of nights in a real bed. He decided to spend them in luxury, in one of the city's most historic hotels, the Ben Lomond Suites.

In 1891, E. A. Reed built a four-story hotel, which he named after himself, at the corner of Washington Boulevard and Twenty-fifth Street. A. Perry, the president and cofounder of the Ogden Bank, rightly reasoned that a rapidly growing city like Ogden needed first-class lodgings, so in 1926 he formed a corporation with three hundred stockholders to purchase the Reed Hotel and completely remodel it.

Perry engaged Utah architects Hodgson & McClenahan to transform the building. Their first step was to raze and refurbish the interior of the Reed while letting the basic structure stand. An eight-story L-shaped tower with 350 guest rooms was attached to the rear of the original hotel.

The new overall design was Italian Renaissance Revival. The exterior of the base, some of the lower floors, and the uppermost stories were faced with terra-cotta. The interior public rooms were adorned in a cacophony of styles, from Florentine flourishes to the LeConte Stewart murals in the sitting area known as the Shakespeare Room. Dark wood paneling was used in the English Room to re-create a chamber in Britain's Bromley Castle. The Georgian Room, located on the mezzanine, had neoclassical ornamentations associated with eighteenth-century Scottish architect Robert Adam. Even the coffee shop was festively festooned in an Arabian theme. There was enough meeting space to seat a thousand for dinner, as well as several small lounges, in-house shops, and a bank. Fireproofing was installed throughout. In all, $1.2 million was spent in the hotel's renovation. The newly rechristened Bigelow Hotel opened to universal acclaim in 1927, instantly ranking it with the top hotels in the state.

In 1933, Marriner S. Eccles, another Utah banker, purchased the Bigelow, added a two-story penthouse, and renamed the building the Ben Lomond Hotel. (Eccles is better remembered for his time in government than as a hotelier. He was instrumental in creating the Federal Deposit Insurance Corporation (FDIC), helped craft the Emergency Banking Act of 1933, and was head of the Federal Reserve for fourteen years, serving under both FDR and Truman.)

The Ben Lomond Hotel was a mainstay of the community for more than forty years. It then passed through a number of owners, including, for a time, Weber County, which used it for government offices. (Weber County still utilizes the hotel's fourth floor.) In the 1980s, the property was acquired by the Radisson chain, which converted the guest rooms into ninety-seven suites and twenty-three condos (the latter of which are all located on the tenth and eleventh floors). The hotel was listed on the National Register of Historic Places in 1990.

After dragging himself the long three and a half blocks from Union Station to the hotel, Jay couldn't have cared less about its illustrious past. By the time he had finally entered the lobby, he barely noticed the crystal chandeliers and marble floor. All he could think about was getting a good night's sleep. He'd start out fresh first thing in the morning. He pampered himself by taking a condo for his two nights' stay, and armed with his key for 1102, he headed for the elevator. Once inside the room, he quickly showered and dropped into bed, a dead weight. He was out as soon as his head hit the pillow.

To quote a cliché, he felt like a new man the next morning. He picked up his car, then, map in hand, headed out toward Golden Spike National Park.

Jay knew that almost nothing he would see there was original. Back in 1869, as soon as the speeches were over and the press photographs were taken, the original spike was removed for safekeeping and replaced with a regular iron spike. (Jay made a mental note that one day he would visit the Cantor Arts Center in Stanford, California, where the original Golden Spike is on permanent display.) Even the mile-long track of rail in the park isn't the real McCoy. The rails across Promontory Summit had been pulled up in 1942 and reused in military depots as part of the war effort. The two steam engines at the park are also replicas of the Union Pacific's coal-burning No. 119 and the Jupiter, Central Pacific's wood-burning No. 60.

During the winter season, the new locomotives are kept in an engine house to protect them from the elements. But on Saturday during the summer months and on special occasions such as the May 10 anniversary, the engines move out onto the park's single stretch of track and cautiously approach one another until they're just a few feet apart. That year, Jay, along with railroad aficionados from all over the country, was treated to the thrill of a lifetime as the mighty locomotives steamed into view.

It was late afternoon by the time Jay got back to the hotel. The sun seemed high enough in the sky, but deep shadows had already begun to fall on the foothills. Jay looked up to the Wasatch Mountains overlooking the city. To the east he could plainly make out Mount Ogden and, to the north, the peak of Ben Lomond, from which his hotel got its name.

What a beautiful setting, thought Jay. Ogden had been founded in 1846 by a fur trapper named Miles Goodyear. The settlement, which he named Fort Buenaventura, was at the juncture of the Ogden and Weber Rivers, about a mile west of the current downtown. The following year, Mormon settlers bought the budding community, by then known as Brownsville. The town's name was changed once again, to Ogden, to honor Peter Skene Ogden, a trader and expedition leader for the Hudson's Bay Company.

By 1869 the population stood at ten to fourteen thousand. Ogden quickly became a railroad hub, earning it the nickname Junction City. At the time, most passengers traveling from San Francisco to Chicago passed through Ogden rather than the much larger Salt Lake City. The Ben Lomond Suites had been built to accommodate many of those travelers.

It had been a long day. As Jay headed back to his room, he decided he needed a long, hot bath. He could use a good soak after so many days jostling across the country by train. He could already see himself drawing the water, making sure it was just the right temperature, and slipping in. It would be heaven!

But as soon as he opened the door to his room, he immediately knew something was wrong. Water was already running in the bathroom! He rushed in, and sure enough, a slow but steady stream was splashing into the jetted tub. Fortunately the drain was open. Had he left the tap on when he took off in the morning? Or had housekeeping made the error?

Well, no real harm done, Jay decided. Within just a few minutes, he had immersed himself into the generous tub and allowed his mind to drift back to what had been a perfect day. The weather, which could be tricky at that time of year, had been on its best behavior. The crowds hadn't been too large, so he had been able to take hundreds of unobstructed photographs of the engine run and the costumed actors pounding an ersatz Golden Spike into place.

Without warning, Jay felt something prod at him, pushing against his back. Was his mind playing tricks, or was it just the water jets? Then, not ten seconds later, he felt what seemed to be invisible hands pressing hard against his arm and side. Something, some unseen force, wanted him out of the tub!

Jay took the hint. He leapt out, quickly toweled off, and lay down on the bed. His mind raced. What had just happened? There had to *some* explanation for what he had felt.

He never came up with an answer. If he had only thought to ask the front desk clerk on his way out the next morning, he would at least have gone away with some clues. It was policy not to discuss such matters, but the receptionist might have shared some of the rumors about the ghosts inhabiting the Ben Lomond Suites Hotel, including the room in which Jay had stayed.

According to an old wives' tale—and there are no specific names or dates ever attached to the story—a woman on her honeymoon accidentally drowned in the bathtub in Room 1102. Ever since, occupants have occasionally been startled to find the water running, even though no one had turned on the faucets. Many people reported feeling unseen hands shoving them in the tub.

Another spirit, the drowning victim's son (from the woman's previous marriage), went to the hotel to pick up some personal effects his mother had left behind. He chose to stay in 1101, next door to the room where she died. Sometime in the middle of the night, overcome with despair, he committed suicide.

Guests and staff alike have heard the soft, incomprehensible voices of both phantoms in those rooms, and housekeeping has discovered unexplainable depressions on the beds that looked as if someone had been lying on them. According to some reports, every so often, the apparitions even materialize.

At least one other room on the eleventh floor is haunted. Receptionists have gotten telephone calls from Room 1106 at times when they knew no one was staying there. As soon as the clerk would speak, the line would go dead. Legend has it that the mystery caller is the spectre of a woman who stayed at the Ben Lomond while waiting for her son to return from World War II. Some sources claim she found out that he had been killed. Regardless, the woman stopped eating and eventually starved to death in that very room. (Yet another variation of the tale says that the anxious mother checked out of the hotel very much alive, but for some reason her apparition has returned to make those pesky phone calls.)

A female spirit has been caught roaming the corridors. She's thought to be Eccles's wife, presumably his first wife, Mary (also known as Maysie), to whom the tycoon was married when he bought the hotel. (Eccles and his second wife stayed more often at the apartments he maintained in San

Francisco and at the Hotel Utah in Salt Lake City.) Even when Maysie isn't visible, people know when she's around by her distinctive lilac perfume. The scent is evident most often on the fifth floor, the top floor, and in the elevators.

A ghost in the lobby has never been seen, but his presence is certainly felt. He's believed to be a night clerk who was stabbed to death by a fifteen-year-old boy while the youth was robbing the hotel in 1976. The sixty-five-year-old spirit apparently hangs out by the reception desk, turning on the sound system to play music in the foyer and fiddling with the phone cords.

A security guard has run across a noncorporeal entity (thought to be female) in the third-floor gymnasium, and guests in Room 212 have been subject to spectral hands shoving them out of the way.

There's been a lot of other paranormal activity in the hotel that's never been pinned down to a particular banshee. There are strange cold spots found throughout the hotel, the sounds of footsteps and closing doors, and the echo of phantom people moving around overhead. Then, too, the elevators sometimes act up. They'll stop on their own at the fifth or the tenth floor, despite the fact that the call button hasn't been pushed for either.

None of the spirits—and we're talking about at least six—is ever malicious, so there's never any danger to visitors. And in a way, it's nice to know they're there. They contribute yet another chapter to the long and continuing story of one of Utah's most celebrated inns, the Ben Lomond Suites Hotel.

Chapter 9

"Here's Johnny . . ."

Stanley Hotel
Estes Park, Colorado

Stephen King may have been inspired to write The Shining *during his stay at the Stanley Hotel, but the paranormal activity that takes place there is anything but fictional. The whole fourth floor appears to be haunted. As are the billiards room, and the bar, and the ballroom, and the . . .*

Cameron couldn't believe it. He was actually checking into Room 217 at the Overlook—rather, the Stanley Hotel—in Estes Park, Colorado. This was the very same room where Stephen King stayed when he visited the hotel and the one that featured so prominently (as the Overlook) in the author's third novel, *The Shining*. Cameron had planned the weekend a full year in advance to be sure the room was available.

Cameron was a King fanatic. As far as he knew, he had read everything the guy had ever published, including the books he wrote under the pen name Richard Bachman as well as the story he released as John Swithen. Cameron's favorites? Well, it was hard for him to pick, but they were probably the early ones: *Carrie,* King's first book, *Salem's Lot,* which followed, and, needless to say, *The Shining.*

As Cameron opened the door to the room, he was immediately struck by the spectacular sight of the Rockies on the other side of the window. (The hotel was only a few miles down the road from the entrance to Rocky Mountain National Park.) This was the view King had talked about in interviews. Soon after falling asleep, King had an unsettling dream that his three-year-old son, Joe, was running down a hotel corridor, chased by a fire hose. (*Perhaps the hallway is the one right outside my room*, Cameron thought.) King woke from the nightmare, got out of bed, lit a cigarette, sat in a chair by the window, and gazed out at the mountains. By the time the cigarette was finished, he had conceived the bare bones of what would become *The Shining*.

The plot of the book is straightforward enough. A former teacher, wannabe writer, and recovering alcoholic with anger issues named Jack Torrance takes a position as the winter caretaker of the Overlook Hotel, which is almost completely cut off from civilization once the snows fall. Along for the stay is his wife, Wendy, and their young son, Danny, who is sensitive to ghostly spirits. While getting ready to leave the property for the season, the desk clerk, Dick Hallorann, tells Danny he shares the boy's paranormal abilities, which the man calls "shining." The hotel turns out to be infested by sinister phantoms, and when they are unable to take control of Danny. The apparitions take possession of Jack, who then attempts to murder his wife and son. Danny uses his shining to psychically call out to Hallorann for assistance. The clerk returns to help Wendy and the boy in the final, violent battle with Jack. They narrowly escape just as the hotel—and presumably Jack—is blown up in a boiler explosion.

After the success of King's first two novels, his publisher was concerned he would be pigeonholed in the horror genre. That didn't worry King. But the stories in both books had taken place in his native Maine. He figured he had to do a bit of reseach if he wanted to set his next novel someplace else, so he spread out a map on the table. He put down his finger randomly and found he had pointed to Colorado. King took the plunge. In 1974 he bundled up his wife, Tabitha, and two children and moved to Boulder.

After about six months, he and Tabitha wanted to have a night out without the kids, so they booked an evening at the Stanley Hotel in nearby Estes Park. The Georgian-style hotel, with its 138 rooms, white walls, red roof, and golden-dome lookout tower, had opened on July 4, 1909. It was built by Freelan Oscar Stanley, who, with his twin brother, Francis, was the inventor of the steam-powered automobile known as the Stanley Steamer.

F. O. Stanley was born into a farming family in Maine in 1849, one of seven children. Inveterate tinkerers, F.O. and Francis came up with the first model of their revolu-tionary vehicle in 1897. Within two years, they had built a factory and were manufacturing up to ten cars a day. Interestingly, they sold the business to an investor, but he was unable to keep the operation profitable. The brothers bought back their own company and once again made it successful.

In the winter of 1903, F. O. Stanley came down with tuberculosis. The prognosis was not good: His doctor told him he would probably die within the year. He suggested that the entrepreneur move to Colorado in the hopes that the fresh mountain air would give him a new lease on life. Indeed, it did. That summer, Stanley and his wife, Flora, trekked to Estes Park and took up residence in a cottage belonging to a friend of their doctor. Within days, Stanley's condition began to reverse itself, and just a few months later he was once again his robust self. Amazingly, despite his doctor's dire prediction, he would live until 1940 to the age of ninety-one.

By the time autumn approached, the Stanleys had already decided they were going to stay in Colorado. They built a mansion similar to the one they had left behind in New England. But that wasn't all. Stanley decided to go into the hotel business.

In the early 1870s, the British Earl of Dunraven had surreptitiously bought up much of what is today Estes Park through second and third parties in order to create a private hunting reserve for himself and his friends. When the scheme became known, other settlers in the area opposed Dunraven. Although he never put his plan into effect, he held onto the property until 1907, when he was forced to sell some six thousand acres. Among the buyers was Stanley.

Many thought Stanley's dream to build a resort hotel on 160 acres in the foothills of the Rockies—7,500 feet above sea level—was foolhardy. At that time, there was no railroad linking Denver and Estes Park, and it was a difficult journey on dirt roads. To prove that guests would have no problem reaching the lodge, Stanley drove one of his own Steamers up to the property.

Stanley designed the hotel himself, and construction began in 1907. It would be a luxury getaway costing about a half million dollars to build—which Stanley was able to pay in cash. There were facilities for tennis, golf, and trap shooting, and a power plant (also designed by the industrious Stanley) to provide electricity. There was running water in all rooms as well as telephones. Built for seasonal use, however, heat wasn't installed in the Stanley until around 1979. (To this day, the rooms, like many homes in the Rockies, are not air-conditioned in the summer, but have ceiling fans.)

From the beginning Stanley's intent was to cater to the rich and famous. Even during the Depression, when business was slow, Stanley wouldn't allow anyone who did not meet his standards to stay there. As a result of its exclusivity, the elite hotel was immediately popular with celebrities and titans of industry. Among the first visitors to the Stanley were Harvey Firestone, J. C. Penney, Dr. William Mayo, John Philip Sousa, "The Unsinkable" Margaret "Molly" Brown, and Theodore Roosevelt. More recently, Cary Grant, Doris Day, Bob Dylan, Billy Graham, astronaut Scott Carpenter, and the emperor and empress of Japan have been guests. As has Stephen King.

The author and his wife arrived at the Stanley Hotel on October 30, 1974, the night before Halloween, unaware the hotel was about to close the very next day for the winter season. They were the only two guests in the entire place and were lodged in Room 217. Dinner in the Cascades Restaurant that night must have seemed awfully strange: They were the only patrons. Their table was the only one that was set, and there was only one meal available on the menu.

After dinner, King's wife went back to their room, but her always-inquisitive husband wanted to roam through the sprawling hotel. With no other guests and no activities going on, King could hear every squeak, rumble, and imagined whisper the old lodging had to offer.

Now it was Cameron's turn. He wanted to inspect the place for himself, like King had. With about two hours to kill before suppertime, he headed up to the fourth story. From there he would descend, floor by floor, until he reached the lobby—looking, listening, trying to catch wind of anything otherworldly that might be in the air.

But nothing. Whether it was because there were so many people around, because it was too light out, or the spirits just weren't feeling playful, Cameron didn't hear or see a thing out of the ordinary. *Oh, well,* he laughingly told himself, *I guess I just don't have the shining.*

Of course, he knew the Stanley was not the Overlook. In fact, not a single frame of the 1980 Stanley Kubrick film version of *The Shining* was shot at the Stanley Hotel, though many scenes from the 1997 TV miniseries were. (The inn also stood in for the Hotel Danbury in the movie *Dumb and Dumber,* but Cameron couldn't care less about that.)

He walked down the last flight of stairs and surveyed the broad lobby, with its gleaming hardwood floors and sumptuous decor. And there at one end was a restored 1906 Stanley Steamer, a reminder of the hotel's founder. (On his way into the hotel earlier that day, Cameron had seen a Stanley Steamer bus that was used to transport tour groups around the grounds. Originally, the vehicles had been used to ferry guests up the mountain from Lyons.)

As Cameron strolled through the foyer, a light strain of music caught his ear. Soft piano music. It wasn't being piped in over a sound system. No, someone was playing it live. He couldn't make out the melody exactly, but it was sweet, wistful. Thinking the music must be coming from a piano bar—he needed a drink after his tiring walk wandering through the entire building—Cameron followed the sound.

Unexpectedly, it led him not to a cocktail lounge but to an open doorway, on the far side of which was the hotel ballroom. It wasn't set up for an event that night, so he was able to see the entire room at a glance. It was empty. Nevertheless, there was that music. Eventually Cameron's eyes fell on a grand piano at one end of the room. The notes were coming out of it all right, but no one was sitting on the bench. Then his eyes dropped to the keyboard: The keys were moving by themselves in time to the piece of music.

Was it possible?!

Cameron stepped into the room, and the instant he crossed the threshold the music stopped. The keys stood still. Whoever or whatever had been playing was gone.

Cameron staggered out of the deserted room and headed toward the front desk. Would they think he was crazy?

"I hate to bother you," he hesitatingly ventured. "This is going to sound really strange, but . . ."

It was then that Cameron noticed the small brochure lying on the desk in front of him. The flyer was advertising the hotel's ghost tour, which was offered every night to guests and the public alike. So the place *was* haunted!

It was too good to be true. Cameron quickly signed up for the tour, and just two hours later he was back in the lobby joining about twenty other intrepid ghost hunters. As the tour progressed, their guide assured them that—as opposed to the ghosts in *The Shining*—none of the spectres currently inhabiting the Stanley Hotel is evil or malicious.

The most frequently seen is F. O. Stanley himself. He most often shows up in the lobby or in the billiards parlor, which was his favorite room in the hotel. Several bartenders have also spied him walking through their lounges, but whenever they tried to intercept the spectre, he vanished.

And as it turned out, Cameron wasn't alone in what he had experienced in the ballroom. Many people have had the exact same thing happen to them. Always, the spectral music and the moving piano keys stop the instant anyone passes through the doorway. Although no apparition has ever materialized there, it's been decided that the invisible musician is none other than Flora Stanley, who liked to play for guests at the hotel. Her ghost isn't the only one to visit the ballroom. Workers in the adjoining kitchen have heard the noise from a phantom party in full swing when the room was actually empty.

Unexplainable footsteps and noises have been heard all over the building, but nowhere do they occur more often than on the fourth floor. When the hotel first opened, adults stayed on the first three floors, but their children and the nannies stayed on the fourth floor. (Cameron suddenly recalled reading somewhere that, during his single night in the hotel, King had seen the ghost of a little boy calling for his nanny.) Today, guests who stay on the top floor sometimes are disturbed by the sound of children laughing or playing in the hallway. But if the occupants open their doors to complain, there's no one in the passage.

Inside the rooms, children's handprints occasionally appear on the mirrors. Guests have returned to their rooms to discover that their personal belongings have moved around on their own. Some rooms are more active than others. In Room 401, children have been heard singing in the closet, and the windows sometimes fly open by themselves. Lights flick on and off for no reason in Room 407, and the closest elevator has a life of its own. People standing outside the hotel have looked up to see the face of a man looking out its window even when the room was unoccupied. For some reason legend has it that the nameless stranger is Lord Dunraven.

The room that has the most paranormal activity on the fourth floor is 418. Guests who stay there are frequently bothered by the sound of phantom children on the other side of the door, and even when the room is empty, the youngsters' noise emanates from inside. Maids will enter the vacant room to discover indentations on the bedcovering, as if someone had been sitting or lying on it. The place has another strange anomaly: If anyone who is sick walks into the room, his or her symptoms will become more acute. Perhaps that's because, according to rumor, Room 418 used to be set aside for children when they were ill.

The hazy spectre of an unidentified man has been spotted in rooms all over the hotel at night. Sometimes guests will awaken to find him looming over them. When discovered, the ghost runs into the closet or simply vanishes. From time to time the spirit has been blamed for stealing jewelry and baggage, though there's no known reason why he would do so.

The identity of the spectral housekeeper in the room where Stephen King stayed—there are suggestions he may have seen her—is well known. Her name is Miss Wilson. She was working in Room 217 during the early years of the hotel when she was injured in a gas explosion. After her recovery, Stanley employed her for the rest of her life. She remained in the hotel's service until she died of an aneurism forty years later—again, in Room 217. She has gone to her mortal end, but her spirit has stayed at the Stanley, hard at work. Guests find their covers turned down or their luggage unpacked and placed in the closet even though housekeeping hasn't been in the room. Miss Wilson can be mischievous as well. Sometimes she pulls the blankets off visitors in the middle of the night.

Room 217 is on the ghost tour when no one's staying there, but Cameron had it all to himself that night. Or did he? Would Miss Wilson be watching over him as he slept?

That night after crawling into bed, he turned on the TV to help him nod off, but wouldn't you know it? The Stanley

Hotel certainly knew one of its chief claims to fame: There on the in-house cable, playing over and over in an endless cycle, was Kubrick's *The Shining*. Cameron turned up the sound. An ax head was splintering a door. A maniacal Jack Nicholson popped his face through the hole. "Here's Johnny . . ."

A perfect end to a perfect day, Cameron thought as he fell into a deep, contented sleep.

Today, the Stanley Hotel is on the National Register of Historic Places, with eleven buildings set on fifty-five acres. In addition to its accommodations for overnight guests, the hotel offers sixteen thousand square feet of space for meetings and special events. Plus, as many a visitor can attest, plenty of room for the ghosts.

Chapter 10
Shades of
the Old West

St. James Hotel
Cimarron, New Mexico

At least two of the ghosts that inhabit the old St. James Hotel in Cimarron, New Mexico, are holdovers from its raucous Wild West days: one, an inveterate gambler gunned down after winning his biggest stake ever, the other, the wife of the original owner. There may be a phantom cowboy and an unattractive spectre known only as "the Imp" as well. But then, who's counting?

Cheryl *was* Annie Oakley. Well, obviously not literally, but she was going to play the famous sharpshooter during what she hoped would be a fun yet spooky murder-mystery weekend in Cimarron, New Mexico.

Cheryl lived in Taos, the ski resort and arts community, about fifty miles southwest of Cimarron. She'd been reading about the getaway staged at the St. James Hotel for a couple of years, and she'd driven by the place a few times, but (as often happens) she didn't think seriously about doing it until she heard rumors that it might be discontinued. New owners would be taking over the 125-year-old former saloon and completely refurbishing it, and who knew if the "games" would continue?

About two weeks before the event, participants received a "subpoena" in the mail, ordering them to appear to take part in an inquest regarding a murder at the lodgings. They were each given a specific character to play throughout the entire proceedings, many of whom, like Cheryl's, were actual historical people who had some tie to the joint. The twenty or so players—and, indeed, they would be role-playing throughout—were expected to provide their own wardrobe, appropriate to whomever they would be portraying.

Everyone would arrive at the hotel early Friday, get settled, and then gather downstairs with the others, in costume, for the festivities to begin. They would be given clues (including lots of red herrings), act out prepared scenes, and have a chance to search for evidence. Finally, the killer would be revealed late Saturday night.

Cheryl made the turn off US 64 and traveled about a half mile down NM 21 into the center of the dusty town just after noon. The rooms were already prepared, so she was able to check in early. She had deliberately chosen to stay in one of the hotel's original thirteen rooms rather than in the ten-room annex that was added in the 1980s. If she was going to do this thing, she was going to do it right. By two o'clock, she had made her way to Room 17. Except for the modern bathroom facilities and bed, the room probably looked very much the way it did back in the 1870s.

The room really was in a time warp: There was no phone and no TV. They *were* available in the newer rooms, but what would be the adventure in staying in one of those? She hung up some clothes, unpacked her toiletries, opened the window to let in the midday breeze, and laid out her cowgirl outfit on the bed for later. Time to explore.

With only nine hundred or so year-round inhabitants, Cimarron is little more than a village. Its roots date back to the western migration of the pioneers in the nineteenth century. Up until the beginning of the 1800s, the land was occupied solely by Native Americans, primarily the Anasazi, the Jicarille Apaches, and the Utes.

Between 1821 and 1880, the Santa Fe Trail was established as the main wagon trail for those hoping to make the exhausting nine-hundred-mile journey from Missouri down to New Mexico. The "highway" was also used by traders, the federal army during the Mexican-American War, fortune seekers heading to the California gold rush, and, later, stagecoaches. The dirt path fell into disuse after the railroad reached Santa Fe in 1880.

One of the main legs of the trail, the Mountain Branch, crosses today's US 64 and passes right through present-day Cimarron. (The Cimarron Cutoff passes farther south.) Many parts of the trail remain visible. Ruts can be seen out near Philmont Ranch and about thirteen miles south of town off NM 21. The closest section to Cimarron is a thirty-yard-wide basin visible from US 64 near where Cheryl had made the turnoff to Cimarron. She made a note to check it out on her way home on Sunday.

The town also dates to the mid-nineteenth century. In 1842, a trapper named Lucien Bonaparte Maxwell fell in love with a local woman named Luz Beaubrien. Her father, Charles, along with Guadalupe Miranda, the secretary of the territory's governor, owned the 1.7-million-acre Beaubrien-Miranda Ranch in northern New Mexico—the result of a land grant from the governor. As a wedding present, Charles gave the couple fifteen thousand acres of property, on which, in 1858, Maxwell built a two-story mansion on the site of what is today Cimarron. The community, nestled in the foothills of the Sangre de Cristo Mountains, received its official charter four years later and took its name from a Spanish word for "wild" or "unbroken."

Charles Beaubrien died in 1864, naming Maxwell as his heir. Maxwell later bought out all of his father-in-law's partners and other family members to ultimately own all of the original ranch. He welcomed settlers onto the property and did little or nothing to discourage squatters, even after gold was discovered in nearby Elizabethtown. In 1870, Maxwell sold everything (by then known as the Maxwell Land Grant Company) except for his house and 1,200 surrounding acres. He moved shortly thereafter to eastern New Mexico, where he died in 1875.

Meanwhile, Henri Lambert, who had been President Lincoln's personal chef, was working in Elizabethtown. He had come west to get rich after hearing about the gold strike but wound up going back into the restaurant trade. The new Maxwell Land Grant Company convinced Lambert to move to Cimarron to open a saloon and restaurant to serve the town's rough-and-tumble mix of cowboys, miners, and frontiersmen.

The Lambert Inn was an immediate success, and it soon became one of the most notorious bars in the Southwest. And one of the most dangerous. Twenty-two bullet holes still riddle the ceiling of the saloon, now the St. James Hotel's dining room. When the pressed-tin roofing was removed during a refurbishment in 1901, more than four *hundred* bullet holes were found in the beams underneath. (The only reason people weren't killed in the overhead rooms was the double layer of wood between the saloon ceiling and the floorboards above.)

Sensing that Cimarron needed a comfortable place for travelers to stay overnight—and for hungover cowpokes to sleep off a night's revels—Lambert added guest rooms to the adobe structure in 1880. At the time, it was considered deluxe accommodations, one of the first hotels west of the Mississippi to have running water.

By the time the railroad bypassed Cimarron in favor of Santa Fe, gold had been depleted in the area mines, and the boom times were over. The population and the number of visitors to the town immediately declined. The hotel struggled on, however. Lambert died in 1913, his wife thirteen years later. Over the next sixty years, the landmark passed through a number of hands and was vacant for several long periods. Along the way, there had also been a name change to the St. James Hotel. Finally, in 1985, a new owner took over, and the hotel was completely restored with heavy carpets over the hardwood floors, plush velvet drapes, crystal chandeliers, and other period furnishings.

The legacy of the St. James Hotel cannot be disputed. The list of occupants and visitors reads like a Who's Who of the Old West: Wyatt and Morgan Earp, Doc Holliday, Jesse James (who always stayed in Room 14 under his pseudonym R. H. Howard), Robert Ford (who had been a member of the James gang before turning against the outlaw and shooting him), Bat Masterson, Kit Carson, Billy the Kid, Pat Garrett, train robber Black Jack Ketchum, and Gen. Philip Sheridan.

Among the most frequent visitors was gunfighter Clay Allison, who liked dancing naked on the bar after having one drink too many. (That bar can still be found in the dining room.) Allison also liked shooting people. According to most accounts, he personally killed nineteen of the twenty-six men who died in gunfights at the saloon.

Rumor has is that William "Buffalo Bill" Cody once worked for Maxwell and, years later, after his time as an

Indian scout, returned and befriended Lambert. By all accounts he became the godfather of the innkeeper's son, Fred.

Supposedly, Cody also met Annie Oakley for the first time in the old Lambert Inn, but the tale isn't true. Their initial encounter was in New Orleans in 1884 when the *Buffalo Bill Wild West* show was playing the Crescent City. Oakley was also in town, performing in the Sells Brothers Circus. But the story about the two circus legends meeting in Cimarron persists, so Cheryl was more than happy to masquerade as Little Sure Shot for three days—even though Oakley may never have set foot in the St. James.

Cheryl spent most of her afternoon visiting the fifteen buildings and other sites in the Cimarron old historic district, all of which dates from the 1860s and '70s. Following a map she had picked up at the visitor center, she started out at the old well in the town plaza. Next came the Colfax County courthouse, the offices of the *Cimarron News*, a placard marking the site of Lucien Maxwell's homestead, and the Old Mill Museum, which had once been a gristmill named the Aztec Mill, built in 1864 for Maxwell.

Having "done the tour," Cheryl hurried back to the crown jewel of Old Town: the St. James Hotel. It was time to get dressed.

A few hours later, with introductions and instructions for the weekend out of the way, Cheryl enjoyed an early dinner with the other participants. This was the second mystery weekend for one of them, and two others, a husband and wife, were already making plans to return in the future.

Cheryl decided to turn in early. The next day would be a long one. She slowly climbed the wooden staircase to the second floor, the boards audibly creaking in a way only heard in old buildings. She made her way down the short hallway to 17, opened the door, clicked on the light, and walked in.

As she undressed, being careful not to tangle the fringe on her buckskin skirt and jacket, Cheryl slowly became aware of the strong scent of roses in the room. *How strange*, she thought. There were no fresh flowers in the room, and roses were definitely out of season. Nevertheless, the odor was unmistakable.

She crossed to the open window and bent forward across the wide sill. She took a deep whiff, filling her lungs with the clean night air. No, not even a hint of roses. The flowery scent wasn't coming from outside. She leaned back into the room.

Though puzzling, the smell wasn't overpowering. In fact, Cheryl decided, it was kind of nice. She walked to the bed, turned the lights out, and within minutes was fast asleep. An hour passed, then two, then three.

Suddenly, Cheryl found herself wide awake, her eyes unseeing in the dark. It only took an instant for her to remember where she was. Cimarron. *This town must really close up at night*, she thought to herself. There wasn't a hint of light coming through the window.

The window. Something was tapping on the open glass. That's what woke her up: a barely audible yet persistent rapping! Not like a twig scraping along the surface. The sound was more precise, measured, like fingers tapping on a desk.

Reflexively, Cheryl pulled her blanket in close for protection. Was someone trying to sneak into the room? But no, the sounds weren't menacing. The soft, rhythmic beats continued . . . one . . . after . . . the other. Finally, she could stand it no longer. Cheryl jumped out of bed, her eyes now acclimated to the darkened chamber, and rushed to the window.

As she crossed the few steps, the raps became more persistent and pronounced. The taps were also getting louder. And louder. Cheryl reached out, grabbed hold of the latch, and pulled the window shut.

Instantly, the sound stopped.

Dead silence.

Cheryl backed away from window in surprise. How could whatever was causing the disturbance have ceased so abruptly? And why? She ran her hand across the pane, then tested its mounting on the frame. Nothing was loose or rattling. There seemed to be no explanation for what she had just experienced.

And, although Cheryl didn't know it, there wasn't one—at least not an *earthly* explanation. But there *was* a supernatural one. The next morning, when she casually mentioned the incident to the clerk working the front desk, the woman said matter-of-factly, "Oh, you were visited by one of our ghosts, Mary."

It turned out that the St. James Hotel was, indeed, haunted by not one but several spirits from its bygone days. And Cheryl had met one of the inn's most frequent otherworldly tenants: Henri Lambert's wife, Mary. Room 17 used to be her bedroom. It was also where she died.

Mary's apparition never appears, but guests who have stayed in the room have reported the unambiguous, unexplainable scent of roses (the flower that Mary favored) permeating the premises. And if the occupants left the window open at night, invariably they would be awakened by the sound of an invisible hand—Mary's—rapping on the glass. The noise would continue unabated until the window was closed tightly.

There have been lots of other paranormal goings-on in the hotel. Mysterious cold spots are felt all over the inn.

Patrons in the dining room as well as a former owner have claimed that every so often the reflection of a cowboy appears in the mirror over the bar. There are also rumors that the unidentified phantom of a short, pockmarked man nicknamed "the Imp" prowls the halls.

Most of the spectral phenomena takes place on the second floor. Electronic equipment often goes haywire, especially cameras. Lights turn on and off without warning, and personal items will sometimes move by themselves or fall off tables and shelves. Smoking isn't permitted in the hotel, but somehow the clearly identifiable aroma of cigar smoke will occasionally waft down the corridor.

By far, the most intriguing spectre at the St. James Hotel belongs to T. J. Wright. According to legends surrounding his malevolent spirit, the twenty-two-year-old cardsharp was staying in Room 18 when he won the deed to the hotel in a high-stakes poker game. But he never collected. Wright was found in his room, shot to death, the next morning. Ever since, dangerous, poltergeist-like activity has broken out whenever anyone tries to go inside. People say a fresh glass of whiskey is left in the room to placate the vengeful wraith. Otherwise, the room is kept under lock and key, and no one is allowed to enter, even for a quick peek.

The St. James Hotel is open year-round. But Cimarron, despite its rich past, is not exactly on the tourist trail. You have to want to go there. As a result, if you do stay at the inn, it's possible you may be the only overnight guest—at least, among the living. You can rest assured you will not be alone.

Chapter 11
The Menger Mysteries

Menger Hotel
San Antonio, Texas

San Antonio's Menger Hotel was built in 1859, so there's been plenty of time for its more than thirty ghosts to check in. The most-frequently recognized are Richard King, who once kept an apartment at the hotel, and Sallie White, a former maid and murder victim.

Myra couldn't believe it. They were here again. This was where she had met Jorge, while attending a conference in San Antonio. On their last night in town they had managed to get away from their colleagues for a few hours and spend an hour or two walking along this very stretch.

The River Walk, wide parallel pathways set a block below street level, follows along both sides of the San Antonio River as it meanders through the center of town. It's one of the city's most popular tourist destinations, filled with great restaurants, festive bars, galleries, and kiosks overflowing with trinkets and souvenirs. And lots and lots of people. But as they made their way through the crowd, Myra barely noticed them. That night, the only thing that registered was the man strolling beside her.

Jorge felt the same way about Myra. He had grown up locally, not more than a mile or two out of the city. He'd been visiting the water path as long as he could remember. But tonight was different. Tonight he was in love.

And to think the River Walk had almost never been built. Jorge had learned all about it in elementary school. After a severe flood in 1921, plans were drawn up to dam and divert the river so that it would no longer flow through downtown. The existing channel would be paved over and turned into a giant storm drain. Work began on the project five years later, but a farsighted architect named Robert Hugman made an audacious recommendation. He suggested that, rather than convert the riverbed into drainage, a controlled stream of water should be allowed to continue to run through the city. Both sides of the river could then be developed with shops and eateries. Eventually the proposal was accepted, and money from the WPA program allowed construction to begin in 1939. The two-and-a-half-mile riverside pathway was completed seven years later. Now, after almost seven decades, it was impossible to imagine a San Antonio without the River Walk.

Myra and Jorge's first stroll along the waterway was one of the most magical nights that either had ever experienced. By evening's end, they knew that they *had* to see each other again, even though she'd be flying back to Denver the next day and he was headed back home to Austin. Their courtship continued, at first by phone and e-mail. But before long, there were visits back and forth, and after a year of mutually pursuing each other, they married.

Jorge made the move to Colorado. They bought a home in the upscale Greenwood Village area, just south of Denver, and two years after that, their son, Ben, was born.

As the couple's tenth anniversary approached, Myra started hinting that their boy was now old enough that she and Jorge could get away for a weekend, just the two of them. Her doting mother would be more than happy to watch the boy, and little Ben couldn't get enough of his grandma.

But where would they go? The more exotic destinations—Hawaii, Florida—were out of the question. They could only take two nights at most. Maybe one of the spas in Colorado Springs, or perhaps a resort up the mountains.

Leave it to Jorge, still wildly romantic, to come up with the perfect idea. They would go to San Antonio. It would be their first time back since they met.

They decided to splurge and took a suite, the King Ranch Room, at the celebrated Menger Hotel. Now on the National Register of Historic Places, the 316-room hotel officially opened its doors on February 1, 1859. It was built by William Menger, who, after emigrating from Germany, came to San Antonio sometime in the early 1840s.

Menger founded a brewery—the first in Texas—with partner Charles Phillip Degen. The company flourished, and Menger soon set up a hotel next to the factory. The first rooms of the original two-story stone building designed by San Antonio architect John M. Fries opened in 1857. Forty more rooms were added the following year, as well as a tunnel to connect the hotel to the brewery. By the time construction was complete in 1859, the hotel was one of the grandest west of the Mississippi.

In the years following the Civil War, the Menger became the most popular hotel in the region. The city grew in leaps and bounds after the railroad arrived in 1877, so the hotel added an east annex in 1881 to accommodate visitors. The building was enlarged again in 1909 and 1951, and the entire place was completely renovated and modernized in the 1980s.

On the weekend of their anniversary, Myra and Jorge took off early on Friday, and by late afternoon they were following the bellman up to their suite. The young man quickly showed them the amenities, then left them to settle in. The rooms were exquisite, from the Victorian-style furnishings to the large four-poster bed. The suite had been named for Richard King, the founder of the fabled King Ranch. For many years he had kept those very hotel rooms as a private apartment.

King was born in New York City in 1824. He came from a poor Irish family, and his father indentured him to a jeweler when the boy was only nine years old. King fled, stowing away on a ship headed toward Alabama. Rather than putting him ashore after he was discovered, the crew adopted the lad and taught him the ropes. King was a fast and eager learner, and he had his steamboat pilot's license by the time he was sixteen. Two years later, he was running a fleet of boats on the Apalachicola and Chattahoochee Rivers.

In 1847, at the urging of his friend Mifflin Kenedy, King traveled to the Rio Grande River to help him ferry soldiers and supplies during the Mexican-American War. The two, along with other partners, continued to transport goods on the Rio Grande all the way up to 1874. During the Civil War, they expanded their trade to ship supplies in and out of the Confederacy, which they managed to do by sailing their ships under the neutral Mexican flag.

Much of what they carried came from their own ranches. King had started buying huge expanses of land between the Nueces River and the Rio Grande in 1853. At the end of the War Between the States, King owned 146,000 acres. By the time of his death, the King Ranch had grown to more than six hundred thousand.

King married in 1854, and the couple had five children. Because his business dealings took him to San Antonio so often, King rented a suite of rooms at the Menger Hotel on a full-time basis. He spent the last several months of his life in the apartment, and he died there of stomach cancer on April 14, 1885. His funeral was held downstairs in the hotel parlor. King was buried in San Antonio, but after his wife passed in 1925, his remains were disinterred and moved to King Ranch to lie by her side.

Though well known throughout the Southwest, King was far from the most famous person to stay at the Menger Hotel. Guests have included Generals Robert E. Lee and Ulysses S. Grant (presumably at different times), Babe Ruth, Sarah Bernhardt, and Mae West.

Theodore Roosevelt first stayed at the hotel in 1892 while in Texas on a hunting expedition. Six years later he made the Menger Bar his headquarters when he came to town to recruit cowboys to join his Rough Riders. (The bar is a replica of the taproom at the House of Lords Club in London, right down to the cherry wood paneling and the gold-plated spittoon.) Roosevelt's final visit came in 1905, during his presidency, to be honored at a banquet.

Myra and Jorge freshened up and made their way out of the hotel. Instinctively, they turned toward the River Walk. No words had to be spoken. Where else would they spend their first night in town?

The next morning, they slept in late. After an unhurried brunch, they made their way across the plaza for the obligatory visit to the Alamo. Jorge had been there many times as a youngster on field trips, but beyond what he was forced to learn in school, he had never really thought much about the place. Myra had peeked into the mission during that conference a decade earlier—how could she not?—but it had really been checklist tourism: been there, done that. This time, however, as they ambled through the grounds, they fully appreciated the enormous sacrifice that had taken place there.

Built in 1724 as the Mission San Antonio de Valero, the structure was used until 1793 by Spanish missionaries to educate and care for the local Native Americans they converted to Christianity. In the early 1800s, it was used by the Mexican army to house a company of soldiers. The Alamo probably got its name from the soldiers' hometown, Álamo de Parras in the state of Coahuila.

During the War for Texas Independence, more than two hundred men, including co-commanders James Bowie and William B. Travis, as well as Davy Crockett, his company of Tennesseans, and a group of Hispanic volunteers, barricaded themselves in the Alamo to engage Mexican forces led by Gen. Antonio Lopéz de Santa Anna. The army laid siege to the mission beginning on February 23, 1836. On March 6, the soldiers finally stormed the fort and breeched its walls. The brave defenders fought to the very last man.

After their visit to the mission, Myra and Jorge spent the remainder of their afternoon arm in arm, leisurely poking in and out of little arts-and-crafts boutiques in the La Villita district. By six o'clock, they were back at the hotel, getting ready for their last night in Fiesta City. Then it was off to a slow boat ride on the river, followed by a light dinner on the waterside patio of Casa Rio, the first restaurant to open on the River Walk. Drinks came next at the Menger Bar—tossing back a few in memory of old Teddy—then up to the room for an intimate evening alone.

Or so they thought.

It was about midnight. The pair were lounging in the outer room, Myra standing by the window, gazing absent-mindedly down at lovers passing on the street below. Jorge was flipping through channels on the TV, even though he had no real interest in watching anything. Myra turned back toward the sofa, and her mouth dropped open. The shadowy figure of a man was walking across the far side of the room, seemingly oblivious to everything around him. Jorge caught Myra's eye, then followed it until he, too, saw the spirit.

The mysterious stranger neither spoke nor acknowledged the young couple. He was handsome, ruggedly built, probably in his fifties, with wavy black hair and a long, full goatee but no moustache. He wore a jacket and vest that seemed to date to the nineteenth century. In a determined stride, the apparition walked straight toward the wall separating the room from the hallway—and passed right through!

As quickly as it had appeared, the spectre was gone.

Myra and Jorge turned to each other and simultaneously cried out an incredulous, "Did you see that?" They had heard that the hotel was haunted. It was no big secret. But they never expected in a million years that they would actually see one of the ghosts. But they knew who it was from one of the old photographs they had seen in the lobby. It was none other than the suite's longtime eponymous occupant, Capt. Richard King.

Apparently the otherworldly experience of our anniversary couple is not all that unusual. For whatever reason, whether it's because King was fond of the suite during his life or because it's where his spirit left his body, he has decided to remain behind at the Menger. His apparition has been seen all over the hotel, but it most often appears in his namesake suite, walking through the wall where a door once stood.

King's ghost is only one of thirty-two different phantoms that have been spotted in the hotel. One is unmistakable: Teddy Roosevelt returns to the Menger Bar off the lobby, where he sits quietly nursing a drink. Bully!

Another spectre is that of Sallie White, a young maid who used to work at the Menger. Her abusive husband attacked her in the hotel on March 26, 1876, fatally injuring her. She died two days later. The hotel paid the $32 for her funeral expenses. Perhaps it's out of gratitude or loyalty that her ghost lingers in the hallways she used to service. She wears a period uniform—a long gray skirt and her hair tied back by a scarf around her forehead—and she's seen carrying clean towels and linen to the rooms.

The identity of the other spirits is uncertain. Staff members have often approached one, an elderly woman dressed in a nineteenth-century-style blue dress and wearing wire-rimmed glasses. She always sits by herself, knitting in the hotel's original lobby. If anyone tries to speak to her, she instantly disappears.

One overnight guest in the hotel reported that an ethereal intruder, dressed in gray pants and a buckskin coat, appeared by the side of his bed. The ghost seemed to be arguing with an unseen spirit. The spectral man demanded, "Are you gonna stay or are you gonna go?" three times, then faded into nothingness.

Oftentimes, the paranormal visitors don't become visible but find other ways to let their presence be known.

Kitchen utensils will sometimes move themselves from one place to another or float in the air. Now and then, heavy footsteps are heard around the building, and at least one pair of weathered military boots such as the ones worn at the Battle of the Alamo have been discovered in a fourth-floor office.

Probably this last claim is just an old wives' tale, since no one seems to know what became of what would be tangible, irrefutable evidence of spectral materialization. But the story does make one wonder if a couple of restless souls from the massacre ever wandered the few hundred yards across the plaza from the mission into the hotel.

The Alamo, it seems, is haunted, too. After Santa Anna captured the makeshift fortress, he commanded that all of the defenders' bodies be thrown into a mass grave and the mission be torn down. He soon left the area, having other battles to fight. The workers who were left behind dutifully buried the dead, but they never carried out the general's second order. It's said that when they tried to break down the Alamo's walls, ghostly hands bearing flaming torches emerged from the stone to stop them. Some heard disembodied voices threatening to kill anyone who touched the building. Needless to say, the men scattered and never returned to the scene. It's been said that, to this day, phantoms occasionally pop out of the walls at night.

Remember the Alamo! As unlikely as all the ghostly tales about it and the Menger Hotel may seem, there have been too many to dismiss out of hand.

Chapter 12

The Belle of
New Orleans

Le Pavillon Hotel
New Orleans, Louisiana

It was quite a day for Dana as she undertook the Herculean task of visiting ten haunted hotels, all within a few blocks of each other. The surprise didn't come until she returned to the hotel where she was staying, where she literally bumped into the apparition of a lost teenage girl.

Dana made her list and checked it twice. She had devised a walking tour of the French Quarter that encompassed almost a dozen different hotels. What made this expedition so special was that virtually every one of the lodgings was supposed to be haunted.

She knew that New Orleans, founded on the banks of the Mississippi River by Jean Baptiste LaMoyne, Sieur de Bienville in 1718, was believed to be one of the most haunted cities in America. Much of the reputation, no doubt, came from its being the unofficial home of voodoo in the United States. The mysterious belief, a blend of religion, magic, and superstition, arrived in the Crescent City with the importation of Caribbean slaves. Soon, it was established in the Cajun culture. Rumors persist that one of its most famous practitioners, Marie Laveau, the Voodoo Queen, who died in 1881, still walks down St. Ann Street in the Vieux Carré. Her spirit also comes back to her old house as well as the area around her mausoleum in St. Louis Cemetery No. 1. In the graveyard, she appears in the form of a large black crow or, on occasion, a coal black hellhound.

Dana would try to stop by the cemetery if she had time, but first: the hotels. She made her plans carefully. She was staying at Le Pavillon, nicknamed the Belle of the South. But she didn't choose it for its plush furnishings and accommodations. She picked it because it was reputed to be the most haunted hotel in the city.

One of its most reliable phantoms is a ghostly middle-aged couple, dressed in 1920s-era finery, who are seen holding hands or walking arm in arm as they wander through the hotel. They are easy to recognize: The man has a mustache, wears a hat, and sometimes carries a cane or umbrella. There's also always the scent of a strong cigar when he's near. The woman has dark hair, wears a blue gown, and carries a purse. They're not believed to have married. Her perfume is sometimes detected in the third-floor room where she used to stay, and the odor of a cigar lingers on the fourth floor, where he roomed. The scent of tobacco is especially strong between the evening hours of seven and midnight.

Their story is a sad one. The two used to meet at Le Pavillon surreptitiously. On one of their trysts, the man died of a heart attack while walking back to the hotel. His spectre showed up in the building almost immediately; hers joined him after her death in the 1960s. They are sometimes seen separately, but they always seem to be together throughout the afternoon.

There are other apparitions in the hotel as well, including a resident hippie. The guy wears 1960s or '70s clothing: a bright shirt with billowing sleeves, bell-bottom pants with a large belt buckle . . . and no shoes. The young man, in his late teens or early twenties, runs down the corridors and sometimes vanishes as he walks through walls. Now and then people catch a glimpse of him in the hotel mirrors as well. He's also a bit of a Peeping Tom. Guests have seen him staring at them from outside the window—even when they're staying on the upper floors. He's the one who's usually blamed when personal objects move about on their own or guests feel their bedding being pulled by invisible hands in the middle of the night.

Then there's the ghost of a little old lady in a flimsy black nightgown who sits down on the bed next to guests—mostly men—while they're trying to get to sleep. Holy succubus!

Dana thought that, with so many ghosts at Le Pavillon, she might get lucky during her two nights there and see one of them. But she also had a backup plan. She had picked up a map at the city's visitor center and pinpointed ten hotels in the French Quarter that were supposed to be haunted. (Le Pavillon is located just a few blocks outside the Quarter.) By starting first thing in the morning, Dana would be able to get to all of the hotels in one day.

She knew that she was probably on a fool's errand. The chances of catching a spook were slim to none. Spirits don't appear on any schedule, and they're least likely to show up in broad daylight. But she figured it was worth a shot. With so many hotels and so many ghosts purported to be haunting them, who knew?

Bright and early the next morning, Dana was up and out. First on her list: the Dauphine Orleans Hotel. She walked the half block up Poydras to Baronne, then turned right. In just five blocks, she hit Canal Street and the beginning of the

French Quarter. As Baronne crossed Canal, it became Dauphine. Just three more blocks, and she was at her first stop.

This was going to be easier than she had imagined. Realizing that the farthest hotel on her list was only about twelve blocks away, Dana relaxed. There was no need to rush. She could take her time and recheck her notes along the way. She reached into her bag, pulled out her journal, and began to read:

Dauphine Orleans Hotel, 415 Dauphine St. The first buildings on this site date back to 1775. The main building was constructed in the 1800s. Like most houses from this time period, it was laid out around a central courtyard. James Audubon is said to have stayed in a cottage on the grounds around 1821 or 1822 while painting part of his *Birds of America*. The hotel bar was once an infamous house of ill repute known as May Baily's Place, which dates back to, at the latest, 1857.

The phantom of a woman—May Baily?—has been spotted moving the bottles behind the bar, and customers sometimes mistake the spectres of ladies dressed in typical nineteenth-century bordello attire for costumed performers. The shade of a Civil War soldier meanders through the courtyard outside the former saloon, and the beds in the guest rooms sometimes shake or bounce up and down on their own, primarily in the very early morning or late in the afternoon.

Dana strolled through the foyer and out into the center court. She looked from end to end, but, as she suspected would be the case, there were no military men there, real or imagined. She could pinpoint Baily's, though: There was a symbolic red light hanging from the wall out front. But it was too early in the day for *any* kind of activity to be going on inside the bar. Unfortunately, there was no way for Dana to check whether the beds were minding their manners in the guest rooms, so it was back out onto Dauphine Street.

She backtracked two blocks toward Canal Street, then turned left onto Iberville. One block down she was at number 800, the Chateau Bourbon Hotel. Now a Wyndham Hotel, the Chateau Bourbon started life as the Orleans Ballroom, built by John Davis in 1817. Plantation owners and other members of high society would dance away the evening on the gleaming floor, with chandeliers of European glass sparkling high overhead. Beginning in the 1820s, masquerade balls were held there, presaging the modern Mardi Gras celebrations.

The Civil War years took their toll, and by 1881 the building was under the ownership of the Sisters of the Holy Family, an order of African-American nuns. They transformed the facilities into a convent, a school for girls (the St. Mary's Academy), a small hospital, and an orphanage. When the sisterhood moved out in the 1960s, the place was once again repurposed, this time into the hotel we see today.

The Chateau Bourbon is far from squeamish about its purported ghosts, and it celebrates them on its Web site. At least seventeen different apparitions have been identified over the past half century. First there is the spectre of a female dancer who twirls all alone on the dance floor of the ballroom, which is now on the hotel's second floor. Her period dress suggests that she is a holdover spirit from the building's earliest days. She's not alone in there, however.

The catering staff has been known to see and hear table-cloths and glassware moving by themselves.

The wraith of a Confederate solider, nicknamed simply "the Man," walks the third, sixth, and seventh stories. Then, too, there are spectral children and women who most likely date to the time the hotel was a convent and school. The youngsters materialize all over the hotel, including inside guest rooms. Even when they remain out of sight, their disembodied voices have been heard. One little girl in particular likes to roll a ball up and down the sixth-floor hallway. There's one person the spectral children try to avoid: They are said to be afraid of an adult female banshee who often shows up in the elevator.

Women have felt an invisible set of lips (thought to belong to a male spirit) kiss them on the cheek. Gentlemen who curse aloud might get slapped on the face by an imperceptible spirit hand.

The ghost whom Dana hoped to meet, and one who seems to be a frequent visitor, is an old man who sits all by himself in the lobby reading a newspaper. He's always smoking a cigar, and people are able to smell the tobacco burning. But if you try to engage the Southern colonel in conversation, he evaporates.

Dana scanned the reception area. There was a young couple checking out and a teenage girl chatting up one of the bellboys. A few folk were sitting in the foyer, but, unfortunately, the elderly entity was not among them.

Reluctantly, Dana stepped out onto the sidewalk. She only had to travel one block down Iberville toward the river until she hit Royal Street. Close to the intersection, she found Hotel Monteleone. Dana was amazed by its size. With six hundred rooms, it was probably the largest hotel in the

Vieux Carré, and some of America's top writers have been guests: William Faulkner, John Grisham, Ernest Hemingway, Anne Rice, and Tennessee Williams, among others.

It's also played host to about a dozen ghosts. To mention just a few, guests have heard a jazz singer vocalizing inside an empty room and two ten-year-old boys playing hide-and-seek in the hallways. Another youngster who appears to be lost will walk up to people and take their hands before vanishing completely. A workman tinkering with the grandfather clock in the lobby during both daytime and nighttime hours turns out not to be real. In addition, doors, especially those of the restaurant, become unlocked on their own, and the elevators will stop on floors where they haven't been called.

But did Dana get to experience anything spooky at the Monteleone? Sadly, no.

Three down, seven to go, she thought to herself as she stepped out the door. At least the rest of the hotels were either on or just a block to one side of Royal. It was time to head into the heart of the Quarter.

By this time, Dana had resigned herself to the fact that she probably would not be having a ghoulie jump out at her. But she was on a mission, and she was going to see it through. She checked her notebook as she breezed through the next four hotels in short order.

Omni Royal Orleans Hotel, 621 St. Louis St. The primary ghost seems to be that of a housemaid dressed in eighteenth-century clothing. The hotel building doesn't date back to that period, so she must be a lingering spirit from an earlier time. She'll show up in the rooms, switch on the lights, run a bath, or flush the toilet.

Hotel Maison de Ville, 727 Toulouse St. In addition to the main house, the boutique hotel has nine guest cottages that are refurbished former slave quarters. Anomalies on the premises include tapping sounds, voices, wet footprints, shifting objects, and invisible hands pulling off bedsheets or grabbing at people's feet as they lie in bed. There are also occasional full-form materializations of both male and female phantoms.

Place D'Armes Hotel, 625 St. Ann St. There are eighty-five guest rooms in the various buildings making up the property, located just off Jackson Square. The hotel was built on the site of a schoolhouse that burned to the ground, killing many children and the teachers. Some of their souls have been emblazoned onto the scene. But perhaps the spectre that's most frequently seen is an aged, bearded man from the 1800s who will suddenly appear, acknowledge the visitors, and then just as quickly vanish.

Andrew Jackson Hotel, 919 Royal St. The inn, with twenty-two guest rooms and suites on two levels, is named for the former president who, as a major general in the War of 1812, defeated the British in New Orleans. Legend has it that the hotel was built on the grounds of an all-boys' school that was razed in the fire that destroyed much of the Crescent City in 1788. Five youngsters died in the flames, which may explain the sound of phantom children playing in the central courtyard in the dead of night. Some guests have claimed that the ghost of Jackson himself has wandered through the building. Various other apparitions have been seen, heard, and felt in the hallways on the first and second floors as well as on the stairwell.

It was time for lunch. Past time. Dana had been so excited about getting under way first thing in the morning that she didn't have a full sit-down breakfast. Instead, she had grabbed a croissant, some fruit, and juice at a convenience store midmorning. But now it was well into the afternoon, and she was starving—and exhausted.

Besides, she needed a break. The hotels, the second-story patio balconies, the wrought-iron railings, and the eighteenth- and nineteenth-century furnishings were all starting to blur together in her mind. She had to let what she'd already seen settle in her brain before she tried to cram in anything more.

Dana headed a block up to Bourbon Street and plopped down in the first inviting restaurant she could find. She didn't even look up to see its name as she entered. She just needed a place to sit down and rest for a few minutes. That, and a po'boy.

So far, it had been a disappointing morning for her. Well, she *had* gotten to see some amazing architecture, and everyone she talked to was very nice and helpful. In many places, staff members had been more than happy to show her around their premises once they heard why she was there. But Dana had yet to see anything, well, otherworldly.

She had just three more hotels to go before making her way back to her own hotel. Fortunately, the Lafitte Guest House, on Bourbon, was just steps away. The land where the bed-and-breakfast now sits was first deeded to Charity

Hospital by the Spanish king in 1793. When the building burned down in 1809, a small combination brick-and-wood house was put in its place. Paul Joseph Gleises replaced it in 1849 with a three-story showcase mansion with an attached annex for the slave (and, after the war, servant) quarters.

He and his wife, Marie, had six children, two of whom died in what is now Room 21. One daughter was felled by yellow fever; the other youngster hanged herself. Although the family moved before the Civil War to Philadelphia, then on to New York, they retained ownership of the property until 1866, when it was sold.

Marie never got over the loss of her girls, and her ghost has returned to keep vigil in the room where they passed. Many guests who stay there are temporarily overcome with unexplainable feelings of intense hopelessness and unfathomable sadness. Visitors to the guest house know when Marie is walking around the inn because lights flicker in her wake. The girl who died of fever hasn't traveled far, either. Her reflection is trapped in a mirror mounted just outside her former room.

Dana snuck onto the second floor and stared into the mirror. Nothing there. Room 21 was occupied, so she couldn't ask to go inside. But it didn't matter. It was getting late, and she still had two more places to cover before dinner.

Next on her list was the Hotel Provincial, which was about two blocks away on Chartres Street. The many buildings (as well as the courtyards and two pools) that make up the lodgings lie on what was a land grant from King Louis XV in 1725, just six years after the founding of the city. The land passed through many hands over the two and a quarter centuries until the first two structures of the present hotel, the 100 and 200 buildings, opened in 1961. The 300 building, added six years later, dates to

1825, and the 400 building was a former retail store, built in the 1830s, before being acquired in 1964.

Perhaps the most interesting section of the hotel, at least for paranormal purposes, is the 500 building, which was made part of the hotel in 1969. Originally, a military hospital stood on the site in the 1720s. The land then passed to the Catholic Church. In 1831 the property transferred back into private hands, and the old structure was replaced by two new buildings that were used for shops and a boardinghouse. They stood until a fire felled them in 1874, when they were replaced by the building found there today.

But here's the spooky part. For some reason the long-gone hospital has imprinted itself onto the area as a residual haunting. Guests have walked into their rooms in the 500 building and been startled to see blood on the bedcovers or wounded soldiers crying out in pain. On at least one occasion, people stepped out of the elevator onto the second floor to see the ghostly tableaux of the hospital in full operation before their eyes. In a flash, the vision ceased to exist.

The most frequently repeated story about the Provincial concerns a phantom solider, dressed in a 1930s-era khaki uniform complete with hat and military ribbons. He appears in various rooms and supposedly loves country music. But the story goes on to say that he likes a particular station. If anyone leaves a radio playing, the dial will mysteriously shift to WTIX-FM 94.3.

Dana stood quietly, hoping to catch a few strains of music floating through the air. But all she heard was the gentle buzz of the French Quarter waking up for the long Saturday night ahead.

She headed the two blocks down Chartres to her final destination, Le Richelieu Hotel. The buildings were part of a private home, which the owner renovated into guest quarters in 1969. Several Spanish soldiers were purportedly executed in 1802 right where Le Richelieu Hotel now stands. Their tortured souls haunt the bar area and the swimming pool. But none were taking a dip as Dana passed through the courtyard.

With her quest complete and far from her hotel, Dana decided to hail a cab to head back to her room for a relaxing soak in the tub, to be followed by a light dinner—if there can be such a thing in New Orleans. Then, if it wasn't too late, she'd drop in at the cemetery to pay her respects to Marie Laveau. If she had any energy left after that, she'd head back to the Quarter to experience Bourbon Street at night. And who knew? Maybe if she ducked into one of the hotels she had visited earlier, a ghost or two might pop out under cover of darkness.

As Dana stepped out of her taxi and headed toward the entrance of Le Pavillon, she unexpectedly felt a jolt at her elbow. She turned to come face-to-face with a young girl. She was about fifteen to seventeen, pretty, with pale white skin, doelike brown eyes, and long brown hair pulled back from her face. The girl was dressed in vintage clothing, all in black: a full dress that fell to her ankles, a broad-brimmed hat, and a shawl, and she held onto a small clutch purse for dear life. Dana hadn't known better, she'd have thought Blanche DuBois from Tennessee Williams's immortal play *A Streetcar Named Desire* had come to life.

"Pardon me," the girl said with a heavy French accent, "I am . . . lost." Dana watched as the sprite floated down to the cab she had just left, spoke briefly with the driver, and stepped inside. In a moment, the car was off.

Dana was halfway across the lobby when, on a whim, she turned and walked back to the concierge. Something— she couldn't tell what—was troubling her about the girl.

"Excuse me, sir," she ventured. "Did you by any chance see that lady in black who just passed by?"

The man smiled broadly. "Oh, you mean our little ghost?"

Dana was stunned. When, that morning before setting out, she had mentally ticked off all the spirits who made their home in Le Pavillon, she had completely forgotten that the hotel was also allegedly haunted by a teenager by the name of Adda (or Ava or Eva, depending where you pick up the story). The girl is said to have lived in the 1840s and was rushing to the docks to meet her family to board a ship when she was killed by a runaway carriage. *No wonder she seemed confused*, Dana thought. *She doesn't know what happened to her or where she is, and she can't find her parents.*

"Yes," the concierge continued, "the poor girl bumps into guests all the time as she wanders through the lobby. Did you smell her perfume? Some people catch a strong whiff of roses or lilacs as she goes by. The ones I pity, though, are the poor cabdrivers. Think what it must be like for them when she disappears from the backseat halfway to the cruise ship terminal."

Dana smiled, slowly at first, then with a broad, contented grin. After years of trying, she had finally seen a ghost, and she wouldn't have known it if she hadn't stopped to ask the concierge. Sometimes you *do* have to rely on the kindness of strangers.

It was time to celebrate. And where better than in New Orleans?

Chapter 13
Puzzle at
the Plantation

The Myrtles Plantation
St. Francisville, Louisiana

If you're looking to stay at a bed-and-breakfast where there's a high chance of running into an apparition, look no further than the Myrtles Plantation. There have been thousands of recorded sightings, and at least a half dozen spirits are regular guests. But which one will come looking for you?

Chloe was almost finished mixing the cake batter. Everything was in place, she thought. Just one more ingredient, and it would be ready to place in the oven.

The slave worked on a large Louisiana plantation that had been founded in 1796 by a judge named David Bradford. Just four years before that the jurist had been an up-and-coming lawyer in his early twenties in the town of Washington, Pennsylvania. By 1793 he had been appointed as deputy attorney general for the county. But then he became one of the most vocal opponents of the federal government's new excise tax on the production of whiskey, and when a warrant was issued for his arrest in October 1794 during the Whiskey Rebellion, Bradford fled down the Ohio and Mississippi Rivers.

He bought five hundred acres outside St. Francisville, a small town located just about twenty-five miles north of

Baton Rogue, Louisiana, in what was then Spanish West Florida. In 1796, he built a two-story antebellum mansion on the highest point of the bayou property—some say on top of an ancient Tunica Indian burial ground. He called his new home Laurel Grove.

Bradford soon established himself as a judge as well as a prosperous planter. After he received an official pardon from President John Adams in March 1799, Bradford sent for his wife and children. (The jurist had left them behind in Pennsylvania until his safety was ensured.) He died at Laurel Grove in 1817; his wife remained at the plantation until her death in 1830.

One of their daughters, Sarah Matilda, caught the eye of Clark Woodruff while he was studying law under Bradford. After the judge's death, Woodruff lost no time in asking for Sarah's hand in marriage. The wedding took place in November 1817 when Sarah was just fourteen years old.

Woodruff loved his wife, but as was often the case with plantation owners in the Deep South at the time, Woodruff took one of his slaves, a woman named Chloe, as a mistress. To make his rendezvous with her easier, he moved the young woman into the main house as his children's servant.

Chloe had a bad habit, though. When she was able to sneak away from chores, she would often eavesdrop on her master's private business meetings in the gentlemen's parlor. Whether it was out of simple curiosity or an attempt to overhear information that she could use against her master is unknown, but Woodruff caught the slave on several occasions and each time gave her a stern warning.

But finally Chloe went too far. She was discovered listening in on a conversation in front of several prominent businessmen, and the plantation owner had no recourse but to punish the slave. He not only banished her from the mansion but also ordered that her left ear be cut off.

Humiliated by the mutilation, Chloe wrapped her head in a bandanna from then on. Working back in the fields, she yearned for her days of relative ease in the big house. She finally came up with a plan to get back into her former lover's good graces.

And so, there she was, standing in front of a hot oven mixing batter. One of the Woodruffs' young daughters was going to have a birthday. Chloe would bake a cake for the celebration, but she would add a secret ingredient: oleander. Though the decorative flower was fragrant and beautiful to behold, the herb was extremely toxic. A small handful of leaves could sicken an adult; ingestion of a single leaf could prove fatal to a baby.

But Chloe's intent wasn't to kill the Woodruffs. Oh, no. She would blend just enough of the poisonous plant into the cake to make the children slightly sick. Then, claiming that she was a native healer, Chloe would offer to nurse the youngsters back to health. Once they recovered, she would be welcomed back into the house with open arms.

The cake was accepted, and it was served to Sarah Matilda and the girls. But Chloe had miscalculated how little of the shrub was necessary to be deadly, and Mrs. Woodruff and her daughters immediately fell violently ill. They began to vomit, developed diarrhea, and suffered seizures. Within hours, the mother and her children were dead.

The judge had been called away from the plantation and was absent from the party. When he returned, he discovered that his entire family was gone. Insane with grief and anger, he stormed into the slaves' quarters, certain that one of them had been responsible. Fearful for their own safety, the other slaves betrayed Chloe. Before long the murderess was captured, and Woodruff had her hanged from a plantation tree for all to see. Then, after Chloe's corpse was cut down, it was loaded down with rocks and thrown into the river.

With Chloe dead, Woodruff had every reason to believe that the slave would soon be forgotten. But that presumed that she would accept her passage to the Next World. Instead, Chloe's spirit almost immediately returned to the mansion.

Her ghost, wearing her distinctive green bandanna, was soon seen inside the house. Furniture began to rearrange itself overnight behind closed doors. During the day, ladies (especially those walking through the parlor where Chloe had eavesdropped on her master) would have one of their earrings pulled off by an invisible hand. Why was only one taken? Well, isn't it obvious? After Chloe was disfigured, she no longer had need of a complete pair.

To this day, a single earring will turn up out of the blue in some unusual spot. Where do they come from? Well, women in the Land of the Living tire of having to wear the same old jewelry. Perhaps it's no different for female phantoms.

As it turns out, Chloe's not the only ghost to walk the grounds. The spectres of her victims—Sarah and the two children—show up in a large mirror that hangs in the manor. Visitors looking at their reflections sometimes see one or more of the ethereal entities standing behind them. As is usual in such cases, when the people turn, no one is there. From time to time the otherworldly guests leave their handprints behind on the glass.

The two little girls can be quite mischievous, and they don't always remain indoors. They've been spotted all over the plantation. On several occasions they've surprised guests in the house who look up to see two small faces peering at them from the other side of the window—even when they're on the second floor. It's no use trying to catch the girls, though. By the time anyone goes outside to look for them, the spectres have disappeared.

As with many ghost stories, there are multiple variations of the Chloe story. One suggests that the slave was actually thrown out of the house because Sarah caught her with her husband in the children's nursery. That version doesn't mention the mutilation of Chloe's ear.

In some accounts, the poisoning was no accident. Chloe planned to do away with the family all along.

The question remains: Did Chloe exist at all? There is no record of her name in the county archives in the lists of Woodruff holdings. And there's another discrepancy in the reports as well. Sarah Matilda died of yellow fever in 1823, and her two children, a *boy* and a girl, died of the same thing a year later, *not* from a poisoned cake.

But a little thing like the truth doesn't matter when spirits are at play, does it?

In 1834, Judge Woodruff sold Laurel Grove to Ruffin Grey Stirling, whose family already owned several plantations in the area. In 1850, Stirling remodeled the mansion, adding a southern wing to the house for his large family and a gallery with a wrought-iron railing along the front of the building. He also increased the size of the property to more than 1,500 acres and bought about a hundred more slaves. It was during this renovation and expansion that Stirling changed the name of the manor to the Myrtles Plantation due to the number of myrtle trees on the grounds. Ruffin Grey and his wife, Mary, had eight sons (six of whom would perish in the Civil War) and one daughter, Sarah.

After Stirling died in 1854, Mary hired Sarah's husband, William Drew Winter, a lawyer, to manage the plantation. Eventually, she gave the young couple the deed to the property. The War Between the States was financially devastating, forcing the family into bankruptcy. They temporarily lost the house in 1868, but Sarah, as the heir to Ruffin Stirling, managed to get it back two years later.

Then, on January 26, 1871, Winter was inside the house when he heard a horse rapidly approaching. A voice from the unknown rider called out to him, and Winter walked onto the veranda to greet the visitor. Suddenly, a shot rang out, and Winter, struck in the chest and mortally wounded, staggered back into the house. He desperately tried to make it up the staircase to bid farewell to his beloved Sarah. She had heard the gunfire and by then was standing on the upper landing. Winter managed to drag himself up seventeen of the twenty steps before he collapsed, dead. Sarah lived for another seven years with the horrific memory of watching her husband die at her feet. (Although at least one newspaper identified the assassin as E. S. Webber, the man was never prosecuted.)

Many who have stayed in the house since have claimed they've heard heavy, disembodied footsteps dragging their way up the deserted staircase. But the mysterious thumping sound never makes it past the seventeenth step.

The Myrtles Plantation changed hands over the next hundred years, and much of the property was sold off. Some of the ghost stories still being told today started in the 1950s when a widow named Marjorie Munson owned the place. Many of the early tales centered on the apparition of an old woman wearing, similar to Chloe's ghost, a green bonnet or beret.

In the 1970s, Arlin Dease and Mr. and Mrs. Robert Ward bought the plantation. They had the mansion restored with 1850s period furnishings, including French-style furniture, stained glass, Aubusson tapestries, and Baccarat crystal chandeliers. The Chloe story, or at least the details about a poisoned cake and the green head wrap, seems to have taken hold during this period.

Frances Kermeen, who has written extensively about her time at the Myrtles Plantation, purchased it on April 1, 1980, and lived there for eight and a half years. The mansion came into the public eye when it opened for tours as a bed-and-breakfast.

As more and more people came to visit the plantation, the number of reported ghost sightings skyrocketed. There have been so many rumors that many guests stay there specifically in the hopes of spying a spirit. Many have been rewarded. Even when the phantoms don't materialize, they sometimes show up in photographs, as anything from streaks of light to full-form figures.

Some people have reported waking up in an upstairs bedroom to find the spirit of a female slave looming over their bed. Other guests have seen the ghost's shadow moving across the walls. According to an old wives' tale, when one of William Winter's daughters contracted yellow fever, he turned in desperation to the local voodoo queen. The priestess, who was a slave on the neighboring Solitude Plantation, was believed to be able to heal the sick and dying with secret herbal medicines. Despite the slave's incantations over the girl for three days, the youngster died. Winter, in fury, hanged the hapless woman from the chandelier in that very room—the same room she haunts to this day. (Some versions of this story give the slave's name as Clio, which sounds suspiciously like Chloe, or Sarah. A few say the girl was Stirling's daughter instead. It's probable that over the past centuries, all of the various legends have become inextricably interwoven, and it's impossible to tell exactly where one ends and the next one begins.)

Other ephemeral figures floating around at the Myrtles include a fussy maid, a little girl (who may or may not be one of the Woodruff girls) bouncing on the bed, and a woman in a dark dress who dances in one of the parlors. Female guests who stay overnight in the former nursery (where Woodruff had his assignations with Chloe) have even been "romanced" by an invisible incubus that may be the spirit of the judge himself.

The apparition of a sixteen-year-old Confederate soldier haunts another room. After being slightly injured, the boy had hid in the Myrtles. When the locals discovered him, they were so incensed that he hadn't gone back into battle that they dragged him from the mansion and hanged him.

In addition to the appearance of all the phantoms, the house has its share of other paranormal phenomena: footsteps, whispered voices, the scent of perfume wafting in the air, cold spots, lights turning on and dimming, and doors that unlock themselves. The Bridal Suite (the Stirlings' former bedroom) is particularly active.

There's one more banshee out there in the bayou. He's a caretaker dressed in khaki pants who tries to turn away visitors at the front gate to the plantation. When the startled guests try to complain, the watchman vanishes. The crabby wraith is believed to be a cantankerous worker from the 1920s who was murdered on the grounds.

So if one day you decide to tour the plantation or perhaps spend a night or two, beware if a cranky old coot tries to shoo you off as you turn up the driveway. Take a close look. You may have already come face-to-face with one of the many wandering spirits populating the Myrtles Plantation.

Chapter 14

Taking the
Cure

1886 Crescent Hotel & Spa
Eureka Springs, Arkansas

Norman Baker, who fancied himself a doctor, turned a former hotel and women's college in Eureka Springs, Arkansas, into a sanatorium to treat cancer. Did his regimen really result in miracle cures as he claimed? Probably not. But a miracle of sorts has occurred at the hotel: Baker, and apparently several others, have returned from the Other Side and taken up residence.

When Wendy decided she needed to get away for a long weekend, all her girlfriends said she *had* to go to Eureka Springs. Not only was the town itself a charmer, but because she worked at the University of Arkansas in Fayetteville, the resort town was only thirty-five miles away.

Eureka Springs is up in the Ozark Mountains, and the small town—it only has about 2,500 permanent residents—is set on a steep hillside. The place is known for its winding roads and quaint Victorian homes, and many of the buildings now house boutiques, art galleries, and crafts shops.

Across the valley from downtown is the Christ of the Ozarks, a seven-story-tall, white concrete statue of Jesus, and the city plays host to an annual production of *The Great Passion Play*, which draws thousands of visitors each spring.

Wendy wasn't heading there for spiritual healing, though. She was giving herself a three-day retreat to undergo another type of renewal. She planned to pamper herself with massages, facials, body wraps—you name it—at the New Moon Spa located in the 1866 Crescent Hotel.

The town owes its existence to the cool mineral springs located throughout the region. In the mid-1800s, a doctor by the name of Alvah Jackson was convinced that his son's enflamed eyes were healed by rinsing them with the waters of one pool named Basin Spring. During the Civil War, the doctor operated a "hospital" in a local cave and later bottled and sold the springwater as Dr. Jackson's Eye Water.

Then, in 1879 a friend of his, Judge J. B. Saunders, claimed that by bathing in the pools he had cleared up a chronic and debilitating skin disease. Within weeks, the word was out, and people flocked to the region for the springs' restorative powers. Is it any wonder that, when a town was founded there on February 14, 1880, it was named Eureka Springs? Within a year, the hamlet grew to a city of more than ten thousand.

Former Arkansas governor Powell Clayton moved to Eureka Springs in 1882, and he tirelessly began to promote the site's bucolic air and scenic beauty. To attract tourists and settlers, the Eureka Springs Improvement Company, spearheaded by Clayton, was established to bring the railroad to town.

His campaign worked. Soon the streets were lined with fashionable houses and hotels. Perhaps foremost among the lodgings was the Crescent Hotel, which Clayton built with several partners in 1886. Architect Isaac L. Taylor was selected to design the hotel, which would sit on twenty-seven acres a mile north of and overlooking the city. The walls were constructed of magnesium limestone quarried from the banks of the White River, and the eighteen-inch-thick blocks were fitted so precisely that no mortar was needed between them. Modern conveniences such as Edison lamps, steam heating, and an elevator were incorporated into the interior, and guests could make use of the hotel's attached stables, which had room for a hundred horses.

The exuberance of the hotel's early years was short-lived. By 1901 it had fallen on hard times, and seven years later it was transformed into the Crescent College and Conservatory for Young Women. But the school couldn't sustain itself either, and it closed in 1924. For four years, from 1930 to 1934, the building housed a junior college. The next two summers it was run as a seasonal hotel. The Crescent Hotel was about to enter its darkest period when, in 1937, it was purchased by Norman Baker.

If ever there were a man who deserved being called a huckster, it was Baker. He was born on November 27, 1882, in Muscatine, Iowa, the youngest of ten children. His hometown, located on a bend of the Mississippi River, was a center of commerce, and after quitting school at sixteen, Baker began work as a tool and die maker. But machinist work wasn't in his blood. Sometime around the age of twenty, Baker saw Doctor Flint, an itinerant magician, perform a mind-reading act, and the young man decided right there and then where his future lay.

In 1904 he framed his own traveling show, fronting a pseudo-psychic named Madame Pearl Tangley. When she quit after five seasons, Baker hired a college girl, Theresa Pinder, as her replacement. She and Baker were married the following year.

The couple returned to Muscatine in the summer of 1914. During the break from the road, Baker came up with an invention that would make him rich. He perfected a new type of calliope run by compressed air that was a vast improvement over the more dangerous and less musical models powered by steam.

Baker gave up the mentalism act, and in 1915 he divorced his wife. He concentrated on marketing his Tangley Calliaphone, which he built and sold for the next seventeen years. His other business interests weren't so legitimate. In 1920, he started a mail correspondence course to teach drawing—even though he had virtually no artistic ability or background himself.

Baker knew that the best way to reach the widest possible audience was on the airwaves. In 1925, he founded radio station KTNT, which he said stood for Know the Truth. In exchange for a promise to promote Muscatine, city fathers provided the station free electricity and water, and they waived its taxes. Baker used KTNT to broadcast his personal views, but one in particular struck a chord with the common man in rural Iowa: distrust of big business, whether it be government, Wall Street, or the American Medical Association.

In 1929, to boost ratings, KTNT investigated a cancer clinic run by Dr. Charles Ozias in Kansas City. Based on what he saw—and despite having had no medical training whatsoever—Baker came up with his own version of the Ozias "cure" and opened a clinic in Muscatine.

The treatments at the Baker Institute consisted of a series of injections (five to seven a day) of what today would be considered holistic medicine—except that it had no possibility of effecting a cure: a liquid solution containing alcohol, glycerin, carbolic acid, and essences of watermelon seed, corn silk, and clover.

In the spring of 1930, the American Medical Association went on the attack. Tired of the shyster slandering them nonstop on the radio, worried that his denunciations of cancer surgery would be taken seriously, and concerned for the people who were losing their lives from what they called "Baker's cancer cure quackery," the AMA called on state licensing boards, Iowa prosecutors, and the Federal Radio Commission to put him out of business. Baker returned fire by suing the AMA for libel and defamation.

But in 1931, the tide turned against Baker. First, the FRC refused to renew his radio license. He lost his court case against the AMA, and he was indicted for practicing medicine without a license. To escape arrest, Baker went to Mexico, where he remained for six years. Finally in 1937 he returned to Muscatine to face justice. His sentence was a slap on the wrist: a single day in jail.

Baker knew that he had no future in Iowa. But a tiger doesn't change its stripes. It just moves on to a new hunting ground. And Baker found one in Eureka Springs, a place already renowned for miraculous healings. The charlatan took over the Crescent Hotel in 1937, renamed it the Baker Hospital, and basically started up the same scam he had operated back at the Baker Institute. For two years he got away with it.

But his actions had not gone unnoticed by authorities. What finally led to Baker's downfall were seven letters he sent through the U.S. mail to advertise his clinic. He was arrested for mail fraud, and in a January 1940 trial he was found guilty on all charges. He was sentenced to four years in the Leavenworth Federal Penitentiary and a mere $4,000 fine. (It was believed that he had bilked cancer patients out of an estimated $4 million.)

Baker was set free on July 19, 1944. He moved to Florida, where he died of cirrhosis of the liver in 1958. His body was returned to Muscatine for burial.

The sanatorium was closed after his imprisonment. In 1946 or 1947, a Chicago consortium acquired the property and turned it back into a hotel. Guests were once again visiting the "Castle in the Air High Atop the Ozarks," as it was advertised. In 1972, the Crescent Hotel got a long-overdue makeover when two businessmen from Wichita, Kansas, bought it and restored the grande dame to its Victorian splendor. Today the hotel is owned by Marty and Elise Roenigk.

Wendy knew little of the hotel's history as she pulled up the drive. She was just happy it was her turn to enjoy the Queen of the Ozarks, as the 1886 Crescent Hotel & Spa is often called.

It was a late autumn dusk as she pulled up the drive, parked her car, and entered the foyer. Minutes later, she was slipping her key into the door of Room 419. Anxious to get settled in, Wendy swung open the door and . . .

Standing there, midway across the room, was a woman, her back to the door. The stranger slowly, silently, spun on her heels and stared directly at Wendy. She parted her lips and pleasantly smiled, as if happy to see a new face.

"Oh! I'm sorry," Wendy cried out in surprise. "I thought, I mean, I didn't know this room was still occupied. The clerk must have made a mistake."

The stranger approached Wendy cautiously, seemingly unsure about how to explain her presence. All she said was, "Are you here for the cure, too?"

"The cure? You mean the spa. Yes. It's my first time." Wendy glanced over her shoulder as she gestured into the hallway. "Perhaps I should head down to the front desk to see about a different room."

She turned back into the room to apologize once again for her intrusion. But the woman had vanished. More puzzled than frightened, Wendy closed the door and went downstairs. She spotted the staff member who had checked her in and started to explain what had just happened.

The young woman's eyes visibly widened. "Really?" she almost squealed. "You actually met Miss Theodora?"

It was *not* the reaction Wendy expected. A manager, overhearing the exchange, glared at the clerk and asked Wendy to step with him to the end of the desk where they could talk discreetly. What she learned in the next few moments was equally thrilling and disturbing: The person she had spoken to in 419 wasn't a guest at all, at least not in the last sixty-some years. It was a ghost, thought to have been a former cancer patient during the time the hotel was the Baker Hospital. Her identity was uncertain, but the staff had named her Theodora, and her appearances—and subsequent sudden disappearances—always followed the same routine. Guests have also discovered they shouldn't say anything to upset her: She's been known to toss people's belongings into the hall if they indicate they don't like the room.

Wendy was dumbfounded. At first she was uncertain whether she wanted to stay in the hotel anymore. Was the entire place haunted? But she had been planning the weekend for some time, the sympathetic manger offered her a very nice alternate room, and, in the end, she decided that no spook was going to come between her and her exfoliating scrubs!

The rest of the holiday was blissfully uneventful, in part because Wendy didn't find out until after her return to Fayetteville that the entire hotel was haunted—by more than a dozen documented spirits, making it one of the most ghost-infested hotels in the United States.

The apparition that Wendy encountered was not the only one from the facility's two and a half years as a hospital. A nurse, dressed in a Depression-era white starched uniform, has been seen on the second floor and, to a lesser extent, the third. She's often spied wheeling an empty gurney down the corridor. The nurse never interacts with any of the living, so she remains anonymous. Interestingly, although the cart is also an apparition, guests hear its wheels turning.

By far the hotel's most notorious phantom is Norman Baker himself. Although he left the grounds in disgrace, some part of him no doubt remained attached to the place. It was, after all, the site of his greatest and most lucrative con. He has been seen shuffling all over the hospital—or hotel, rather—most notably outside of what is now the recreation room, wearing a befuddled expression. He's almost always dressed in a white linen suit with a lavender or purple shirt.

There are resident spirits from every incarnation of the Crescent Hotel. A lone girl presumed to have been a student during the building's days as a conservatory strolls through the gardens behind the hotel. According to legend, she died when she jumped, fell, or was pushed from the roof. She may or may not be the same phantom as a secretive "Lady in White" who shows up in the garden and on balconies.

A male spectre occasionally descends the main staircase, appears at the bottom of the steps, or shows up in the lobby bar. He's a mutton-chopped man dressed in a Gay Nineties black swallowtail tuxedo jacket, gray striped formal pants, a high-collared shirt, ascot, white gloves, and top hat. The ghost is often mistaken for a specially wardrobed member of the staff or a costumed strolling actor. Many now think that he was Dr. Ellis, a one-time house physician.

Several spirits are connected with the hotel's main dining room and kitchen. A gracious but ghostly gentleman in 1890s attire makes the rounds during dinner, chatting with patrons. One moment, he's telling them that he's waiting for his lady friend to join him; the next moment, he's disappeared from sight.

Both staff and visitors have peeked into the Crystal Dining Room when it was closed and have seen a party of phantoms, all dressed in Victorian-era clothing, supping at one of the corner tables. Not only that: There were spectral servers attending them. Even when ghosts don't materialize in the room, sometimes their reflections appear in one of the mirrors.

A chef has reported seeing the apparition of a little boy in knickers and wearing old-style, wire-rimmed glasses running through the kitchen. At times, pots and pans come to life and move about on their own.

At least one group of teenagers has reported being followed into the elevator by a waiter dressed in turn-of-the-twentieth-century garb. They assumed he was from room service because he was carrying a tray of butter. He stood quietly, expressionless, not acknowledging the youngsters' presence, but when the lift stopped on the third floor and the kids got out, so did the waiter! He followed them partway down the hallway, but when the teens gathered up the courage to turn and confront him, the ethereal image had evaporated.

Then there are the apparitions that don't seem to be pegged to a particular point in time. A tall man with a beard knocks on random doors and, when they're answered, asks, "Are you waiting for me?" before popping off into the aether.

Colored lights and floating orbs streak through the North Penthouse, which was once "Dr." Baker's private residence. A Native American has been spotted roaming the fourth floor, and a crying woman carrying a baby blanket aimlessly wanders the passageways throughout the building. Visitors have rushed up to a man in his late teens or early twenties who has collapsed onto the lobby floor, only to have him vanish at their feet. Overnight guests have felt invisible hands tugging at their sheets and blankets in the middle of the night. And there's even a phantom house cat scurrying about.

Everyone agrees that the second floor is the most haunted area of the hotel. Unexplainable wisps of cold wind often whip down the long hallway on the second level. Many believe the chill emanates from Room 218, which seems to be the most haunted room of all. It has an ephemeral intruder thought to be Michael, an Irish stonemason who died after falling several stories and crashing to the floor of the unfinished room during the hotel's construction. Mostly he stays in the room out of sight, but some have seen his hand emerge from the bathroom mirror or heard his mournful wail.

Room 218 is plagued by other paranormal activity, which may or may not be caused by Michael's ghost. The lights and television turn on and off without assistance. Doors and windows swing open and closed, and the toilet flushes on its own. Disembodied footsteps can be heard in the room. The most frequent anomaly, pounding noises, comes from inside the walls.

(Michael is also thought to be the entity haunting Room 202 and, for some reason, 424. A very few people have also seen the worker outside the hotel, wandering throughout the property.)

Ancient tales suggest that the Shawnee and other Native American tribes were aware of the medicinal powers of the nearby mineral springs and considered the spot to be sacred. There are those today who believe the pools and underground aquifers have a mystical aura or spiritual energy that attracts supernatural elements to the Ozark valley.

Is that why the ghosts return, or are they drawn back to the hotel itself? Heaven knows the place has seen its share of joy and sorrow, celebration and death. No doubt many souls formed deep emotional ties to the Crescent Hotel, and some of those links may have been strong enough to allow the spirits to transcend death. The truth may never be known.

Chapter 15

The Whistler

Blackhawk Hotel
Davenport, Iowa

Who would suspect the unassuming Blackhawk Hotel in Davenport, Iowa, of harboring ghosts? Yet it does. Several. One of them, "the Whistler," is only heard in the dead of night. Another spectre plays the piano in the ballroom. A third, an ethereal woman, walks the halls. And is it possible that the mature, well-attired apparition is none other than Cary Grant?

Another night out of town on business. When Susan took the job as the regional manager of a sales firm in Decatur she knew she'd be on the road. She just didn't know how much.

In an era of teleconferencing, she hoped that most of her work could be done behind her desk, making calls, answering e-mails, and only attending conventions when absolutely necessary. She hadn't fully appreciated that, as the public face of her company in that part of the country, meeting clients face-to-face was an essential part of doing business.

So here she was in Davenport, Iowa. The city was established in 1836 and named for George Davenport, an army officer in the War of 1812 and an early settler in the region. The town became the county seat in 1840 and was Iowa's military headquarters during the Civil War. The city really began to blossom economically just after the turn of the twentieth century, and several of the downtown structures were built at that time—including the Blackhawk Hotel, where Susan was staying.

It's nice now and then to get into an old, historic place like this, she thought as she made her way up to her room. Most of the places she stayed were sleek, bland, and interchangeable, so it would be fun to overnight in a quirky spot with a little character.

The Blackhawk Hotel dated to 1915. It originally had just seven stories, but four more floors were added the following decade. In all, there were about four hundred guest rooms and suites.

During its heyday, the Blackhawk Hotel was the best lodgings in town. Bandleaders such as Stan Kenton and Guy Lombardo were attracted to its ballroom, the finest in the Quad Cities (as several towns in the area straddling the Mississippi River are collectively known). The hotel was also the stopping point for every celebrity or notable politician who came through, including Jack Dempsey, Carl Sandburg, Herbert Hoover, and Richard Nixon.

When Susan visited in the late 1980s, the Blackhawk was pretty much the only game in town. And it certainly had a pedigree. Hadn't Cary Grant stayed there less than a decade earlier?

The iconic film star was born Archibald Leach in Bristol, England, in 1904. He came to America with the Bob Pender company of acrobats and physical comedians in 1920. With their tour over, the Pender Troupe appeared in the cast of a musical, *Good Times,* on Broadway. Afterward, the Pender group returned to the United Kingdom, but Leach stayed. The handsome, charming youth was soon back on the Great White Way, where he performed in five more musicals over the next eight years. He then joined a repertory company at the Muny in St. Louis, performing in at least seven shows there in 1931 alone.

That same year, Leach moved to Hollywood, where Paramount Pictures put him under contract and gave him the name by which he's known today. Over the next thirty-five years, Cary Grant made more than seventy movies and became one of Tinseltown's biggest box office stars. He retired when he was still on top, cementing his debonair image in the public's hearts and minds forever.

In 1982, sixteen years after he'd retired from films, Grant stunned his friends by announcing that he was returning to the stage, albeit in a one-man theatrical reminiscence complete with Q&A called *A Conversation with Cary Grant*. Over the next four years, he made thirty-six appearances with the show.

Grant was to appear at the Adler Theatre in Davenport, Iowa, on November 29, 1986. Unlike the old show business adage, that show would *not* go on.

The night before it was scheduled, Grant and his fifth wife, Barbara Harris, checked into their suite in the Blackhawk Hotel and spent a relaxed evening alone. The next afternoon, the couple strolled through downtown Davenport with Doug and Vicki Miller, who had codeveloped and financed the show. Then, shortly after four, Grant arrived at the theater.

The Adler Theatre, less than a block away from the Blackhawk Hotel, started life in November 1931 as the Orpheum Theatre. It had been planned by the Radio-Keith-Orpheum vaudeville chain (RKO) as far back as 1926. Somehow, despite the Depression, the $2 million movie palace got completed. The interior was decorated in the art deco style then in vogue. The lobby was replete with ebony and marble furnishings, and the ceiling was covered in gold leaf.

The Orpheum Theatre lost its luster and appeal as audiences fled to the suburbs in the 1950s and '60s. It showed its last movie in 1973 and only managed to stay open through the rest of the decade by booking an occasional touring show or concert. In 1983, the performance space was incorporated into RiverCenter, a massive new convention-meeting complex. Over the next three years, the playhouse, renamed the Adler Theatre, was restored top to bottom, from its original crystal chandeliers down to its English carpets.

The Adler Theatre had its grand reopening on April 16, 1986, with a Burt Bacharach concert featuring the Quad City Symphony Orchestra. It was into that space that Cary Grant sauntered on November 29.

A first run-through went fine. The show would open with an eight-minute film montage, ending with a clip from the 1970 Academy Awards telecast in which the actor received his honorary Oscar from Frank Sinatra. Mirroring what was happening on the screen, Grant would leisurely walk onto the stage. He'd take his place on a stool situated far downstage (at his request) so that he could be as close as possible to his fans.

While a few technical adjustments were being made, Grant retired to his dressing room. Once there, he unexpectedly became ill. He thought his headache and nausea would pass, but when it worsened it became clear he had to be taken back to his hotel. Ever the professional, Grant refused to go to a hospital because he didn't want to cancel that night's performance. But when his condition didn't improve, two doctors were summoned. They alerted St. Luke's Hospital immediately. By the time the ambulance arrived, Grant was already in a coma. He was taken first to the emergency room, and then to the Intensive Care Unit, but he never regained consciousness. Cary Grant, eighty-two years old, was pronounced dead from a stroke at 11:22 p.m. His body was flown back to Los Angeles by chartered jet, but some say he's never left the Blackhawk.

Susan had heard as much. Supposedly the misty outline of an elderly, gray-haired man appears from time to time in the halls. No one's ever gotten a good look at the spectre's face to identify him, but legend has it that the apparition is probably Cary Grant returning to the place where he spent his last night on Earth.

Susan wasn't about to let some silly old wives' tale keep her from getting a good night's sleep. The long drive into town and the afternoon meetings had taken a lot out of her. She had more people to see the next day, so she decided to turn in early, around nine. After a few pages of light reading, she reached over and switched off the light on the nightstand. Within minutes, she was sound asleep.

Normally, she went through the entire night without stirring. For some reason, however, that night she woke with a start. She was so surprised to find herself awake at four o'clock that it took her a few moments to remember where she was. Right—she was in Davenport, in the Blackhawk Hotel.

As she sat there, puzzled, she realized that the room was unnaturally cold. She pulled the blankets up around her shoulders. Were September evenings really this chilly in Iowa?

Then, off to her left, she heard a faint noise in the darkness. White noise, like radio static. And, quietly, underneath the buzzing, just barely audible voices. The sound was indistinct enough that she couldn't make out words, but it was definitely people talking.

Curious, Susan stepped out of bed and walked toward the door. The murmuring was coming from the other side. Susan gently wrapped her fingers around the knob, gave it a jerk, and thrust her head out into the corridor. The place was deserted.

Susan was confused. She was sure the sound had come from outside the room, but perhaps she had been mistaken. She crossed to the window and peeked out. There was enough illumination from the streetlights that she could clearly see the sidewalks were empty. No, the sound wasn't coming from outdoors either. It was only then that she realized the buzzing sound had stopped.

Susan closed the curtain and climbed back into bed. She had barely laid her head on the pillow when the delicate droning and hushed tones started up again. She tried to put them out of her mind when, without warning, a sharp, loud whistle, like a master summoning his dog, cut through the dark.

That did it! In a flash, Susan jumped out of bed, changed into street clothes, grabbed her iPod, and headed down to the lobby. She had been planning to get up in an hour or so anyway to get an early start. She'd come back to the room to change after it got light.

Later, after breakfast, Susan struck up a conversation with the girl behind the front desk. She told her about the strange experience she had had in the middle of the night and asked whether anyone else had ever reported anything similar. Keeping a tight smile and without answering her directly, the clerk said she was sorry there was a problem with the room and offered to change it. Susan replied that she'd consider it, but for now she'd stay where she was.

Whether the front desk clerk knew about any purported ghosts in the hotel, Susan had no way of knowing. The girl certainly wasn't saying anything one way or the other. But when she got back in the late afternoon, Susan found out everything she wanted to know. The shift had changed, and a young man was on duty. Susan figured it wouldn't hurt to ask him, and she got an earful.

"Oh, you ran into the Whistler."

The Whistler? Susan thought to herself. So *that's* what she heard.

"Well, that's what we call him. He was some kind of scientist who lived in the hotel during World War II. He worked in a shop across the street and used a walkie-talkie to communicate with someone back in the hotel. But sometimes he'd just lean out the window and get the guy's attention by whistling."

To illustrate, the clerk spread his lips and made a crackling noise through his teeth, imitating the sound of a walkie-talkie, and then followed with a crisp whistle. It was eerily similar to what Susan had heard the night before.

The Whistler didn't return to visit Susan on her second night in town. But if she had stayed a bit longer, she might have seen the other two ghosts that inhabit the Blackhawk Hotel.

The wraith of a woman, dressed in a red or blue evening gown—she apparently has a choice of ensembles on the Other Side—often appears drifting down hallways throughout the hotel. Because of the woman's attire, it's assumed that she's probably heading toward the ballroom—which is where the other spirit hangs out. Guests at the Blackhawk sometimes hear piano music floating out of the ballroom when it's not being used. But the phantom musician, whoever it is, has never been seen.

It's unknown whether future visitors to Davenport will have a chance to be spooked by the spectres. In the 1990s, a gaming consortium called Isle of Capri bought the Black-hawk Hotel and rechristened it the President Casinos Black-hawk Hotel. By then, the inn was starting to look a little long in the tooth, and the company agreed to upgrade the facilities. They also promised to build another hotel down on the waterfront.

But the new hotel never came to pass, and not much was done to the old place, either. In the dead of winter, February 2006, a fire broke out in the Blackhawk when a meth lab that had been secretly set up in one of the rooms exploded. Although the flames were contained to that floor, other stories suffered severe water and smoke damage. Soon thereafter several water pipes froze and burst, forcing the hotel to shut down completely.

It took almost three years of political wrangling for a renovation proposal to be approved. In the end, Isle of Capri sold the building to Restoration St. Louis. Work on the hotel began in January 2009, and an official ribbon-cutting ceremony announcing the project was held the following April. If everything remains on track, the Blackhawk Hotel will have reopened for business by December 2010.

During the hotel's closure, everything's been quiet inside its ruined chambers, and no one knows if its ghostly guests will be there when it reopens. Then again, all the ruckus may awaken the dormant spirits from their long sleep. Only time will tell.

Chapter 16

Pfister Returns

The Pfister Hotel
Milwaukee, Wisconsin

Charles Pfister, who founded his eponymous hotel in Milwaukee back in the 1890s, never seems to have left. But his spectre may not be alone. Unseen spirits play tricks in many of the rooms. In fact, at least one visiting baseball player has refused to stay there overnight ever again.

Ira found the place amazing every time he walked in.

He had lived in Milwaukee for only about a year, but work had already taken him to the Pfister Hotel to attend more meetings and banquets than he could remember. Nevertheless, every time he entered the foyer he was once again stunned by the hotel's opulence. Ira had stayed in any number of luxury hotels during his travels, but the Pfister had a certain elegance few others could match.

Of course, that was Charles Pfister's plan from the very beginning.

In 1818, a French Canadian explorer named Solomon Juneau founded a small village near present-day Milwaukee. Two more pioneers, Byron Kilbourn and George H. Walker, went on to establish their own hamlets along the Milwaukee River, and in 1846, the three towns merged to form the present city. By that time, German immigrants were flooding into the area, so much so that the city got the nickname Deutsches Athen, or "German Athens."

One of those immigrants was Guido Pfister. Born in Hechingen, Germany, in 1818, Pfister was a tanner by trade. He came to the United States in 1845, settling in Buffalo, New York, before moving to Milwaukee in 1847. He set up his own tanning and leather store, which was immediately successful. In 1872, he partnered with Charles Vogel, and within just a few years their tanning company, Pfister and Vogel Leather, was producing more leather than just about any other manufacturer in the Midwest.

Pfister had many interests besides the tanning trade. He became president of the German Exchange Bank and a trustee of the Northwestern Mutual Life Insurance Company. He was also a director of the Milwaukee and Northern Railroad Company, the Northwestern National Insurance Company, and the Milwaukee Merchandise Insurance Company.

He also believed that Milwaukee needed a first-class—a world-class—hotel. He wanted a magnificent building—indeed, someplace where people would feel privileged to stay: a "grand hotel of the West." But he also hoped that folks from every social stratum would feel free to mix and mingle there.

Guido Pfister didn't live to see the hotel. He died in 1889 at the age of seventy-eight before a single stone was laid. His son, Charles, shared his vision, however, and he and his sister, Laura Vogel, immediately set about to fulfill their father's dream.

Charles hired architects Henry Koch and Hermann Esser to design an eight-story Romanesque Revival structure to be located on East Wisconsin Avenue just three blocks off Lake Michigan. Guido had estimated that the hotel would cost $500,000. Charles authorized $1.5 million—in 1890s dollars!

Pfister insisted that, wherever practical, Milwaukee workers be employed and Wisconsin materials be utilized in the building, including the distinct cream-colored brick on the exterior. (In 1843, two brothers, George and Jonathan Burnham, had opened a brickyard in town using a particular local yellow clay. Other factories followed their lead, and, soon, so many buildings were constructed with the pale blocks that Milwaukee got a second sobriquet: Cream City.)

The exterior of the limestone-and-brick Pfister Hotel is almost plain. The interior is anything but. The front doors open into an enormous, three-story lobby topped by an Italian-style fresco on the ceiling. Many of the staircases, the decorative pillars, the huge fireplace, and the floors are faced with marble. As a final touch, Pfister filled the lobby, hallways, and other public areas with dozens of pieces of Victorian artwork from his own collection—more than eighty in all, making it the largest display of Victorian art in any hotel.

The Pfister Hotel had its grand opening on May 1, 1893. At the time, it was arguably the most luxurious hotel in the country. It was also one of the most modern. The Pfister was one of the first—if not *the* first—hotel to run completely on electricity (provided by its own generator), and there were individual thermostats in every room. It also had the most up-to-date fireproofing available.

The hotel was only one of Charles Pfister's many endeavors. He was an even better businessman than his father. He started working in his father's tanning company in 1876, and he eventually became president and treasurer. He also followed in his father's footsteps in railroad, insurance, and banking. He became a power broker in city and state politics, too, almost always on the side of the Republicans. In 1900 he became the owner and publisher of the *Milwaukee Sentinel,* and he used the newspaper to boost his own interests as well as the image of the city. He finally sold the journal to William Randolph Hearst in 1924.

Pfister died just three years later. But he's never really gone. Pfister's pride and joy was his namesake hotel, and he's apparently stayed there to make sure that everything is kept in tip-top shape.

Ira didn't know about Pfister's ghost when he crossed the main lobby heading toward the ballroom. His mind was on the upcoming event. He had been asked to provide a few words after dinner, and he hated public speaking. But he was one of the managers of his company, and making presentations came with the territory.

As he passed the grand staircase leading to the upper atriums, he couldn't help but notice the two large Italian bronze lion statues, nicknamed Dick and Harry, at the foot of the steps. For the first thirty-three years of the hotel's existence, they had stood silent guard outside the main entrance.

Ira's eyes crept heavenward toward the amazing frescoed ceiling, but for some reason he found his attention being drawn to a portly gray-haired gentleman, elegantly dressed in a business suit, who was staring down from the first landing. As Ira studied the stranger, he realized the man was not looking at him at all, at least not specifically. Rather, he was smiling benignly, surveying the entire surroundings in a single, fixed gaze, taking in all three levels of the atrium at one time. And he was content.

Ira wondered who the old guy was. He certainly wasn't the concierge. Ira had passed him as he came in. And the cut of the unknown gentleman's clothes wasn't quite modern enough for him to be the manager of such a prestigious hotel. *Oh, well*, Ira thought as he hurried toward the Imperial Ballroom. *It's not my concern.*

The cocktail hour was over, and seating for the banquet was beginning as Ira rushed into the room. He instantly felt guilty. He thought he had arrived in plenty of time to schmooze: Heck, that was half the point of coming to these things. How long had he been staring at that man in the lobby?

Ira was quickly greeted by the host and hostess, who showed him to his seat at one end of the head table. He made small talk throughout much of the dinner, and then began to collect his thoughts as the first speaker began. Thanks for inviting me. It was an honor to work on behalf of such a fine organization. Yada, yada, yada.

Ira's mind drifted. *This room has seen some amazing things*, he thought. Indeed, the hall had been inaugurated with a banquet honoring President William McKinley and his cabinet.

Unconsciously, Ira's eyes once again glanced skyward. The gold and beige ballroom was built on two levels, with its ornate ceiling towering thirty-two feet over the dance floor. Halfway up was the minstrel's gallery, where, in past times, musicians would have been seated to play.

There he is again! Ira's eyes froze as he caught sight of a solitary figure standing in the musicians' alcove. It was the same man he had seen just an hour or so earlier on the staircase. The kindly intruder said nothing; he just hovered there, fixedly, looking down at the crowd, with the same slight grin on his face. The man *had* to have something to do with the hotel!

Curiosity finally got the better of him. Ira tapped the shoulder of the gentleman seated next to him, someone he knew to be a longtime resident of Milwaukee.

"Excuse me, Stan, do you happen to know who that person is standing up there on the mezzanine?" As Ira pointed, both men looked up at the railing. Whoever had been standing there was gone.

The episode was quickly forgotten as the speeches progressed, and the evening finally drew to a close. It was only on his way out of the hotel that Ira noticed a portrait hanging in the lobby. It was the same person Ira had seen on the stairs and in the gallery niche. Why would the hotel have an oil painting of *him?*

Ira rushed over to the concierge desk. "Excuse me, could you tell me who's in that painting over there?" he asked as he gestured toward the artwork.

"That?" the man replied incredulously. "You must be new to Milwaukee. That's Charles Pfister, who founded the hotel. Why do you ask?"

Ira didn't know how to answer.

Almost every U.S. president beginning with McKinley has either stayed at or visited the Pfister Hotel. It's also been home away from home for such notables as Sarah Bernhardt, Bob Hope, Elvis, Bruce Springsteen, and Jay Leno, just to name a handful.

In 1962, Ben Marcus (of the Marcus Corporation) bought the Pfister Hotel and immediately set about refurbishing it to its original stately grandeur. In the mid-'60s, he added a modern twenty-three-story tower adjoining the north side of the hotel, raising the guest room count from 200 to 307. The entire structure was once again renovated in 1993. The building is now registered as a Historic Hotel of America by the National Trust for Historic Preservation.

So far, Pfister's phantom has not shown up in the tower where the new rooms are located. But there have been many, many reports of Charles's ghost appearing on the hotel's original marble staircase, the musicians' gallery in the ballroom, and in a storage area on the ninth floor. A few have seen him in one of the elevators and walking his dog. Pfister never interferes with visitors or staff. Instead, he appears to be politely overseeing operations, making certain that everything is running smoothly.

Pfister may not be the only spirit haunting the hotel. Guests have reported hearing knocking sounds in the walls, and TVs and air conditioners have a habit of turning themselves on and off. A phantom dog has been heard yapping and racing up and down the corridors. Is it the same one that's been seen with Pfister?

People from every walk of life have experienced ghosts around the hotel. Interestingly enough, some of the most recent reports of paranormal phenomena have come from baseball players when their teams come to town to play the Milwaukee Brewers.

An incident that occurred to Carlos Gomez, the Minnesota Twins outfielder, was widely reported by the Associated Press in July 2009. A few years back, while coming out of the shower, the ballplayer was sure that he heard voices in the other room. But when he went to investigate, he found the place empty. Then, as he started getting dressed, his iPod, which was sitting on a tabletop, came to life and started to vibrate. Every time Gomez turned it off, it would start up again. In another version of the story, the ballplayer heard the iPod playing static as he came out of the washroom. But when he picked up the iPod to examine it, music started playing. But only for a few moments. It then switched back to static.

When Gomez's team returned to the Pfister on their next road trip to Milwaukee, he made sure that he had a roommate—and brought a Bible. Now, he just wishes the team would stay at a different hotel.

Gomez isn't the only one who has insisted on doubling up. At least two different pairs of teammates playing for the Florida Marlins also opt for sharing rooms when they're at the Pfister.

Pablo Sandoval, the Venezuelan-born player for the San Francisco Giants, is said to have encountered strange anomalies at the hotel as well. When Jim Tracy (now manager of the Colorado Rockies) was managing the Los Angeles Dodgers, he would often hear suggestions from his players that it might be best to move to a less-spirited hotel. It's said that Adrian Beltre of the Dodgers, for instance, was known to sleep with a baseball bat by his side when he stayed at the Pfister because of all the strange noises in the dark. (For whatever reason the Dodgers no long use the Pfister Hotel when they're in town.)

Brendan Ryan, shortstop for the St. Louis Cardinals, was witness to a strange light orb that floated through his room. He was also subject to another common ghost phenomenon: The room got inexplicably chilly.

In an AP interview, Phil Rozewicz, the Brewers clubhouse manager, related a story about an unnamed out-of-town rookie who was put up at the Pfister along with the rest of his team. The new player woke up in the middle of the night to find that his blinds were up and the window was open. He shut them both and went back to bed, but early the next morning he awoke to find them open again. The next night he slept in the lobby. Eventually he moved to a different hotel.

To this day some of the Brewers won't overnight at the Pfister if business requires that they stay downtown.

Do *you* dare visit? Why not? The spectres, whoever they are, have never done anyone any harm. And, in a way, it's comforting to know that the founder of the hotel is still there, watching over the staff and making sure guests have a pleasant stay.

Chapter 17

Apparitions in
the Adirondacks

The Sagamore
Bolton Landing, New York

At least a half dozen ghostly guests have taken up residence in the exclusive Sagamore Hotel in Bolton Landing, New York. Two ladies and a gentleman each travel alone; an arguing couple turn up in the dining room. Then there's the impish boy whose antics disrupt players on the golf course.

Pam and Johnny needed the getaway more than either of them cared to admit. It had been a rough winter, with almost twice as much snow as usual, and by January, Johnny could be depended upon to defiantly yell out, *"What* global warming?" whenever a new blizzard hit. When the spring thaw finally came, both of them were anxious to get out of the house and just take off.

They didn't have to travel far. Living a few miles outside Albany, they already knew where they wanted to go: straight up I-87 into the Adirondacks. The vistas would be incredible at that time of year, what with flowers peeking out of the vast meadows and the first melts filling the creeks and waterfalls to capacity, all topped by the stunning white peaks of the mountains. And then there would be the lake.

At nearly thirty-two miles across, Lake George was, in their opinion, one of the most perfect places on Earth. The narrow lake's clear waters, up to three miles deep in places, were perfect for boating, fishing, swimming, or just plain idling along the shore. The region's dense forests and hillsides offered trails for beginner to advanced hikers. And the small lakeside towns exude all the charm and friendliness that any visitor could hope for.

It's little wonder Thomas Jefferson wrote to his daughter in 1791 that Lake George was "without comparison the most beautiful water" he had ever seen. He described the lake as being "interspersed with islands, its water limpid as crystal, and the mountain sides covered with rich groves."

The first Europeans to see it were Samuel de Champlain and his men. The French explorer mentioned the lake in his personal log on July 3, 1609, but he didn't name it. Thirty-seven years later, a missionary, Isaac Jogues, christened it Lac du Saint-Sacrement. After the British victory in the Seven Year's War, the lake was renamed to honor King George II.

Pam preferred what the native Abenaki and Algonquin tribes living in the region had called it: Horican, meaning "tail of the lake," perhaps in a reference to its position with respect to nearby Lake Champlain. Horican was also the name used by James Fenimore Cooper, one of her favorite authors, in his 1826 novel *The Last of the Mohicans*. Pam remembered being swept up into the tale of romance as a child, and driving through the very region where the story was set brought it all back to mind.

Johnny was a fan of Cooper, too, but he mostly recalled the book's battle scenes, kidnappings, and massacres. He had been amazed when he found out that part of its plot may have been based on a very real event: the 1777 Native American killing of a young woman named Jane McCrea. The attack had happened nearby. She had been traveling to meet her fiancé, who was stationed at Fort Ticonderoga near the north end of Lake George.

Pam and Johnny wouldn't be heading all the way to Ticonderoga that night. They had taken a room at the outrageously luxurious Sagamore, which was located on a small island off Bolton Landing. They'd even splurged and taken a veranda suite with a lake view. It cost about twice what they normally spent for rooms when they went on holiday, but the Sagamore was special. It also had a *Mohicans* tie-in! *Sagamore* is an Americanized version of the Algonquian word *sakimawa*, meaning "chief." And Cooper used the word throughout his writings.

Johnny exited the interstate onto NY 9N. After stopping for a light snack in the village of Lake George at the southernmost tip of the lake, he and Pam leisurely began the remaining ten-mile drive to their destination.

By the early 1900s, Lake George had become one of the premier tourist destinations in the Northeast. It was particularly attractive to the super-rich, who built large mansions on a section of Lake Shore Drive (then Bolton Road) bordering the waters' western coast. The several-mile stretch soon became known as Millionaires Row. The stone houses, which the owners self-effacingly called "cottages," were huge, with up to a dozen bedrooms each and acres of property attached.

The Sagamore hotel was the brainchild of Myron O. Brown, the manager of Mohican House, an early lakeside lodge. He convinced four millionaires—William B. Bement, George Burnham, Robert Glendenning, and E. Burgess Warren—who summered in the Adirondacks that they should invest in a newer, more lavish hotel. They formed the Green Island Improvement Company and bought a small islet, the seventy-two-acre Green

Island, just offshore from Bolton Landing. (Another backer, John Boulton Simpson of New York, joined them soon after.)

The Wilson Brothers, architects from Philadelphia, designed the Sagamore in a Queen Anne style. They built the hotel on the south end of the island, and it opened on July 3, 1883, to rave reviews. From its inception the hotel was intended for wealthy, discriminating patrons only. Riff-raff need not apply. The inn was soon filled to capacity—up to four hundred guests—especially during the busy summer season when the well-heeled sought to escape the heat and grit of the cities.

Fire struck the building in 1893 and again in 1914, but each time the damage was repaired and the hotel opened anew. By 1930, the exclusive resort was showing its age, but it was rejuvenated thanks to an influx of capital from two of the hotel's corporate shareholders, Dr. William G. Beckers of New York and William H. Bixby of St. Louis.

Starting in the Depression years, many of those owning houses on Millionaires Row sold off their property. By mid-century, most of the homes had been torn down or transformed into hotels, though three of the estates still exist. By the end of World War II, the clientele who visited Lake George had also changed as middle-class families became more mobile and could afford to get there.

Through it all, the Sagamore eked by, but eventually it was forced to close its doors in 1981. Two years later, Norman Wolpin, a real estate developer, teamed with Kennington Ltd. of Los Angeles to form Green Island Associates. The new consortium completely restored the fading lady. Since then, additional guest accommodation buildings have been added to the property: several condominiums, the seven Lodges, and even the Tudor-style Wapanak Castle that houses twelve. Taken together, the new units add another 250 rooms to the one hundred available in the main historic building. Today, the hotel is managed by Ocean Properties of Delray Beach, Florida.

Johnny and Pam drove across the short bridge connecting the village of Bolton Landing to Green Island. Though the two weren't frequent guests at the hotel, the familiar building with its glimmering white facade, red tiled roof, and gables was always a welcome sight.

After checking in, the pair headed toward the elevator. They entered the lift, signaled for their floor, then turned to the front as the doors closed. Slowly they became aware that they weren't alone. They looked over their shoulders and were startled to see a man standing behind them. Odd that they had hadn't noticed him when they entered. They must have been so excited about getting to their suite that they had been completely oblivious to the fact that someone was already in the car.

The fellow was portly but fashionably dressed in an expensive brown suit with a gold watch fob attached to his vest. His most distinguishable feature was his huge handlebar moustache—a style that was popular at the turn of the nineteenth century.

"Oh, I'm sorry. I didn't see you there," Pam gasped.

The stranger met her gaze as a wry smile crossed his lips. No sooner had he nodded a silent acknowledgment than the elevator slowed to a halt. It was Johnny and Pam's floor. The young couple stepped out of the car, and the doors gently slid shut.

The rest of the afternoon passed peaceably enough, but for some reason they just couldn't get the man they had seen in the elevator out of their minds. That night, as they headed for dinner at La Bella Vita, one of the hotel's six restaurants, they decided to inquire about him at the front desk. His wardrobe and grooming were so unusual that they figured the staff would know him. Perhaps he was one of the employees, hired to wear period costumes and mingle among the guests to enhance the hotel atmosphere. It was then that Pam and Johnny got the shock of their lives. The man they had seen was a ghost. And he had a name: Walter.

The startled couple was told that the first person to see the apparition was a female staff member who entered an empty elevator only to bump into an invisible presence lurking inside. As the young woman stared, a male figure slowly became visible. The phantom looked exactly the way Johnny and Pam had described. He also reeked of cigars, which the pair had noticed, too. In time, employees had decided that the phantom was probably trying to find his way down to the Trillium bis, a restaurant that used to be a gentlemen's smoking lounge. They also named him Walter, even though all attempts to identify the spectral visitor had been in vain.

Intrigued by the ghostly legend, Johnny and Pam decided to ask around. By the time they left on Sunday, they discovered that the Sagamore is home to at least five other spirits. Two of them were married, and their apparel suggested they came from the first decade the hotel was in operation. The spectres would come down from the second floor and make their way into the Trillium bis. Some accounts say that they would sit patiently for a few moments in the restaurant's reception area before completely disappearing. Most versions of the story have them entering the dining room and breaking into a fight. The husband would violently throw his wife to the floor. Then, as she reached up to grab at him, they both faded into nothingness.

There haven't been many reports of the arguing couple—and fewer of Walter, as well—since the wing in which the Trillium bis was located was converted into guest rooms. But that doesn't mean the spirits aren't around somewhere.

Pam and Johnny should be very happy they didn't run into one of the other phantoms at the hotel, because it shows up in people's suites in the middle of the night. The spectre is a woman, but nobody knows who she is—or was. Dressed all in white, she materializes by people's beds and leans over them. When the startled guests awaken, she blows her icy breath onto their faces. Other tenants never see the phantom, but they are aware she's in the room. Many are so uncomfortable that they're being watched by invisible eyes that they toss and turn throughout the night and are unable to get to sleep.

Another story concerns a sous chef who, several years ago, suddenly quit after making an almost unbelievable claim. He said he was at his station in Mister Brown's Pub when a tall blonde woman, dressed in elegant white evening attire, came into the kitchen. She marched up to the chef, spoke with him briefly—what was said has not been recorded—then stepped forward and walked right through him. Shocked, the chef looked behind him just in time to see the mysterious creature vanish from sight. He turned in his apron on the spot.

Finally, there is the boy. The Sagamore has an eighteen-hole, par 70 championship golf course that was designed by Donald Ross in 1928. The spectre of a mischievous young lad dressed in 1950s clothing has been seen sneaking around the course, which is located across the causeway on the mainland. According to legend, when the boy was alive he used to earn spare change by finding lost balls and turning them in at the pro shop. Unfortunately, one day he didn't check before he ran out into the street, and he was struck and killed by a car. Death doesn't seem to have slowed the boy down, however. These days, he doesn't wait for the balls to go astray. He'll pick them up as soon as they hit the fairway and hide behind a tree. Then when the players approach, he'll laugh and throw the balls at their feet.

Sightings of all six of the Sagamore's ghosts have occurred often enough that their tales have become part of the hotel's legacy. Although the resort doesn't necessarily encourage the reputation, some sources place the Sagamore on the list of Top Ten Haunted Hotels in America. What better reason to visit Lake George and the Sagamore for oneself?

Chapter 18

The Bohemian Spirit

Hotel Chelsea
New York, New York

Ah, la vie bohème. *The legendary Chelsea Hotel calls itself "a rest stop for rare individuals." They're absolutely right. After all, what's more "rare" than a ghost? At least three famous phantoms are known to walk the hotel's halls. More spectral activity takes place in its ninety-seven rooms.*

Meagan couldn't believe it. She was finally in New York City! She had dreamt about this moment for years.

She hoped to see her name in lights on the Great White Way one day, but she was still Midwestern sensible. Before moving lock, stock, and barrel to the Big Apple, she thought it would be best to first take a wee bite. She wanted to make sure she liked the place. But if the energy and excitement that overwhelmed her as she stepped out of Port Authority were any indication, the city had already won her over.

She decided that for her first weeklong foray she would overnight at one of the city's old, historic hotels rather than in some bland, faceless Hilton or Sheraton. Something with a little more character, a trifle off-kilter, yet clean and safe for all of that. As soon as Meagan saw the hotel's name pop up on Travelocity, she knew where she had to stay: the Chelsea.

Even back in Nebraska, Meagan had heard about the fabled hotel. It was impossible for any real performer *not* to know about it. Dozens upon dozens of artists, designers, writers, directors, and musicians, some of them the top in their fields, have stayed there over the decades.

As she walked into the lobby, Meagan was immediately struck by the offbeat ambience of the place. The cacophony of furnishings and mismatched furniture screamed bohemia; the walls were filled with artwork, from oil paintings and sketches to sculpture. (She would discover that the art continued up the walls lining the winding staircase as well.) After a minimum of fuss, she made her way up to her room—she had chosen a cozy one-bedroom for her short exploratory visit of the city—and began to unpack.

As the mid-eighteenth century approached, the "city" of New York was confined to the southern tip of Manhattan. In 1750, Capt. Thomas Clark, an officer in the French and Indian Wars, settled along the Hudson River about two and a half miles father north. His homestead, which he named Chelsea, was located near what is today Twenty-third Street between Ninth and Tenth Avenues.

The city continued to expand. Meanwhile, the Clarks' daughter, Charity, married Benjamin Moore, the Episcopal bishop. Their son, Clement, became famous as the author of the poem "A Visit from St. Nicholas," or, as most people know it, "The Night Before Christmas." Clement took advantage of the burgeoning demand for real estate, and by around 1850 he had subdivided and sold off the family's property to form the district known as Chelsea to this day.

In 1884, the Hotel Chelsea opened on West Twenty-third Street between Seventh and Eighth Avenues in the thriving theater district. It was the first co-op apartment building in

New York City, designed for long-term residents, although some rooms were available for short-term lease. At the time of its construction, the twelve-story building was the tallest in Manhattan, and it remained so until 1902.

Several features made the place highly attractive. The building had a striking Queen Anne–style redbrick facade. Hallways on the guest floors were tiled in marble. No two apartments were alike; some were particularly spacious, with up to seven bedrooms. Many had balconies with wrought-iron railings. All had tall doors and windows, and some had ceilings that reached ten to twelve feet high.

Meagan tested her bed. It was comfortable, with a bright, new comforter on top. Many of the room fixtures, such as the bathroom taps, were certainly mid-twentieth century, but there was a modern flat-screen TV on the bureau.

And the room had Wi-Fi . . . which was amazing since the walls seemed particularly thick. No wonder musicians—and perhaps more pointedly, their neighbors—loved the rooms. No sound would bleed between them. If it weren't for the noise of the city coming through the windows, the place would be quiet as a morgue. (As the thought came to mind, Meagan shuddered. Could she be any more ghoulish?)

The original hotel cooperative was short-lived. The company went bankrupt in 1903, and the building was put up for sale. Two years later it reopened as a hotel. The Chelsea continued to welcome long-term tenants, however—a tradition that remained until very recently. (Today the maximum stay at any one time is three weeks.)

Soon there was an ever-changing whirlwind of guests passing through. The hotel's reputation as a haven for artists started almost immediately. Early visitors included actresses Lillie Langtry and Sarah Bernhardt (who traveled with and slept in her own coffin rather than use hotel beds) as well as writers O. Henry and Mark Twain.

The parade of performers and artisans who have called the Chelsea home beginning in the 1950s really cemented its reputation as a sanctuary—and even asylum—for creative souls. Willem de Kooning, Jasper Johns, Robert Mapplethorpe, and Diego Rivera were just a few of the visual masters who lived and worked there.

Stage and film personalities who have darkened its door include Jane Fonda, Milos Forman, Elliott Gould, Ethan Hawke, Dennis Hopper, Eddie Izzard, Elaine Stritch, and Uma Thurman. Some of Andy Warhol's "Superstars," including Edie Sedgwick, frequented the hotel, and he directed his 1966 film *Chelsea Girl* to chronicle their time there. Author Arthur C. Clarke was living at the Chelsea when he met with Stanley Kubrick to collaborate on the screenplay for *2001: A Space Odyssey*.

The hotel's musical heritage is even more amazing: Bob Dylan wrote "Sad-Eyed Lady of the Lowlands" while living there. A stay prompted Joni Mitchell to write "Chelsea Morning." Dee Dee Ramone took up residence and wrote songs for the Ramones in his near-soundproof room. His time there also led to his writing a novel, *Chelsea Horror Hotel*. Then there's Leonard Cohen, who composed "Chelsea Hotel No. 2" about his tryst in his apartment with an unnamed woman, though the lyrics almost certainly refer to Janis Joplin.

Others from the music industry to choose the Chelsea were Canned Heat, Alice Cooper, the Grateful Dead, Jimi Hendrix, Madonna, Edith Piaf, Patti Smith, Virgil Thomson, Rufus Wainwright, Tom Waits, and Frank Zappa. The list goes on and on.

But the most notorious musical couple to stay there were Sid Vicious, the bass guitarist for the Sex Pistols, and his girlfriend, Nancy Spungen. Theirs was a dictionary definition of a codependent, destructive relationship, and it ended, eventually, in both of their deaths.

The English punk rocker was born Simon John Ritchie in 1957. His friend John Lydon gave him the stage name Sid Vicious partly as a joke when Lydon's pet hamster, Sid, "vicious"ly bit Ritchie. After working with two other bands, Vicious was hired to replace Glen Matlock, who left the Sex Pistols in 1977. His first performance with the group was in April that same year.

Sometime in November, Vicious started seeing American groupie Nancy Spungen. She was a heroin addict, and soon the rocker was also addicted. Their unstable antics ultimately destroyed the group, which disbanded in January 1978. Vicious continued on a solo career, but by then his body was clearly falling apart.

On the morning of October 12, 1978, Vicious awoke in his apartment, Room 100, at the Chelsea Hotel. Spungen lay dead on the bathroom floor, having bled to death from a wound to her stomach caused by Sid's knife. Vicious was arrested for her murder but somehow managed to be released on bail. Ten days later he attempted suicide, and in December he was sent to Riker's Island for fifty days for assaulting Patti Smith's brother Todd.

By the time he got out on February 1, 1979, Vicious had gone through rehab and was clean. But between that night and the next morning, he died of an overdose, having shot up with almost pure heroin.

Despite the fact that his time with Spungen was marked by bouts of extreme violence, Sid Vicious denied to the end that he had killed her. He swore that he had no memory of the night because of the amount of drugs he had taken, but he offered several alternate possible explanations for her death: Perhaps she fell on the knife during their argument. Maybe some unknown outsider stabbed her during an attempted robbery or a bad drug deal.

Meagan knew Sid Vicious's ghost was rumored to be back at the Chelsea. His highly identifiable spectre has been seen in and lingering around the elevator. He doesn't engage with strangers, though, so no one can be certain about the true reason for his return. Maybe he is trying to find the real killer. And Vicious isn't the only spectre said to haunt the halls!

The Chelsea has been a temporary sanctuary for some of America's most famous writers, including Brendan Behan, Charles Bukowski, William S. Burroughs, Quentin Crisp, Simone de Beauvoir, Allen Ginsberg, Edgar Lee Masters, Arthur Miller, Jean-Paul Sartre, Gore Vidal, and Tennessee Williams. In one of the apartments, Jack Kerouac wrote much of the original manuscript of *On the Road,* famously on a single, long roll of paper. Charles R. Jackson, author of *The Lost Weekend,* ended his own life in his Chelsea Hotel room on September 21, 1968. But the two writers who have chosen to return to the Chelsea after death are Thomas Wolfe and poet Dylan Thomas.

Wolfe was born October 3, 1900, in North Carolina. His form was the autobiographical novel, and he's best remembered for his magnum opus *Look Homeward, Angel.* (The work is now just as well known for its theatrical adaptation by Ketti Frings.) Wolfe first visited New York City in 1923, when he made his first attempt to have his plays produced on Broadway. The following year, he accepted a brief position teaching English at NYU, and he was in and out of Manhattan for the rest of his life. His pied-à-terre was often the

Chelsea Hotel. The celebrated author developed pneumonia while visiting his brother in Seattle in July 1938, and that September he was admitted to Johns Hopkins in Baltimore for military tuberculosis of the brain. He died there on September 15, 1938, just shy of his thirty-eighth birthday.

Wolfe only lived temporarily at the Chelsea, but he obviously developed some strong connection with it—enough to draw him back from the Afterlife. Perhaps his transparent figure has come back to walk the hallway on the eighth floor because he stayed in Room 831 while he was in Manhattan working with his editor, Scribner's Maxwell Perkins, on the manuscript for *Look Homeward, Angel.*

Dylan Thomas probably spent less time at the hotel than Wolfe, and who knows how much of it he was able to recall? By the time the Welshman first toured the United States to perform poetry readings he was already a major alcoholic. It's well documented that upon returning to Room 206 at the Chelsea after a night of binge drinking at the White Horse Tavern on November 3, 1953, Thomas proclaimed, "I've had eighteen straight whiskies. I think that is a record." (He exaggerated, according to eyewitnesses, but not by much.)

The poet's most enduring work is *Under Milk Wood,* which was originally presented as a radio play on the BBC. Thomas performed it solo for the first time at Harvard on May 3, 1953. Just eleven days later, he read the play with other actors at the Poetry Centre in New York. He returned home to England for four months, then came back to Manhattan.

He was already sick—he had lifelong respiratory problems—when he returned to America on October 20. He managed to get through a series of personal appearances, including more readings at the Poetry Centre and a recorded symposium at Cinema 16. Thomas was suffering severely by the night of his bender at the White Horse Tavern. Air pollution was also considerable in the city, and Thomas begged out of social obligations on November 2 and 3. By midnight on November 5 he was unable to breathe. Thomas was rushed from the Chelsea Hotel to St. Vincent's Hospital about two o'clock, where doctors discovered both acute bronchitis and pneumonia. The poet died there on November 9, 1953. Though it's widely assumed the cause was alcoholism—and it was certainly a contributing factor—he actually died of a swelling of the brain due to a lack of oxygen from the pneumonia.

Dylan Thomas may be buried back in Wales, but for some reason his soul has stayed at the Chelsea. Guests will catch his translucent figure careening down the corridors throughout the hotel. To paraphrase his most famous single verse, perhaps he does not want to "go gentle into that good night."

(Some say that he also haunts the White Horse Tavern, where he'll buy people a round of drinks at his favorite table in one of the corners. Or an empty beer or whiskey glass will show up there, thought to be a sign of his presence. Staffers have also heard noises down in the basement that they credit to Thomas.)

According to some residents, playwright Eugene O'Neill and industrial titans J. P. Morgan and Andrew Carnegie also roam the Chelsea halls. And unidentified apparitions have been reported in the lobby bar, the Star Lounge.

But most of the paranormal activity is of the traditional kind: People stumble upon unexplainable cold spots or feel a sudden chilly breeze. Objects move on their own, and the lights, TV, and bathroom water taps turn on or off by themselves. Disembodied voices and footsteps echo in the roomy apartments and down empty hallways. And a few visitors feel the hand of an unseen spirit touch them. Some of the anomalies might be explained away by the expected creaking of an old building. But the rest?

Given the amount of passion, drama, and tragedy that the hotel has seen, it's surprising that more spectral phenomena don't occur. During her short stay, Meagan never encountered anything otherworldly. She certainly didn't see any ghosts—that is, unless the long-haired rock-and-roller with the purple fingernails standing by the lift was Sid Vicious back from the dead.

But she didn't care one way or the other. She'd be coming back to the Big City—maybe even staying at the Chelsea Hotel again. And, if she did, she'd be happy to share it with the boys.

Chapter 19
Entities at
the Inn

The Inn at Jim Thorpe
Jim Thorpe, Pennsylvania

The calm, pastoral settings of the Lehigh Valley, the gateway to the Pocono Mountains, belie the number of spooks that inhabit Jim Thorpe, Pennsylvania. Many of the phantoms have taken up residence in a graceful hotel dating back to the mid-nineteenth century: the Inn at Jim Thorpe. Tourists usually visit for a day or two at a time. The spirits stay for eternity.

Russell burst through the door, and as he barreled into the room a cold blast of November air swept in behind him, hitting the shop owner square in the face.

"Barrett, you're not gonna believe it. I saw one! I just saw one of the ghosts over at the hotel."

Barrett Ravenhurst, the proprietor of the Emporium of Curious Goods in Jim Thorpe, Pennsylvania, looked up, bemused. He had known Russ for a long time, and the young man had been trying to see one of the spirits said to haunt the Inn at Jim Thorpe for years. If he finally spied one, or thought he had, well, it was a big deal indeed.

Ravenhurst and his store were well known in those parts. He was raised in Lehighton, six miles down the road. For thirty years he made his profession as a magician, and it was his interest in the relationship between magic and faith that led to his earning a doctorate in comparative religion. His study of Wicca—the earth-centered belief most commonly identified with witchcraft—led Ravenhurst to annual pilgrimages to Salem, Massachusetts. While there, he visited a friend's New Age store and decided that a similar one might thrive in the arty, laid-back community of Jim Thorpe. (The Salem shop—The Cat, The Crow and The Crown—is owned by Laurie Cabot, who in the 1970s was made the Official Witch of Salem by decree of Governor Michael Dukakis.)

In 1987, with partner Rick Brong, Ravenhurst opened his own shop in two connecting storefronts on Broadway, the main street through Jim Thorpe. Within just a few years the Emporium had become the largest boutique of its kind in northeastern Pennsylvania. And just what does it carry? Books, of course—more than five hundred titles on all sorts of metaphysical subjects, such as alchemy, spell casting, and the Kabbalah. Soothing oils, pungent incense, aromatic plants. Antiques. Wiccan items, ceremonial athames, and ritual wear including robes and capes. All in all, an eclectic, eccentric collection suited to the tastes of occult enthusiasts.

And, as if that isn't enough, the shop is haunted, home to a large, gray ghost cat. For sixteen years, before buying an elegant twenty-two-room Victorian mansion in Lehighton, Ravenhurst lived in an apartment above the Emporium. Frequently he would catch the phantom feline out of the corner of his eye, but whenever he would turn to directly face it, the cat would disappear.

The spectral animal didn't keep to the upstairs, however. It showed up almost as frequently in the shop itself. Brong has spied the cat as well—sort of. While looking at a curtain hanging in a passageway, he saw the bottom edge of the cloth lift up, then drop again, just as if something had crawled under it.

They've nicknamed the otherworldly umbra "Spooky."

Now, when the shop is opened in the morning, if anything has been knocked over or fallen off a shelf, the owners simply chalk it up to Spooky. Ravenhurst and one of the clerks have both felt the invisible creature rub up against their legs at one time or another. Many customers have also commented on it over the years. More than a few have seen it lying on the counter and gone over to pet it, only to be startled by having the cat vanish right before their eyes.

One time Ravenhurst was surprised to hear four teenage boys who had wandered into the store calling out to the cat. When it ignored them and walked away, they called out to Barrett, "Hey, mister, do you know you have a cat in here? It went behind the counter." Ravenhurst didn't bother to explain what they had actually seen. That particular counter was up against a wall, and the ghostly cat had walked straight through it.

It wasn't a sighting of the phantasmal kitty, though, that Russell wanted to share with Barrett. It was his unexpected detection of an apparition in the 150-year-old hotel catty-cornered across the street.

Jim Thorpe is nestled along the Lehigh River in the southern foothills of the Pocono Mountains. Anthracite coal was discovered nearby around the turn of the nineteenth century, and in 1818 the Lehigh Coal and Navigation Company founded the small community as a railroad hub and shipping center. It was originally named Mauch Chunk, a derivation of the words for "sleeping bear" in the language of the Lenni-Lenape tribes that lived in the area.

By the middle of the twentieth century, the easily accessible coal had been mined, and the region fell into an economic slump. Fortunately, there was a budding tourism industry. Aficionados of fine period architecture sought out the preserved mansions that industrialists had built just outside of town. Hikers, cyclists, and rafters came for the mountainsides, trails, waters, and clean air. It was only ninety miles from New York City, seventy from Philly, and a mere twenty miles—a hop, skip, and a jump—to Allentown.

The hamlet also became a mecca for artisans—painters, sculptors, craftspeople, and weavers galore. And with the New Age thinking that arose in the 1970s, it had also become a perfect place for Barrett Ravenhurst to set up his shop.

By then the town was known as Jim Thorpe. After the death of the celebrated athlete in 1953, Thorpe's widow agreed to bury the Olympic legend in Mauch Chunk, even though he had never visited the place. The town erected a large granite monument over his grave and renamed itself Jim Thorpe in his honor. The tomb stands there to this day and has, indeed, become one of the town's major tourist attractions.

Thorpe's grave isn't haunted, but the hotel in town that bears his name is decidedly so. It dates to 1833, when local businessman Cornelius Connor built the White Swan Hotel to cater to the needs of the region's increasing number of visitors. At the time of its construction, it was one of several large hotels in Mauch Chunk.

Sixteen years later, in 1849, a massive fire swept through downtown, destroying many of the buildings, including the White Swan. Connor immediately rebuilt the structure, this time naming it the New American Hotel. Its exterior had a New Orleans look about it, with a second-floor veranda surrounded by wrought-iron railings and potted plants hanging from the eaves. Among the notables to stay in this new facility were President William H. Taft, Gen. Ulysses S. Grant, John D. Rockefeller, William "Buffalo Bill" Cody, and Thomas Edison.

The economic downturns of the mid-1900s were difficult on the hotel, and the inn fell into disrepair. By the 1960s and '70s many residents were staying there on a reduced-cost, month-to-month basis.

Enter John Drury. In 1988, he bought the New American Hotel. Having previously renovated the Chestnut Hill Hotel outside Philadelphia and the Keswick Theatre in Glenside, he completely restored the New American. He kept the basic French Quarter exterior and Victorian interior but fully modernized the forty-five rooms and suites.

Drury rechristened the hotel the Inn at Jim Thorpe, and his son David was made the general manager. An outstanding combination of old and new, the Inn at Jim Thorpe has been placed on the National Register of Historic Places.

With as many incarnations as the hotel has had, it's only fitting that the inn is haunted. Were the spirits awakened by all of the hubbub during the reconstruction? Or have they been there all along? The rumors of their presence have only become common knowledge recently—thanks in large part to the new owner's willingness to publicize guests' claims on the hotel's Web site.

Certainly all of the locals, like Russell, had heard the legends for years. Finally on that chilly afternoon, his efforts were rewarded. He didn't know why, but that day on a whim, he poked his head into the lobby. He wasn't thinking about the spirits. Don't they only show themselves at nighttime? But something had compelled him to go inside.

A friend working behind the desk waved hello as Russ quietly strode into the room. She knew why he was there; he had once confided that he hoped to someday see one of the phantoms. Russ smiled sheepishly at her, passed to the far side of the room, looked around, and then turned to walk back out the entrance. He thought he heard his friend call, "See anything?" But his eyes were glued to a spot on the foyer wall. An indistinct but definite shadow had appeared, a human shape.

Russ jerked his head around to see if there was anyone standing behind him or a light source that could be causing the shadow. But no, except for him and the young lady on the other side of the check-in counter, the place was empty. There didn't seem to be anything that could be causing the shade's appearance.

Russ turned back to the shadow. Surprisingly, it was still there. Then the hazy image started to move, slowly, floating across the bare wall. As Russell stared at it in wonderment, the figure faded away to nothing. Just before the image vanished, however, he had the presence of mind to quickly raise his cell phone and snap a picture.

"Russell. What's going on?" called the girl behind the desk. "You're white as a sheet."

Russ rushed out without answering. He knew the first person he had to tell was Barrett. He would accept what he had to say without question or reservation. Seconds later Russell was in the Emporium.

Barrett tried to calm Russell down, told him to take a deep breath or two, and then listened carefully to his tale. Although Barrett had never been fortunate enough to spy one of the inn's apparitions himself, many, *many* people had told him similar stories. Usually the paranormal activity in the rooms are the usual things that go bump in the night: cold spots, objects moving on their own, or the faint scent of smoke (thought by locals to be a ghostly reminder of the White Swan fire).

A few of the inn's rooms are particularly haunted, however. In 211, for example, the television switches itself on and off. Elsewhere on the second floor, people hear the sound of invisible children laughing, and the odor of cigar smoke lingers in the air. Towels find their way into the toilets to stop up the plumbing. Men, for some reason, are particularly susceptible to having their personal property moved about by spirit hands. It's been reported that one man woke in Room 203 to discover his cell phone had relocated itself to the inside of the mini-bar.

Pesky shadows and orbs turn up in 305, and Room 315 is subject to chairs turning themselves over. But if guests want to increase their chances of seeing an apparition, they should ask for 310 at check-in. According to an old story, a nurse attended her long-term patient there, and she's been known to get upset when guests climb into bed. Some unlucky occupants have felt her icy fingers closing around their limbs, and, as if that weren't enough, on occasion her shimmering spectre, dressed all in white, has appeared. And she's not the only phantom to show up in 310. There's also a tall man with greasy combed-back hair who materializes from time to time.

There's one apparition who allows herself to be seen all over the hotel. It's a woman dressed in late-nineteenth-century clothing, but her identity is unknown because she has no facial features. She'll drift down hallways or turn up inside guest bedrooms, but if she realizes she's being watched, she'll quickly pass through the nearest door, even if it's closed and locked. Visitors who have success in spying a full-form spirit are few and far behind, however. Most people, if they spot anything at all, are like Russell and only glimpse shadows or capture a ball of light in one of their photographs.

As Russ rattled on to Barrett about his ghostly encounter, he finally remembered taking a picture of the shadow with his phone. He scrolled through the photos to see what, if anything, had turned up. Dim but definitely there in front of the hotel wall, a tiny globe of light was floating about five feet off the floor.

Russell slowly turned the screen to Barrett. The two stared at the remarkable image. Barrett had seen several such photos before, but never one from just across the street. Right then and there he made a mental note to pick up a small pocket camera on his way home. Next time, he thought, if anyone brought evidence of ghosts cavorting at the inn into the Emporium, it was going to be him!

There is one more haunting in Jim Thorpe that's worth noting: Cell 17 of the Old Jail.

In the 1860s and '70s, the Molly Maguires was a secret, militant organization of Irish coal miners that operated independently of their union. Conditions in the mines were deplorable; safety measures were lax or nonexistent. Every day the men risked their lives down in the hole for a miniscule salary. The Molly Maguires used violent means, including arson, kidnapping, and murder, to draw attention to the coalmen's plight and to force owners to fix the problems and raise the workers' pay.

Instead of acquiescing, the mine keepers brought in the Pinkerton Agency to infiltrate the mob. Many of the criminals were arrested, and ten were sentenced to die. On June 21, 1877, six men were publicly hanged in the Carbon County prison in Pottsville. Another four were hanged in Jim Thorpe (still Mauch Chunk at the time) for the murder of two mine bosses.

Among the quartet was Alexander Campbell. Before he was led to the gallows, he pressed his handprint into the wall of his cell, number 17, and he laid a curse of sorts on the building. He swore on his innocence that the handprint would never go away. Indeed, all attempts to remove the mark have been futile. Visitors to the prison, which now operates as the Old Jail Museum, can just make it out.

Chapter 20

The Fellow on the Thirteenth Floor

Biltmore Hotel
Coral Gables, Florida

Thomas "Fatty" Walsh was no stranger to violence. A hit man for the mob, he moved to Florida and became part owner of a Jazz Age speakeasy on the thirteenth floor of the Biltmore Hotel in Coral Gables, Florida. Despite being killed there, he's apparently decided to stick around to schmooze with hotel guests.

"The strangest thing just happened to me."

The concierge looked up. Midforties, dressed in a smart pantsuit, with her hair styled in a severe corporate cut, and wearing just the smallest hint of makeup, the woman was clearly a no-nonsense type. Her statement, neither defensive nor demanding, was a simple statement of fact. And she wanted answers.

She had taken one of the suites in the hotel's signature ninety-three-foot tower, which had been modeled after the Giralda Tower in Seville, Spain. Accompanied by the bellman, she had entered the tower's private elevator and pressed the 10 button. The doors silently slid shut, and the lift started its smooth ascent. She watched patiently as the floor numbers lit up as the elevator rose: 7, 8, 9.

But then, rather than stop at ten, the lift took on a mind of its own. It passed her floor without slowing down, continuing on to eleven, then twelve. Finally, at thirteen, the elevator came to a standstill. The doors parted.

The suite, which took up the entire level, was completely dark, save for what light was coming through the windows. The room was dead silent, and an almost eerie, uneasy calm filled the space.

The woman glanced over at the bellman standing beside her. Though she knew it was clichéd to think the words, his face was white as a ghost. Was he concerned about a small elevator malfunction? Or was he bothered by the suite number? Very few hotels have a thirteenth floor because of the superstition associated with the number—or rather the hotels *have* them but just don't *number* them thirteen.

What was more puzzling: The doors stayed open for what became an uncomfortably long period of time. Just as the woman was about to step across the threshold into the foyer of the suite, the doors finally began to close. The bellman, who had recovered his composure, quickly punched the 10 button, the elevator made its short descent, and within seconds it stopped at the correct floor.

It was only after she had settled into her apartment that the woman made her way down to the lobby to query the concierge about the odd behavior of the elevator and the staff member's reaction. What she heard made quite a story.

It all dated back to the early 1900s, when Florida was undergoing a rapid land boom. George E. Merrick, a speculator and developer, was one of the men at its center. Besides founding the University of Miami, he also laid out many of Miami's surrounding suburbs, including Coral Gables.

The upscale residential hamlet, nicknamed the City Beautiful, was planned from the start as a haven for the well-to-do. Huge mansions soon sprang up beside the wide, palm- and banyan-lined boulevards. Merrick realized that a showcase luxury hotel was necessary to cater to the needs of affluent visitors to the resort town.

In 1924, he convinced John McEntee Bowman, head of the Biltmore chain, to join him in building a landmark hotel in the community. The project was announced at a gala dinner on November 25, 1924. It would be glorious even by Biltmore standards. Plans called for a $10 million, four-hundred-room hotel on 150 acres that would also feature ten tennis courts, a polo field, an eighteen-hole golf course designed by Donald Ross, and a 23,000-square-foot, 700,000-gallon swimming pool—the largest hotel pool in the continental United States.

Bowman entrusted the job to the architects Leonard Schultze and S. Fullerton Weaver, who had previously designed New York City's Grand Central Station and Biltmore hotels in Atlanta and Los Angeles. (The last of these would become a haunted hotel after the notorious 1947 murder of the so-called Black Dahlia, described in Chapter 4.) The sprawling Coral Gables edifice would be Mediterranean revival, a blend of Spanish and Italian influences. And it would have a signature tower. Each of the suites located there would take up an entire floor and have several bedrooms and bathrooms as well as access to a private elevator.

The hotel made its debut on January 15, 1926. For the opening, railcars dubbed the Miami Biltmore Specials ferried members of high society from the Northeast down to Florida. Fifteen hundred guests rode up the arched driveway to the hotel and gasped as they entered the breathtaking lobby. There was a high vaulted ceiling covered with frescoes, tall marble columns, travertine and terrazzo floors, mahogany railings, leaded glass chandeliers, and a lushly decorated courtyard and fountain. Three orchestras, including one led by Paul Whiteman, were engaged for the festivities.

The Biltmore was an immediate success, and from the Roaring Twenties up to the war years, it was one of the most fashionable destinations in the entire country. Notable guests included royalty (the Duke and Duchess of Windsor), presidents (Franklin Roosevelt), magnates (the Vanderbilts), and Hollywood celebrities (Bing Crosby, Judy Garland, and Ginger Rogers).

It also drew its share of shady underworld figures, perhaps most notably Al Capone, who liked to entertain on the thirteenth floor, now known as the Everglades Suite. Also, in 1929, Thomas "Fatty" Walsh was gunned down in that very room. Police files of the subsequent investigation seem to have disappeared, but here's what happened according to the general consensus:

Walsh was already well known in crime and law enforcement circles by the time he moved to Florida from New York. He was into the narcotics trade and was an "associate" of gangsters Dutch Schultz and Charles "Lucky" Luciano. For a time he and Jack "Legs" Diamond were bodyguards of Arnold "The Brain" Rothstein. Not long after Rothstein was murdered in 1928, Walsh made his way to the Sunshine State.

There, he quickly fell into the scene at the Biltmore Hotel, where police were turning a blind eye to an illegal speakeasy and casino being run on the thirteenth floor by Ed Wilson. For a time Walsh and Wilson became partners, but the collaboration was short-lived. The suite was packed and business was in full swing on the night of September 7, 1929, when a heated argument broke out between the two men.

Walsh was an "enforcer" himself, so he should have known better than to turn his back on another mobster— even if he was his partner. But Walsh didn't fear for his life. He was in the middle of a roomful of people. What was the guy gonna do? Shoot him?

But apparently that's what happened. When Walsh turned to walk away, Wilson pulled out a gun and shot him twice in the back at point-blank range. Walsh staggered a few steps up to the coral rock fireplace and dropped to the floor, dead.

Some guests may have used a secret escape route that had been installed behind a bookcase in case the joint was ever raided. Or perhaps the shocked onlookers waited patiently as the single elevator made the several trips that would have been necessary to vacate the premises. Regardless, the room was emptied in minutes. Walsh's body was later discovered where it fell, covered with a sheet. Despite the fact that there must have been several witnesses to the murder, no one was ever arrested.

Though the 1930s brought the Depression years, the hotel managed to remain open. Just as ballrooms turned to the novelty of dance marathons to draw in visitors, the Biltmore found unusual ways to stay afloat, made possible in large part by its famed swimming pool. Sunday afternoons were set aside for aquatic shows that drew crowds of up to three thousand. The programs featured little Jackie Ott, who dove into the pool from an eighty-five-foot platform, and synchronized swimmers, one of whom, Esther Williams, would become a star in Hollywood. (Although he didn't perform in the shows, a pre-*Tarzan* Johnny Weissmuller was a swimming instructor at the hotel at the time.) The Biltmore also sponsored golf tournaments, beauty pageants, fashion shows, and, believe it or not, alligator-wrestling exhibitions.

During World War II, the War Department took over the hotel and converted it into the Army Air Forces Regional Hospital. Most of the windows were covered with concrete for their protection, and, fortunately for future generations, the marble floors were covered with linoleum. It remained a veterans' hospital until 1968, and during those last years, the University of Miami's School of Medicine was operated out of the building.

The city of Coral Gables took possession of the Biltmore in 1973, but the structure sat unoccupied for a full decade until the decision was made to do a full $55 million restoration. The hotel's grand reopening took place on New Year's Eve, 1987.

In 1992, the Seaway Hotels Corporation was granted a contract to manage the facilities. As part of their commitment, the celebrated property underwent a complete $40 million refurbishment, raising it to contemporary world-class standards. A spa and fitness center were added, and as part of the repair and modernization of the legendary pool, Ott's old high-dive tower was replaced with a stunning waterfall. The city spent an additional $3 million upgrading the golf course. Today the Biltmore Hotel has 275 guest rooms, 130 of which are suites. In 1996, it was given National Historic Landmark status.

It was during the decade that the magnificent lodgings stood vacant that it gained its reputation for being haunted. Dennis Hauck, author of the indispensable *Haunted Places: The National Directory,* cites the rumor that townsfolk standing out on the hotel's golf course supposedly were able to see weird, unexplainable lights in the deserted tower and that spooky noises, including macabre laughter, would echo from within the uninhabited walls.

Surprisingly, a few psychics and paranormal groups were allowed to enter the premises to investigate. They never spotted an apparition, but at least one team captured heavy breathing, a loud sigh, and the sound of tapping, like an elderly person walking with a cane, on audiotape.

Sightings and reports of paranormal activity began in earnest after the hotel was reopened to guests. And what tales they are!

A phantom couple repeatedly appears and disappears as the pair dances to the strains of unheard music in the ballroom. In the clubhouse building, a spectre wearing a top hat has been spotted playing the piano. A Woman in White—paranormal jargon for a female spirit dressed all in white—has shown up in several rooms throughout the hotel. It's believed that she committed suicide by leaping from a high window in the tower.

Doors in the hotel will open and shut by themselves (especially for servers heading back into the kitchen), lights operate on their own, and lampshades go missing. Now and then mysterious, illegible handwriting will show up in the condensation on steamy bathroom mirrors.

Most of the paranormal activity that takes place on the thirteenth floor is attributed to none other than Fatty Walsh. Fortunately, despite his occasionally brutal livelihood, the gangster was a rather convivial man in life. He's never been destructive or hurt anyone in death.

Guests catch the unexplainable scent of his cigar smoke in the air, and the room is prone to sudden cold spots. Items left on shelves or tabletops fall to the floor or shift without being touched, and those staying overnight have heard muffled laughter or sensed an unseen entity moving around in the room after the lights are turned out.

It's said that the most famous person to experience one of the room's anomalies was President Bill Clinton. He was attempting to watch a football game on a television in the suite, but the set seemed to have no signal. Then it started to switch on and off by itself. The president didn't attribute the experience to the paranormal, but he did choose to go elsewhere to watch the game.

Walsh really likes to play tricks with the private elevator to the tower—or perhaps he just wants visitors. Guests have said the lift will bypass their own floor and go up to the thirteenth floor, even though a special key is now required above the eleventh floor. On one occasion, the doors stayed open at the thirteenth floor for such a long time that the couple inside decided to investigate. As soon as the woman stepped out of the car, the doors slammed shut behind her, and the elevator immediately started back down to the lobby with her husband inside. She was rescued, but not until after several panicked minutes standing alone in the haunted suite.

According to Sarah Parvis, who wrote the children's book *Haunted Hotels,* on another occasion the elevator came to an abrupt halt when a guest inside opined aloud that Fatty Walsh deserved the end he got. Only after she profusely apologized did the elevator start up again.

Finally, a few guests on the thirteenth floor have stated that they spied a female apparition there. Fatty Walsh had the reputation of being a real ladies' man. Has he been lucky enough to find a companion in the Hereafter? Perhaps all it will take is a night in the Biltmore Hotel to find out for yourself.

Chapter 21
The Wedding Wraith

Fairmont Banff Springs Hotel
Banff, Alberta, Canada

Tragedy struck when a bride coming down the staircase in the Fairmont Banff Springs Hotel in Banff, Alberta, Canada, tripped and died in the fall. The spectral bride still walks the corridors of the historic inn, waiting for the wedding day that will never come.

As she appeared at the top of the grand staircase, the young woman was everything a bride should be. Statuesque in a sumptuous white gown, she paused briefly. Family and friends involuntarily burst into applause. Even the staff, long jaded to such extravagant events, couldn't help but turn an admiring glance in her direction.

The Banff Springs Hotel had been festooned for the happy occasion. Lit candles lined the steps, sparkling as she started her descent. She smiled benevolently, waving ever so gently. It was, as the old saying goes, the happiest day of her life.

But joy can turn to horror in the wink of cruel fate's eye. According to some versions of the tale, she lost her balance and stumbled. Other more gruesome accounts say she panicked when the hem of her dress or the long, flowing train brushed against one of the candles and caught fire. Regardless of the cause, the result was the same: The bride, whose name has been lost to history, fell, tumbling ever more fiercely downward until she stopped, dead, at the foot of the stairs.

The dress was to die for—literally!

As she spilled, the screams of the startled spectators cut through the strains of the lighthearted waltz that was drifting in from the ballroom. Those sounds have long since echoed into the mists of time. But the bride who was not to be has never left the building. Her apparition, dressed in her bridal gown, now dances alone, silently, to unheard music on the ballroom's empty dance floor. She doesn't always stay downstairs, however. Her spectre has also been spied roaming the hallways outside the guest rooms.

A spectral bride who has lingered because of such tragic circumstances should be enough of a burden for any hotel to endure. But it's haunted by two other ghosts as well. The identity of the first one is unknown, but he's easy to spot. He's dressed in full Scottish regalia and carries a bagpipe. There's no mistaking him when you see the spectre coming down the hall.

The third spirit is a former bellman by the name of Sam McAuley. He was happily retired from the hotel in 1967, and he passed on to his reward just a few years later. But he liked serving at the hotel so much that he's come back to help out. Guests will open their doors to see him standing outside in the hall, or the phantom may show up to assist people who have forgotten their keys or locked themselves out.

The lodgings, now the Fairmont Banff Springs Hotel, are located in Banff National Park in Alberta, Canada. It was constructed between 1887 and 1888 by the Canadian Pacific Railway at the urging of the CPR's president, William Cornelius Van Horne. Designed by architect Bruce Price, the

Scottish Baronial–style inn opened to rave reviews on June 1, 1882, at the height of the summer tourist season. It was an immediate success—so much so that the CPR was able to convince the government to set aside the surrounding land as a national park to protect the vistas.

Improvements and additions were made to the hotel in 1911 and 1914. Then in 1926 a major fire completely destroyed the wooden structure. A much larger hotel was built on the same spot two years later. It has been upgraded over the years, including the installation of heat in 1968 to allow it to operate through the winter. Today the Banff Springs Hotel offers almost 850 guest rooms and suites.

The hotel's setting is breathtaking. Van Horne personally picked out the location nestled in the Rocky Mountains, surrounded by hiking trails, waterfalls, and thermal springs. The nearby resort community of Banff, which retains its early-twentieth-century charm, is within easy walking distance.

In many ways, the story of the hotel and the CPR is that of Canada itself, which was founded in 1867. Parliament immediately recognized that for the country to prosper there had to be adequate transportation linking its provinces. In fact, British Columbia demanded a rail line to the east before it would agree to join the Confederation. With the privately owned Canadian Pacific Railways, the government hoped to meet that need and eventually create a true transcontinental railroad. Construction of the first leg began in 1875, but the real work across the plains and over the Rockies took place between 1881 and 1885.

The man overseeing the operation was Van Horne, an American rail executive who had made a name for himself as the manager of the Michigan Central Railway and the

Chicago and Alton Railway. Van Horne was a visionary. He realized that the CPR needed to do more than just lay tracks. The line could be a conduit for telegraph service. It could own a fleet of ships to transport the goods that arrived and departed from both coasts. And to promote rail travel across the country, the CPR could build and manage a series of hotels along its route.

Under a division known as Canadian Pacific Hotels the CPR constructed two types of inns. Some were city hotels near the various passenger stations. The others, like the Banff Springs Hotel, were resorts located near scenic wonders, designed primarily to attract tourists. All of them were constructed of granite and featured copper roofs built in a European chalet style.

Van Horne died in 1915, but the CPR continued to embrace his plan to build luxury hotels to accommodate its customers. Eventually more than thirty hotels were constructed under the Canadian Pacific Hotels banner.

Today the railway no longer operates any of them. About a dozen have been torn down, are no longer open, or have been renovated into other types of facilities. The others have been sold—sixteen of them to the Fairmont Hotel chain. Among these are three haunted properties: the Banff Springs Hotel, the Hotel Vancouver, and Toronto's Royal York.

Hotel Vancouver, the CPR's first undertaking, is located in Vancouver, British Columbia, 360 miles to the southwest of Banff. The present-day building is the third hotel in the city to have that name. The first, which opened its doors on May 16, 1888, was a five-story redbrick building that more resembled a house than a hotel. The second took four years to build and opened in 1916. During the Second World War, the Canadian government transformed it into office space, and the structure was subsequently razed in 1949.

The current fifteen-story Hotel Vancouver took eleven years to build, although no work was done during five of those because of the Depression—little wonder since the hotel's final price tag was $12 million. The government-owned Canadian National Railway began the project, but it was completed in May 1939 under a partnership with the Canadian Pacific Railway. The hotel was finished just in time for King George VI and Queen Elizabeth's visit to the city. In the 1990s, the accommodations, by then a Fairmont property, were given a $70 million makeover. Like all of the other hotels constructed by the CPR, it is notable for the copper-clad, peaked, ornamental towers on the roof.

Businessmen and tourists from all over the world pass through the Hotel Vancouver's doors, but one visitor has decided to stay. It's the spectre of a Jennie Pearl Cox, who was a frequent guest to the ballroom in the early 1940s. She died in a car crash in front of the hotel in 1944, dressed in an elegant red gown.

She used to love taking the elevator to the top floor to gaze out over the city lights, and she's still doing it today. People often spot her apparition, still dressed in her long red gown—which is why she's been nicknamed the Lady in Red. Her phantom most often floats down the corridors of the fourteenth floor, the uppermost one with guest rooms. The elevators also frequently make unscheduled stops on that floor. Now and then, the Lady in Red appears inside a guest room. Bellmen will occasionally open the door of a suite only to discover the room already "occupied" by her.

Perhaps most frighteningly, she makes use of elevators that don't exist. When the hotel was constructed, several elevator shafts were built, but, in the end, only a few of them had lifts installed. There are dummy doors to the empty shafts in the lobby and on the fourteenth floor, but they're locked and never open. That doesn't stop our girl! She'll ride a nonexistent elevator down to the lobby and pass right through its sealed door, startling guests and staff alike. (On at least occasion, an employee saw the doors open to allow the ghost to emerge—which should have been impossible since they are bolted from the inside.)

Toronto, of course, is one of the major stops at the eastern end of the Canadian Pacific Railway. The biggest city in Canada and the provincial capital of Ontario, Toronto had about a million residents when the CPR built one of its flagship hotels in the center of the city. When it opened on June 11, 1929, the Royal York Hotel advertised itself as the largest hotel in the British Empire. Originally on the waterfront, it had a commanding view over Lake Ontario.

The Royal York comes complete with a handful of ghosts. One, a dapper, gray-haired gent wearing a stylish maroon smoking jacket, strolls the hallways of the eighth floor, but he never interacts with people as he silently passes by. He or another elderly man also shows up in the main ballroom.

There is a second dance floor in the hotel, the Crystal Ballroom, located in the penthouse. It is currently closed awaiting renovation, but that doesn't stop the elevator from going up to it despite not being called—at least not by anyone living. Guests in the rooms directly below the ballroom hear loud music and a party in full swing overhead. The work crew, especially, have experienced their share of anomalies up there. Maintenance has entered the empty hall to find the chandeliers swinging, and occasionally their electrical tools will stop working without any reason, or the current will fluctuate or cut out completely.

One particular spectral visitor, a former employee, is never seen, but his screams and footsteps resonate in the stairwell around the nineteenth floor. According to rumor, he hanged himself from the staircase railing back in 1994.

Invisible children, laughing and playing, are heard running up and down the halls throughout the hotel, and a phantom bellhop shows up in some of the rooms. Then there's the other "normal" ghost activity associated with old places like the Royal York: cold spots, unexplainable gusts of wind, lights that go on and off by themselves, and other elevators that stop wherever they like.

The Fairmont Banff Springs Hotel. The Hotel Vancouver. The Royal York. Why not visit them all? Three great hotels; three perfect opportunities to catch a ghost, eh?

Chapter 22

The Legend of Castle Leslie

Castle Leslie
County Monaghan, Ireland

Ghosts run rampant at Castle Leslie, an old family estate turned hotel in County Monaghan, Ireland. The spirits include a young man who was killed in World War I, the woman who rebuilt the house in the late 1800s, a mysterious Woman in White, and, perhaps most frightening of all, a levitating bed said to have belonged to a sixteenth-century cannibal.

For those who are not in the know, it's possible to be disappointed upon arrival at Castle Leslie—that is, if the person is expecting a medieval castle or something out of a fairy tale. There is no drawbridge, no moat, and no battlements or high towers.

At one time a more traditional castle probably stood on the spot, but the house now located on the thousand-acre estate is a large, sprawling, multilevel mansion. The manor retains the name *castle*, though, in the sense that it has been the Leslie family stronghold for generations. *Many* generations. The land has been the ancestral home of the Irish branch of the Leslies since the seventeenth century.

Today, Castle Leslie is open as a hotel for overnight guests. It also serves as an exclusive venue for conventions and other special events. Two celebrity weddings took place there in 2002: Liza Minnelli married David Gest on March 16, and Sir Paul McCartney wed Heather Mills on June 11. (Unfortunately, both marriages have since ended in rather public, bitter divorces.) The castle has also welcomed such varied visitors as W. B. Yeats, Mick Jagger, and Prince Pierre of Monaco.

Yet, for those who want privacy, Castle Leslie is secluded enough, located as it is outside the village of Glaslough in County Monaghan just a few miles from the northern border of the Republic of Ireland. It's a long seventy-five-mile drive from Dublin. But it's well worth the trip—especially if you're a ghost hunter.

All the spirits who haunt the place are thought to be part of the extended Leslie clan. The family traces its roots back to Attila the Hun, but the first member to come to the British Isles was a Hungarian noble named Bartholomew Leslie. He settled in Scotland and became the protector of Queen Margaret, at one point saving her life from drowning.

In 1633, Bishop John Leslie, the bishop for the Isles of Scotland, was translated (that is to say, was transferred) to a parish in County Donegal, Ireland. At the age of sixty-seven, he married a local girl and began to raise a family. Leslie wasn't just a priest. He was also a warrior in the Reformation, and he and his forces successfully fought off Cromwell's army at the Battle of Raphoe. In 1665, Leslie, by then Bishop of Clogher, bought Glaslough Castle from Sir Thomas Ridgeway with a gift of two thousand British pounds he received from King Charles II for loyalty to the Crown. The clergyman met his maker six years later at the age of one hundred.

By the mid-nineteenth century, it became obvious that the old manse had to be replaced. That task fell to John Leslie, who would go on to become Sir Leslie, first Baronet of

Glaslough. His wife, Constance, though good-natured by all accounts, was particularly insistent on the project.

Around 1878 Leslie commissioned architects Lanyon, Lynn, and Lanyon to design the new residence. While the Scottish Baronial castle was being constructed, the Leslies toured the Continent. Leslie was a fine pre-Raphael–style painter, so when the house was finished, he decorated its interior in Italian Renaissance style. The furnishings included many sixteenth- and seventeenth-century pieces that the couple had acquired while in Italy.

The Leslies moved to London in 1910, though they maintained the estate back home. Sir John died six years later. The ghost stories surrounding Castle Leslie started in 1925 with Lady Constance's death. Purportedly, the very day that she breathed her last in England, servants back in Ireland saw her strolling around the mansion.

And, apparently, she's never left.

John and Constance's son, also named John, inherited the castle. (He would take his father's title and become Sir Leslie, second Baronet.) He married Leonie Jerome, whose older sister wed Lord Randolph Churchill, the father of Winston. In 1943, Leonie took to her deathbed. Her husband made sure that nurses attended her twenty-four hours a day. On the last night of Leonie's life, an elderly though handsome woman came into the chamber. She leaned over the fading Leonie, muttered a few quiet words in her ear, then turned and walked out of the room.

Before morning, Leonie had passed in her sleep. After the funeral, family members collected in the dining room. The visiting nurse who had been on duty that final evening innocently mentioned that Leonie had been comforted when the woman whose oil portrait hung on the dining room wall came in to talk to her. Everyone was stunned. The person in the painting was Lady Constance, who had died eighteen years earlier.

Since that night, Lady Constance has become a fairly regular visitor to Castle Leslie. Most often her spirit shows up in the bedroom known as the Mauve Room. Even when she can't be seen, people know when she's around because personal items shift without anyone touching them. When doors on the second floor open or shut on their own, the ghostly activity is also usually attributed to Constance being playful.

The ghost that's seen most often in the castle is not Constance but one of its favorite sons—a young man by the name of Norman Leslie. An officer in the rifle brigade, he was killed in France at the start of World War I. Two nights before his death in 1914, his mother woke to see Norman standing at the foot of her bed. He smiled lovingly, then vanished into thin air. He was spotted again by one of the estate's gamekeepers, outdoors in daylight. The spectre was standing by a sundial in the garden for almost a minute before disappearing. It was later learned that this second materialization occurred at the exact time Norman died in battle.

These days, Norman's spirit most often shows up in his old bedroom. He's also seen in another bedchamber, the Red Room, and most of the paranormal anomalies that occur in the two rooms are attributed to him. But not all of them. From time to time an unidentified woman dressed head to toe in white floats through Norman's room as well.

The scariest ghostly activity in the soldier's former bedroom is centered on its antique bed. Quite a few people who have slept in it have felt an invisible, heavy weight pressing down on them. Even stranger: The bed has been seen to shake on its own—and sometimes levitates!

According to family folklore, the bed used to belong to Sir Goddard Oxenbridge, who lived at Brede (pronounced *Breed*) Place in East Sussex, England, from around 1478 to 1531. Oxenbridge, who was extraordinarily tall, was known as the Giant of Brede, and he has carried a heinous reputation through the ages. Allegedly, he was a cannibal who would butcher and eat young children in the belief that consuming their flesh would allow him to live forever. Eventually—again, according to legend—the locals revolted and killed him, finally slicing his body in half and throwing his remains into a lake. The bed turned up at Castle Leslie because the family is distantly related. But for some reason the evil nobleman's phantom has followed the bed, and he's not happy where it is. He keeps making it tremble and float in hopes that it will be returned to his old estate.

(Brede Place was built in the fourteenth century, probably by one of the knights of Edward III. It still stands, and people say it's haunted by Sir Goddard's spectre. Fortunately, the gruesome stories about his abnormal appetites seem to have no basis in fact. Oxenbridge was of high social standing, a knight of Henry VIII, and a great benefactor of St. George's Church, where he's buried. Besides the Giant of Brede, two other spirits infest his manor. One is Father John, a priest, whose bones were accidentally disinterred on the grounds in 1830. The other is Martha, a maid from the sixteenth century who hanged herself in the garden. Brede Place remains a private residence, but its present owner sometimes opens it for tours.)

A year after Leonie Jerome died, her husband also expired. Subsequently, the castle passed through the hands of several family members. Samantha Leslie and her husband, Jack, who live in the mansion, are now managing it.

It was Sammy, as Samantha calls herself, who transformed Castle Leslie into a hotel. She realized that in a twentieth-century economy and beyond, the money received from tourism would ensure that the grounds remain in family hands. At first, she merely opened a tearoom in the old conservatory, but its success convinced her that her larger plan was viable.

Between 1995 and 1997, she converted fourteen of the castle's bedrooms into guest rooms, each one unique in its decor. Drinks are served in the Drawing Room and the Fountain Garden during cocktail hour, and dinner by candlelight is available in the original dining room.

In addition to the main house (which now has twenty guest rooms), the castle also has an attached cloisterlike hallway known as the Long Gallery, where hazy figures and dark, hooded shapes have been spied. The corridor leads to a one-story wing containing a library and billiards room. Behind the castle are the traditional English gardens, which open onto the estate's vast parklands. Besides the glades and picturesque streams, the property holds three lakes—Kilvey, Dream, and Glaslough.

Following a ten-million-euro renovation, the estate also boasts many remodeled outer buildings, including a stable mews and a thirty-five-room Hunting Lodge, plus several new cottages, all of which are available as guest accommodations. But if catching one of the family ghosts is what you're after, your chances are best in the castle.

The spectral appearances of Lady Constance and Norman Leslie at the castle when they were still alive but clearly far away, in London and France respectively, are examples of a paranormal phenomenon variously known in psychical research as an out-of-body experience (or OBE), astral projection, or bi-location. The concept suggests that it's possible, in very rare instances, for the "astral body" or "spirit double" of an individual to separate itself from the person's physical body and travel to another location. Sometimes the double only hovers over or near one's own body, but it's also been known to wander long distances. Many people who have experienced astral projection are later able to describe verifiable events that took place at the other spot, even though they would otherwise have had no way of knowing about them.

Constance and Norman's astral projections seem to be a particular type of OBE known as a crisis apparition, in which a person's spirit is released at the time of sickness, trauma, an accident, or impending death to talk to or visit someone, usually a loved one. Often the individual who sends out the spirit is under heavy medication or unconscious at the time the OBE occurs.

There's an ongoing debate in paranormal circles regarding crisis apparitions that occur when a person dies. Because it's almost impossible to pinpoint the exact moment that death occurs, the question arises: Was the person alive at the time the spirit body was seen, in which case the phenomenon was an out-of-body experience, or was the person already dead? If it was the latter, what materialized was not an astral body but, by definition, a ghost. It sounds like splitting hairs, but spirit researchers take such things very seriously.

Believe it or not, they sit around and discuss such minutiae as this: Lady Constance's phantom shows up in an elegant evening gown. Norman Leslie appears dressed in his World War I army uniform. But why aren't they naked? If a ghost is a person's soul returning after death, does that mean that their clothing was also once alive?

Fortunately, the hauntings at Castle Leslie don't ask us to speculate on such matters.

Chapter 23

The Hellfire Horror

The George and Dragon
Buckinghamshire, England

Two centuries ago, a misguided prank pulled on a naive barmaid led to tragedy in a cave used by the Hellfire Club in England. Her phantom has returned to the George and Dragon Inn, where she awaits the arrival of the mysterious lover she had hoped to meet the night of her doom.

Michael was in London, hard at research on his new book, when he ran across an oddly familiar name—the Hellfire Clubs. He hadn't thought about them in years. They were some of England's earliest underground gentlemen's clubs, dating back to the mid-1700s.

Michael's mind began to race as a plot involuntarily began to write itself: A modern-day tale of sex and debauchery based on the notorious eighteenth-century bacchanals of a shadowy backroom organization. It had all the right ingredients to be a best seller. Sure, the club had appeared in a few out-of-print novels a few decades back, but it was one of the few secret societies Dan Brown hadn't got around to yet. Dollar signs flashed before Michael's eyes.

If he remembered correctly, one of the branches moved to Buckinghamshire, about thirty miles outside of London, and began to meet in a series of caves. A few clicks of the mouse confirmed it. And the best part of all? The tunnels still existed and were open to visitors! It was all Michael could do to resist the temptation to jump into a car and drive there that very night.

But somehow he managed. He would go up the following weekend, and in the meantime he'd read everything he could find on the enigmatic association. What he discovered was encouraging: There were some solid facts on which to build a story line. But almost everything else about the club, including the members' names and what they did, was so shrouded in mystery that Michael could easily weave any kind of yarn he wished.

Here's what he found out:

In 1719 London, Philip, Duke of Wharton, called together a few of his friends to make a highly unorthodox suggestion. He proposed forming a private association that would forego the niceties and proprieties in other social organizations in the city. At his club, members could say or do pretty much whatever they pleased, whether it was drinking from dusk to dawn or mocking the church. It would be known as the Hellfire Club.

Outsiders knew nothing much for certain about what went on at the meetings, which were usually held on Sunday at some tavern or in a member's home. But whatever took place, it *had* to be scandalous: Both men *and* women were able to join. Rumors started that they were devil worshippers and took part in anti-Christian rituals, clothed as figures from the Bible. They feasted on foods with such provocative names as Devil's Loin, Breast of Venus, and Holy Ghost Pie.

It's unlikely that any such activities actually took place, but the group became so infamous that King George I outlawed it in 1721. Nevertheless, several similar groups sprouted up in secret. One of them was started by Sir Francis Dashwood in 1746. He was born the son of a rich merchant in 1708 and inherited his barony upon his father's death when the boy was just sixteen years old. At eighteen, he took the Grand Tour of Europe. Such excursions were intended to be at least nominally educational, but he spent most of his time indulging himself with drink and women.

In 1734 Dashwood formed his first gentlemen's club, the Dilettanti. Its stated purpose was to study ancient Greece and Italy, but the antics that took place at meetings were anything but serious. Just two years later, the twenty-six-year-old was thought to be attending one of the clandestine Hellfire Clubs in London.

Finally, in 1746, Dashwood formed his own version of a Hellfire Club, although he never used that name. It was variously known as the Order of the Knights of Sir Francis, the Order of the Knights of West Wycombe, and the Brotherhood of St. Francis of Wycombe. Originally, it met at a London inn, the George & Vulture, on Lombard Street. But in 1751, Dashwood restored a ruined monastery, the Medmenham Abbey, on the Thames just a few miles from his ancestral home in West Wycombe. He moved his club meetings there, and members took on the title of the Monks (or Friars) of Medmenham. Again, as with Wharton's Hellfire Club, what took place within the monastery's walls is up for debate, but much can be inferred from the inscription Dashwood had engraved in the stained glass at the monastery's entrance: *Fais ce que tu voudras*, or "Do what thou wilt."

Starting in 1748, Dashwood had begun to pay local workers to expand a natural cave in West Wycombe into a network of tunnels. He claimed he wanted to quarry the chalk as well as provide employment for area farmers after a series of bad harvests. That may be true. But he also had the workmen create a series of small chambers in which his "monks" and "nuns" could meet. The work took four years to complete.

Michael was set by Friday afternoon. He motored the short distance out of London, passing through High Wycombe, then the three miles more to the little hamlet of West Wycombe. The village was picturesque to a fault, with High Street (the main road through town) lined with cottages, taverns, and redbrick row houses, many of them dating from the sixteenth to the eighteenth centuries.

He had already made a reservation for the night at the historic George and Dragon. The current structure was built in 1720, but an inn has stood on the site since the 1400s. The place was easy enough for Michael to find. A wooden signboard out front was gaily painted with a depiction of the beloved saint fighting the mythical creature.

Minutes later, Michael had dropped his overnight bag onto the bed in his small but cozy room and headed out to explore. The caves had closed at four-thirty, but even if they hadn't, he would have waited until the next morning to go in. He wasn't about to rush his way through. He wanted to soak in every turn in the tunnels, run his hands over the walls, and shoot photos. Any detail might be important for his book. He'd be at the entrance when the Hell-Fire Caves opened at eleven.

That night, the soft mattress and downy pillow had Michael drifting off to sleep in no time. Hours passed, until around three in the morning, when he suddenly awoke with the uncomfortable feeling that he wasn't alone. The curtains were parted, and the light of the full moon cast a warm glow into the room. Michael's eyes trailed to the petite vanity table across from the bed. Sitting at the low bench, with her back to him and staring into the mirror, was a girl, possibly in her late teens.

The stranger was completely silent. She was studying Michael through his reflection in the mirror, and when he jolted upright, she quickly stood and turned to him. The girl was dressed in a simple white frock, cut in what was clearly some long-ago fashion. A narrow cloth band was bound around her temple. Was it pink? It was hard for Michael to make out.

He stayed glued to the spot. He didn't want to call out to her and wake the household. Besides, how could he explain the young woman's presence in his room? As he tried to decide what to do, the lass slipped up to the bed and, without saying a word, laid the back of her right hand on his cheek. Michael flinched away involuntarily: Her skin was like ice. Who *was* this creature?

It was only then that he allowed himself to really focus on her face. The girl was beautiful. And there was a longing in her eyes. Not of desire, but some sort of plea for help, a call for salvation. The gaze was heartbreaking. As Michael continued to stare at her, she tilted her head and looked toward the window. A mournful smile of resignation crossed her lips. And then, without warning, she disappeared.

Though still shaken the next morning, Michael headed toward the Hell-Fire Caves located at the foot of the Chiltern Hills. Built to resemble a Gothic church, the entranceway led to a half mile of passages that connected almost a dozen rooms of various shapes and sizes. The last chamber was a full three hundred feet below the surface.

As Michael was paying for his ticket, he decided to make sure there was no time limit and that he could double back from room to room if he wished.

"Take as long as you want," the attendant said. "But you might be leaving sooner than you think."

"Really? Why's that?"

"Well, some people get claustrophobic. The passages are pretty tight. A few are only about two meters tall. And then there are the ghosts."

Ghosts? Michael hadn't counted on that. A supernatural twist for his murder-mystery novel? This was getting better and better.

It turned out that the Hell-Fire Caves are rumored to be haunted by three different ghosts. One is an unidentified man dressed as a monk. Another has been recognized as Paul Whitehead, a poet and fellow libertine and lifelong friend of Sir Francis Dashwood. He was so close to Dashwood that he provided fifty British pounds in his will to have his heart placed in the Dashwood Mausoleum after his death. Whitehead's heart has long since vanished, but the original urn in which it was kept now sits in a niche inside the tunnels. No wonder his spectre also appears there.

"Then there's that servant girl, Suki," the man at the gate continued. "You know, the one who used to work up at the George and Dragon? I hear she also turns up there from time to time."

Michael was speechless. So the inn *was* haunted. He hadn't dreamt the ghostly girl who appeared in his room in the middle of the night. It had been Suki! He shuddered at the thought. The girl had been dead more than two hundred years.

The legend never specifies a precise date, but sixteen-year-old Suki probably worked as a servant and barmaid at the George and Dragon in the early eighteenth century. Located on the route between High Wycombe and Oxford, the pub saw its share of thirsty and tired travelers. One of them, a handsome nobleman not that much older than Suki herself, took a liking to the girl. Whenever he passed through town, he made sure to stop in to see her, and they would flirt outrageously for hours—so much so that it soon became apparent to three village lads.

Perhaps the boys were jealous. Or they were upset that Suki was putting on airs and acting above her station. Maybe they were just feeling mischievous. Whatever the reason, they decided to play a prank on her. They composed a letter, supposedly from the young aristocrat, and had it delivered to Suki.

She probably should have been suspicious. But the letter's contents swept her off her feet. The man of her dreams was coming to take her away from the dreadful, dead-end life she was living.

But, the letter insisted, they had to elope. She must tell no one. She should dress in her finest clothes, what would become her wedding gown, and meet him at midnight in the small cave at the edge of town. She knew the place well. She and her friends had played in it as children.

That night, she said she was sick and begged off work early. Once in her room, she dressed quickly, packed her few belongings in a tatty valise, and started out for the cave under mantle of night. She passed stealthily, making sure none of the gossipy folk of the teeny village saw her, and before long she was in front of the gaping crater. She crept inside, pressed herself against one of the walls, and waited.

Torture. It seemed like days before she heard the rustling at the entrance to the cave. Was it him? She spied the flickering light of a lantern. She stepped forward.

No! Rather than her savior, what appeared to her were the jeering faces of the three hooligans who always taunted her so at the bar. She instantly realized what had happened. She had been tricked! Made a fool of! How could they be so cruel?

Suki cried out, a wail that must have echoed out of the cave all the way to the village. A screaming match ensued. No doubt she lunged at the laughing boys, her fists flailing helplessly against them. What had started out as a bad joke escalated and, according to a plaque posted in the Hell-Fire Caves, "stones were thrown." One hit Suki on the head, and she dropped to the ground, bleeding and unconscious. The boys did have the courage to gather her up in their arms and rush her back to the George and Dragon. But there was nothing that could be done for the poor girl. By morning, she was dead.

Michael must have spent hours in the Hell-Fire Caves, checking out every nook and cranny. He surveyed every carving made in the walls and photographed all of the chambers from one angle or the other. The rooms had the most evocative names: One area, Franklin's Cave, was made up of crisscrossing passages. It was named for Benjamin Franklin, who befriended Dashwood and visited the caves during his time in England as a diplomat before the Revolutionary War. Then there was the large, semicircular Banquet Hall, where orgiastic feasts were said to have occurred. Next came a triangular channel, thought by today's New Agers to have been deliberately cut in that design to represent a female's loins. The Miner's Cave followed. Then, after walking by a tiny pool called the River Styx, Michael reached the holy of holies, the

Inner Temple, where only the most devoted members of the Hellfire Club were ever allowed.

Even though Michael didn't see any of the ghosts who purportedly wander the tunnels, he couldn't get the sad story of Suki out of his mind. When he finally returned to his lodgings that afternoon, the proprietor confirmed the ticket seller's tale—including the fact that Suki haunted the inn as well. The owner was surprised to hear that Michael was just finding out about her. The prospect of running into Suki's ghost was one of the reasons why people chose to stay at the George and Dragon. The phantom is most often seen in the upstairs guest rooms, wearing a bloodstained bandage from her wound. (That explained to Michael why her scarf had looked pink!) Suki shows up on the staircase as well and occasionally is seen emerging from one of the large supply closets in the kitchen. She's also blamed when personal items get lost and for the unexplainable cold spots around the hotel.

Michael was stunned when he was told that Suki wasn't the only spirit haunting the inn. There's also a Woman in White, often called the White Lady, who floats through the garden in the hotel courtyard. Then, too, guests have heard disembodied footsteps on the main staircase that were so loud it was assumed they had to belong to a male phantom rather than one of the spectral women.

Michael anxiously awaited Suki's return that night, but she never appeared. Though disappointed, he had more than enough memories to start an outline for his novel. What should he call his murder mystery—secret society—symbol quest—ghost story? *The Hellfire Horror*. Yes, that had a nice ring to it. He only hoped that Suki would approve.

Chapter 24

The Uninvited Guest
in Room 333

The Langham
London, England

London's most haunted hotel, the Langham, is home to several ghosts, including a German soldier, a Victorian-attired spectre, and even Napoleon III. If you want to increase your chances of meeting one of the phantoms face-to-face, ask to stay in Room 333.

It took James Alexander Gordon several seconds to figure out why he wasn't in his own bed. He should have been back in his house on the outskirts of London, not in some dreary, unfamiliar hotel room.

Oh, that's right, he thought as his mind cleared. He wasn't in a hotel—at least, the building wasn't one anymore. He had a BBC broadcast first thing in the morning, and he wouldn't have been able to make it to the studios on time unless he stayed overnight in the city. Fortunately for him, the station kept several rooms on the third floor of a place they owned across the street from their headquarters for this exact purpose.

And Gordon knew he shouldn't be complaining. That building was a former luxury hotel, the Langham, and it had once been the most fashionable lodgings in the entire country. Room 333 must have seen its share of famous, highborn, and well-to-do guests over the century the hotel was in business. And he wasn't paying a penny to be there.

He looked over at his small travel alarm clock on the dresser and realized that he had only been in bed a couple of hours. He had five hours or so before he had to be up, so if he was lucky, he might be able to get in a few more winks before dawn.

He fluffed his pillow and lay back down. But just as he was closing his eyes, he became aware of a soft glow of light coming from the other side of the room. He turned to see a luminescent mist, and as he watched, it coalesced into a ball, a radiant orb hovering in midair. Slowly, bit by bit, the shining globe took on a shape, a definite form: It was human! A man!

The apparition was dressed in evening attire with a distinctive Edwardian cut, a fashion from some sixty years earlier. The figure had no legs, and it was floating about two feet higher than if its feet had been touching the ground. (Gordon discovered later that the level of the floorboards in the guest rooms had been raised some years back to accommodate new heating ducts.)

"Who are you? What do you want?" Gordon yelled, at the spectral creature, terrified.

It was only then that the shape seemed to notice the man in the bed. It turned to Gordon and stared at him with empty, unblinking eyes. Gordon's heart began to race. Rather than answering, the phantasm raised its arms, zombielike, and began walking toward the bed.

That did it! Gordon jumped out from under the covers, grabbed up his shirt and trousers, and ran out of the room, slamming the door behind him. Within what seemed like seconds, he was in the lobby, panting, half-dressed, try-ing to explain what he had just seen to the commissionaire behind the front desk.

"With all due respect, Mr. Gordon," the attendant replied, "I really don't think we have ghosts here at the BBC. And, even if we did, no, I would *not* like to accompany you to your room to search for one."

What could Gordon do? His wallet was sitting on the nightstand upstairs. So, with no option to go elsewhere, he resigned himself to taking the lift back to his room. When he got there, he instinctively placed his ear against the door. What did he think he would hear? The spectre hadn't made a sound.

Summoning every bit of courage he had, Gordon turned his key and carefully pushed open the door. He didn't want any surprises! He stepped inside, leaving the door slightly ajar behind him. As his eyes adjusted to the light, he could see that the iridescent figure was indeed still there. But now it was faint, motionless, nonthreatening. The spectre didn't turn toward him this time; it didn't even bother to acknowl-edge Gordon's presence. It simply hung in the air, growing dimmer, until it finally passed out of sight.

The ghost, whoever he had been, was gone.

The next day, when Gordon confessed to his fellow broadcasters what had transpired, a few of them discreetly admitted that they, too, had been visited by the same entity in that room. All of them agreed that if they ever had to overnight in the former hotel again, none of them would stay in Room 333.

London's first great hotel, the 165-room Great Western Railway Royal Hotel, debuted in 1852. It was another twelve years before it had a rival in the Charing Cross Hotel. But considering the size of London and the reach of the British Empire, it was surprising that neither of them, nor any other lodging in the city, could favorably compare with the grand hotels in Europe.

The Langham Hotel Company sought to change that. In 1862 it had commissioned architect John Giles to design just such a place. Its cornerstone was laid in July 1863, and on June 10, 1865, the Langham was officially opened by His Royal Highness the Prince of Wales, Edward VII. The hotel was named for Sir James Langham, who had previously owned a mansion on the site.

The hotel instantly overshadowed any other in England. The public rooms boasted marble columns, Moorish-inspired murals on the walls, Persian tapestries, floor mosaics, and high, decorated plaster ceilings.

It was the first hotel in London to offer air-conditioning and hydraulic lifts. There was hot and cold running water in every room, supplied by a 365-foot artesian well dug under the basement. The place had more than six hundred rooms in the building, which included the two-hundred-some guest rooms and thirty-four suites. There were almost three hundred water closets—fourteen of them available to the public. The Langham became the first in the country to have electricity in every room, and telephones arrived in the 1890s.

The Marylebone quarter, where the hotel is located, was one of the poshest areas of the city. As a bonus, the property's elevation was almost a hundred feet higher than the Thames, making the district safe from flooding and the diseases that festered in the then-marshy land along the river.

Unfortunately, the hotel's first manager, the Earl of Shrewsbury, though an Admiral of the Fleet, was not a very good hotel administrator. That, coupled with an 1866 financial panic and other factors, caused the Langham Hotel Company to go bankrupt in 1868. An investment company was able to purchase it at fifty pence on the pound and, with the expertise of the hotel's new manager, American Confederate Cap. James Sanderson, the Langham's fortunes turned around. Almost immediately the hotel was once again *the* place to see and be seen.

Among its notable guests during this period and up until World War I were playwright Oscar Wilde, romance novelist Ouida (who for four years operated a salon out of her suite), and Henry Morton Stanley (the explorer of "Dr. Livingstone, I presume" fame). Sir Arthur Conan Doyle, though not an overnight guest—he lived nearby—stopped in regularly, and the Langham appears in several of his Sherlock Holmes tales.

Composer Antonin Dvorak stayed there often, beginning in 1884. He created a minor scandal when, on one visit, he asked to share his double room with his adult daughter. The Victorian-era hotel politely refused, presumably because of the seeming impropriety.

American guests included poet Henry Wadsworth Longfellow and inveterate traveler (oh, and author) Mark Twain. As for royalty, the Prince of Wales continued his patronage, and Emperor Louis Napoleon III, in exile from France, settled into a suite on the first floor.

Several new luxury hotels opened around the turn of the twentieth century to challenge the supremacy of the

Langham, such as the Savoy, Claridge's, the Carlton, and the Ritz. Many of them became temporary hospitals or government buildings during the First World War, but Langham's managed to stay open as a hotel. Due to lost revenue, however, it became faded and fell into disrepair. Renovations were performed in the 1920s, but the hotel never quite recovered its glamour.

Meanwhile, the BBC, which had its main offices across the street, needed additional space. Around 1934, it offered to buy the Langham. The parties never came to terms, though, and the hotel soldiered on. During this period, such celebrities as Noël Coward, Gracie Fields, Charles Laughton, and Mrs. Wallis Simpson were guests.

During World War II, the hotel's mezzanine became a first aid post. Because tourists stayed away from London, most of the Langham's tenants came from the military. Others were working at the BBC, such as writer (and, during the war, newscaster-commentator) J. B. Priestly. The French general Charles de Gaulle stayed there briefly after escaping a defeated Paris. Then, within the course of three months, between September and December 1940, three bombs fell on the Langham, causing massive damage, especially to the west wing.

The BBC tried once again to purchase the Langham in 1943, and two years later it finally succeeded. The famed hotel closed its doors, and the network moved into the south and west wings, the main floor, and the basement. Most of the hotel furnishings were sold off, but several rooms on the third floor were maintained for visiting correspondents and presenters who needed to stay in the city for a night or two.

Most of the legends about the Langham's being haunted sprang up during the BBC's residency. Besides the phantom in 333, another ghost allegedly walks the third floor: a gray-haired man wearing a Victorian-era coat and a cravat neatly tied around his neck. According to the tale, the filmy phantom was a doctor who killed his wife on their honeymoon night at the hotel.

Spectators outside the building have looked up to see a hefty man in an early-twentieth-century German army uniform standing at a window on the fourth floor. It's thought the spectre was a German prince who committed suicide by leaping from that very window just before the outbreak of World War I.

A pronounced cold spot sometimes appears in the room the BBC used as its library. Some people swear they've seen the spectral image of an aristocrat's footman in the room. The anonymous ghost would have to predate the hotel, however, because the apparition is dressed in blue livery dating from the 1700s.

The identity of the other ghostly presence in the hotel is well known: Louis Napoleon III. For some reason the spirit only shows up in the building's basement. Logically, he should materialize on the first floor or perhaps in the hotel courtyard. (During his stay at the Langham, the ruler famously fashioned an unusual twenty-foot-high sculpture in the patio and named it *Le Fernerie*.)

But of all the spectres that have been reported at the Langham, by far the most frequent nighttime guest is the gleaming ghost in Room 333. As recently as 2003 a woman checked out of the hotel without notice because, as she later explained by letter, some unseen force was shaking her bed and wouldn't let her sleep.

In 1982, the BBC sought to tear down the building but instead wound up moving to a new location. Then, in 1986, the Ladbroke Group bought the structure with the intention of turning it back into a hotel. And that's just what happened. The company acquired the Hilton International brand the following year, and, after a combination restoration and renovation, the hotel was reopened on March 4, 1991, as the five-star Langham Hilton. Among its first regular visitors was Diana, the Princess of Wales.

In May 2004 the hotel acquired a new owner, Great Eagle Hotel Group. Now the luxury accommodation with 380 guest rooms and suites is the flagship hotel of Langham Hotels International. It is known simply as the Langham, or, to differentiate it from the company's Hong Kong and Boston facilities, the Langham, London.

Rumors about the Langham ghosts continue. The hotel is centrally located, just outside Regent's Park and close to the Oxford Circus Underground, so dropping in for a traditional afternoon tea will give anyone who wishes a chance to look around. But if you want to see a ghost, your odds will improve if you stay the night—especially if you ask for Room 333.

Chapter 25

The Singapore Spectre

Raffles Hotel
Singapore

Everything at the world-famous Raffles Hotel in Singapore is all very proper, a holdover from the island's days as a British colony. Then why is an unattended young girl allowed to roam the halls? Well, just try and stop her. Normal rules of behavior don't apply for people visiting from the Great Beyond.

"Well, I never . . ."

Mrs. Beatrice Evelina Buxton-Smyth drew a sharp breath and slightly tilted her nose upward—the universal sign of disapproval—as she spied the young girl at the end of the hallway. The child was all by herself, and she was skipping. Skipping! That might be appropriate behavior in some schoolyard playground, but certainly not in the corridors of one the most prestigious hotels in the world.

"Where are that girl's parents?" the matron sneered derisively to her valet as he showed her to her room. "She should not be allowed out in public with no chaperone. It just isn't done. Furthermore, it's a breach of taste allowing her to be seen . . . what? Frolicking?"

Beatrice turned back to look down the length of the hall. The girl was gone. The entire passageway was empty.

"Well, it doesn't matter now. She had the good sense to go back to her room."

"Yes, ma'am," the young man answered flatly. He hadn't seen anyone. But he knew his place and realized it would be better not to offer an opinion, much less disagree with a guest (or "resident," as the hotel preferred to call them). Besides, he had been assigned to her by the hotel as a personal valet for the length of her stay, so he didn't want to get off on the wrong foot.

Kai had been working at the Raffles Hotel for about three years. Most of the people he attended at the historic venue were from money—you almost had to be to afford to stay at the hotel—but few were so boorish about it. But he understood that those of a certain generation were brought up with a stricter set of values than was the norm today. There were artificial rules in place, especially for women, as to what was socially acceptable in public. Breaking any of those "standards" of decency would have been a serious breach of etiquette.

But condemning a little girl for playing quietly in the hall? Really?

Mrs. Buxton-Smyth, or Bea as she allowed her intimates to call her, knew that she was a living anachronism. She wore hats. And gloves. If she occasionally thought someone was NOCD ("Not our class, dear"), well, so be it.

Kai politely, if briskly, showed off the suite's amenities, reminded Mrs. Buxton-Smyth that he was at her beck and call, then saw himself out. Curious, he couldn't help but look down to the end of the corridor where his new mistress claimed to have seen a young girl playing. Had there actually been someone there? Or was the place, as some of the other staff had told him, really haunted?

The Raffles Hotel in Singapore dates to 1887, when the island nation was still part of the British Empire. In 1819, Sir Thomas Stamford Raffles, operating on behalf of the British East India Company, had founded a trading post at the mouth of the Singapore River. The hamlet's name came from the Malay word *Singapura,* meaning "the Lion City."

The intent was to gain a foothold against the Dutch, who were the principal European players in the region. Plus, being located on the Malacca Strait at the tip of the Malay Peninsula, a British settlement also would hold an important strategic position militarily.

Raffles had already spent extensive time as the governor of Java and Bencoolen (also known as Bengkulu), Indonesia. He introduced several of the laws and institutions that had been successful there into Singapore. Among them, he set up schools and churches and allowed them and other organizations to operate in the local languages rather than enforce the use of English. To attract foreigners and investment, he built roads and a European-style town, carefully separating his new city on the other side of the river, away from the native population. By 1820, there were more than six thousand inhabitants in Singapore.

His duties elsewhere forced Raffles to cede governorship of Singapore to others, but in early 1823 he took control. He quickly regulated land ownership, set up a police force, and put new trade laws in place. He also drafted a constitution that forbade slavery and gambling. Amazingly, the document protected Singapore's multiethnic population, making it illegal to pass any laws based on race—a truly enlightened position for the early nineteenth century. In July 1823, he set sail for England, never to return. He died of a stroke (then called apoplexy) in London three years later.

Although Raffles had never spent more than eight months at a time on the island, he is nevertheless considered the Father of Singapore.

Raffles's legacy is such that his name has been attached to dozens, if not hundreds, of buildings, businesses, clubs, roads, transportation hubs, and even plant and animal species. (The adventurer and statesman was a noted botanist and zoologist.) Of all the landmarks with which Raffles is associated, the Raffles Hotel is arguably the best known internationally. Of course, Raffles himself had nothing to do with it.

Up until the 1880s, the land next to the sea was the most exclusive area for Westerners living in Singapore. Raffles had reserved the oceanfront property for them, and they returned the favor by building a row of fine houses along Beach Road, which followed the coast. As a result, the local Chinese nicknamed the road *ji chap ken,* or "Twenty House Street." During the 1880s, however, most of the residences were sold off, and they were either transformed into or replaced by boardinghouses or restaurants.

One of the better homes, known as Beach House, dated to the early 1830s. It was located prominently at No. 1 Beach Road at the corner of Bras Basah Road. In 1870, an Arab spice merchant named Syed Ahmed Alsagoff purchased the house. Seventeen years later, the Alsagoff family leased it to four Armenian brothers, Martin, Tigran, Aviet, and Arshak Sarkies, to open a hotel. (The brothers had already founded the Eastern and Oriental Hotels in Penang, Malaysia, and wished to expand into Singapore.)

Thus, in 1887, the ten-room was rechristened the Raffles Hotel. In 1899, the house was razed and architect Regent Alfred John Bidwell designed a new, three-story building in a French Renaissance style to replace it. (His firm, Swan and Maclaren, is responsible for several other prominent structures from early-twentieth-century Singapore.)

Over the next twenty years under Tigran's management, three new wings were added to the hotel. Besides expanded guest accommodations, other additions included a veranda, a dining room (the Tiffin Room, named for tiffin, a light midday meal), a ballroom, a bar, and a billiards room. At some point, a short, wide staircase was affixed to the front entrance because seawater sometimes came right up to the door (and occasionally into the lobby) at high tide. (This problem was alleviated when, years later, land was reclaimed from the ocean on the other side of Beach Road, which moved the water's edge farther from the hotel.)

The Raffles Hotel was in its heyday, and stories abound from that period. In 1902, the last indigenous tiger on the island escaped from captivity and, in its flight, wound up in the hotel's Bar & Billiard Room. Mr. C. Phillips, the headmaster of the Raffles Institution (a boys' school next door), ran over and shot the animal with his own rifle, making the species extinct. Sometime between 1910 and 1915, bartender Ngiam Tong Boon created the now-famous cocktail, the Singapore Sling, in the Long Bar.

The hotel went bankrupt in 1931 due to the worldwide effects of the Great Depression. Two years later, investors bought the hotel, and it then operated comfortably until World War II. During the Japanese occupation of Singapore, which began in 1942, the hotel was called *Syonan Ryokan*, or "Light of the South." It was the headquarters for the transport and supply division of the Japanese Imperial Army, and it also housed high-ranking military. Upon the Japanese surrender in 1945, many of the officers stationed there committed ritual suicide in the hotel. Then, for a time, the building was used as a transit stop for liberated prisoners of war. Finally, the hotel resumed normal operations.

The hotel closed for three years in 1989 for a renovation costing more than $100 million. Except for some modern conveniences, the public rooms were restored to the way they looked in 1915 at the height of the hotel's grandeur. The 103-suite Raffles Hotel, known as the Grand Lady of the Far East, reopened to universal approbation on September 16, 1991. Since then, more guest rooms, a shopping arcade, and a museum displaying ephemera from the hotel's past have also been added.

Beatrice Buxton-Smyth had checked in shortly after two in the afternoon. Tea time was fast approaching, and even though she was a bit tired, she felt she had to attend. It was tradition, and that was her way. If something was supposed to be done, it was done. For example, she didn't really care for the taste of tiffin curry, but she would be having some during her stay because the Raffles Hotel was famous for it. She would eat at the buffet in the Palm Court one day, because it was the thing to do. Each night at eight, as the grandfather clock in the lobby struck the hour, the pianist in the Writers Bar would play Nöel Coward's "I'll See You Again." She would be there to raise a toast to the composer's memory.

(Coward was a frequent guest to the hotel. The Writers Bar was named for the many famous authors who visited, from Joseph Conrad and Somerset Maugham to James Michener and Rudyard Kipling.)

Having finished her afternoon obligation, alone as was her wont, Beatrice made her way back to her suite. She had just arrived at her door when a sweet, lilting voice singing a simple melody reached her ears. Normally, her immediate reaction would have been annoyance. How dare anyone disturb her? And singing in the halls? How rude!

But then she recognized the tune . . . and the words. It was an old nursery rhyme she had sung as a girl. Involuntarily Beatrice smiled. She hadn't thought about that song for years.

The sound was coming from right behind her. It must be that youngster she had seen playing in the corridor earlier in the day. The song was so lovely that the child's earlier indiscretion was immediately forgiven. In fact, she wanted to thank the girl for bringing back such a wonderful memory.

She turned, expecting to see that same innocent, joyful face, but as she did, the sound instantly stopped. The hallway was empty. Beatrice looked both ways down the long passage. There had been no time for anyone to duck into one of the rooms, and there was no place that the girl could be hiding. Yet whoever had been singing to her had somehow disappeared.

If Beatrice had shared her experience with her valet, Kai, he could have told her all about the phantom waif. According to legend, the spirit was a little British girl who attended a boarding school that used to stand on the property. She only appears in the rear of the building, never in the lobby or lounges. Usually she's seen traipsing up and down the hallways, but she occasionally tugs on women's skirts by the elevator. Sometimes people are only aware of her presence because they hear her disembodied voice singing nursery rhymes.

Kai had lived in Singapore all his life and knew its history well, so he realized that the facts surrounding the story didn't add up. Most versions of the Raffles legend don't name the girl's old school, so its existence is impossible to confirm. The variations that do mention an academy by name cite the Chinese Girls' School, which was an outgrowth of Singapore's earliest primary school started by Maria Dryer, a British missionary. The trouble is that the CGS was located, first, on North Bridge Road, then on Sophia Road, but never on Beach Road. Besides, the students at that school were native girls and were taught in Malay, so it's unlikely any of their spirits would be singing English folksongs. In addition, it's well documented that the main section of the Raffles Hotel replaced Beach House, not a school.

But, then, the ghost doesn't have to be the phantom of a former student, does she? She could be the spectre of any one of the children who ever visited or lived at Beach House. Or she may be the lingering soul of a one-time guest at the Raffles Hotel.

But if Beatrice had asked Kai, he would have just repeated the old wives' tale that's been passed down through the years. Most of the reports are recent, beginning after the hotel was refurbished back at the end of the 1980s. But some sightings go all the way back to just after World War II. So who's to say when the little girl walked the earth? All anyone knows for certain is that she obviously loves the place too much to leave.

Appendix A
Bookings

Even a cursory visit to a bookstore or library will offer the reader dozens of books that can provide information on the hundreds of haunted hotels found worldwide. These range from general listings, such as *Haunted Places: The National Directory*, to more specialized volumes that deal with a single city, state, or local region. What follows is a representative sampling of the ones I've consulted while writing *Haunted Hotels*.

I've also visited Web sites too numerous to mention, primarily for historical background about a hotel, its builder, or the city where the venue is located. I include here several metasites that contain directories of haunted locations and provide links to other Internet sites dealing with ghosts, the occult, and the unexplained. The official sites of individual hotels mentioned in the stories in *Haunted Hotels* are noted in Appendix B.

BOOKS

Austin-Peters, Tracie. *Welcome to Haunted Las Vegas, Nevada*. Atglen, PA: Schiffer Publishing, 2009. The book's 160 pages explore the paranormal playgrounds located on the Strip and elsewhere in the desert city that claims to be the Entertainment Capital of the World.

Christensen, Jo-Anne. *Haunted Hotels*. Edmonton, AB: Ghost House Books, 2002. Thirty-six hotels and inns are

profiled by region, including America's Northwest and
South, California, Canada, and Great Britain.

Cobb, Todd. *Ghosts of Portland, Oregon.* Atglen, PA: Schiffer
Publishing, 2007. Cobb traces the footsteps of many of
Portland's most famous spectres, including the screaming
girl beneath St. John's Bridge, self-moving furniture
in the White Eagle Bar, and the restless spirits in the
Shanghai Tunnels.

Coulombe, Charles A. *Haunted Places in America.* Guilford,
CT: Globe Pequot Press, 2004. Its fifty chapters include
ghost legends from a variety of venues, from theaters
and college campuses to churches, restaurants, and
private homes. There are also haunted hotels, including
five that appear in this volume: the Golden North Hotel,
the Stanley Hotel, the Menger Hotel, the 1886 Crescent
Hotel and Spa, and Florida's Biltmore Hotel.

Dresbeck, Rachel. *Insider's Guide to Portland, Oregon.* 5th
ed. Guilford, CT: Globe Pequot Press, 2007. Includes
information on Portland's Heathman Hotel.

Dwyer, Jeff. *Ghost Hunter's Guide to Los Angeles.* Gretna,
LA: Pelican Publishing Company, 2007. Dwyer provides
short sketches of about a hundred haunted venues
in Southern California, from Santa Barbara down to
San Diego. They include such sites as the Hollywood
Roosevelt Hotel, the Knickerbocker Hotel, the Oban
Hotel, the Georgian Hotel, the Alexandria Hotel, the
Queen Mary, the Hotel del Coronado, Marilyn Monroe's
crypt in Pierce Brothers Westwood Village Memorial Park,
and Hollywood Forever Cemetery.

Guiley, Rosemary Ellen. *The Encyclopedia of Ghosts and
Spirits.* New York: Facts on File, 1992. This one-volume
encyclopedia is a classic. It collects stories about

phantoms, primarily ones from America and the United Kingdom, along with essays of important figures in ghost folklore as well as paranormal research and Spiritualism.

Hauck, Dennis William. *Haunted Places: The National Directory*. New York: Penguin, 1996.

———. *The International Directory of Haunted Places*. New York: Penguin, 2000. Hauck's national directory, and with its smaller international companion volume, list almost three thousand haunted locations, plus sites where UFOs and mysterious creatures have been sighted around the world. The books are considered essential to any ghost hunter's library.

Hotel del Coronado Heritage Department. *Beautiful Stranger: The Ghost of Kate Morgan and the Hotel del Coronado*. Coronado, CA: Hotel del Coronado Heritage Department, 2002. The book is available only through the Hotel del Coronado's Signature Shop or though its Web site, www.delshop.com.

Jacobson, Laurie, and Marc Wanamaker. *Hollywood Haunted*. Santa Monica, CA: Angel City Press, 1994. The best-known work on Haunted Tinseltown. Chapters include investigations of the Alexandria, Hollywood Roosevelt, and Oban Hotels.

Jonas, Shirley. *Ghosts of the Klondike*. Skagway, AK: Lynn Canal Publishing, 1996. A collection of ghost tales about the colorful characters who populated the Alaskan Panhandle during the days of the Yukon gold rush, including "Mary" at Skagway's Golden North Hotel.

Kermeen, Frances. *Ghostly Encounters: True Stories of America's Haunted Inns and Hotels*. New York: Warner Books, 2002. Kermeen profiles forty haunted hotels and bed-and-breakfasts, including (in great detail) the Myrtles Plantation, which she owned, lived in, and operated as an inn for almost a decade.

_____. *The Myrtles Plantation: The True Story of America's Most Haunted House.* New York: Grand Central Publishing, 2005. This 336-page paperback by a former owner of the Myrtles Plantation details the many ghost legends surrounding the antebellum mansion.

Oberling, Janice. *Haunting of Las Vegas.* Gretna, LA: Pelican Publishing, 2008. A 224-page paperback surveying the haunted hotels, parks, and landmarks of Sin City. This new book supplants her earlier *Las Vegas Haunted* (2004, self-published under the Thunder Mountain Productions Press banner). Oberling is also the author of *Haunted Nevada* (Boca Raton, FL: Universal Publishers, 2001) and maintains the Web site www.hauntednevada.com.

Ogden, Tom. *The Complete Idiot's Guide to Ghosts and Hauntings.* Indianapolis: Alpha Books, 2004. This expanded edition contains first-person accounts of ghost sightings, some published for the first time, in addition to better-known tales from around the globe. Chapters separate the stories by the types of venues the spirits haunt.

_____. *Haunted Cemeteries.* Guilford, CT: Globe Pequot Press, 2010. A collection of twenty-five tales of terror taking place in cemeteries, churchyards, and other burial sites around the world.

_____. *Haunted Highways.* Guilford, CT: Globe Pequot Press, 2008. A collection of campfire-style tales based on popular ghost legends of hauntings that take place on highways, lanes, and trails.

_____. *Haunted Hollywood*. Guilford, CT: Globe Pequot Press, 2009. Twenty-five spooky stories of TV and movie stars, their homes, and many of Tinseltown's most famous landmarks.

_____. *Haunted Theaters*. Guilford, CT: Globe Pequot Press, 2009. Thirty-five spine-tingling tales of ghosts inhabiting playhouses and opera houses in the United States, Canada, and London.

Parvis, Sarah. *Haunted Hotels (Scary Places)*. New York: Bearport Publishing, 2008. This thirty-two-page illustrated hardbound edition introduces young readers to eleven hauntings, each described in about four paragraphs.

Revai, Cheri, and Heather Adel Wiggins. *Haunted New York*. Mechanicsburg, PA: Stackpole Books, 2005. A series of short sketches detail sixty-one haunted sites in New York State.

Schoenberg, Dr. Philip Ernest. *Ghosts of Manhattan*. Charleston, SC: Haunted America, 2009. Schoenberg, who offers walking ghost tours of New York, discusses legendary haunts in the Big Apple, including the Hotel Chelsea.

Smith, Barbara. *Ghost Stories of the Sea*. Edmonton, AB, Canada: Ghost House Books, 2003. This collection of spooky tales includes the story of the *Queen Mary*.

Williams, Docia Schultz. *History and Mystery of the Menger Hotel*. Plano, TX: Republic of Texas Press, 2000. Williams, a city guide and resident of San Antonio, traces the 150-year history of the Menger, profiles its famous guests, and follows its many phantoms. She is also the author of *When Darkness Falls: Tales of San Antonio Ghosts and Hauntings* (1998) and coauthor with Reneta Byrne

of *Spirits of San Antonio and South Texas* (1997), both
published by Republic of Texas Press.

Wlodarski, Robert, Anne Nathan-Wlodarski, and Richard
Senate. *A Guide to the Haunted Queen Mary*. West Hills,
CA: G-Host Publishing, 1995. This small paperback
goes into greater detail than many other tellings of
the hauntings at the ship-turned-hotel located in Long
Beach, California.

ONLINE ARTICLES

Associated Press. "'Haunted' Milwaukee Hotel Spooks
Baseball Teams." FOX News, July 11, 2009. www.foxnews
.com/story/0,2933,531633,00.html.

Kaduk, Kevin. "Fear of Haunted Hotel Has Marlins Bunking
Up in Milwaukee." *Big League Stew* blog on *Yahoo!
Sports*, May 14, 2009. http://sports.yahoo.com/mlb/
blog/big_league_stew/post/Fear-of-haunted-hotel-has-
Marlins-bunking-up-in-?urn=mlb,163523.

WISN 12 News. "Ballplayers Say Pfister Hotel Haunted."
WISN.com, May 27, 2009. www.wisn.com/
news/19586075/detail.html.

VIDEOS AND DVDS

America's Most Haunted Inns. Ardustry Home Entertainment,
producer, and Luminence Films, distributor, 2004. This docu-
mentary by Robert Child profiles several ghost-ridden spots in
Bucks County, Pennsylvania. Owners and managers of the various hotels and bed-and-breakfasts are interviewed on camera,
and psychic Cathe Curtis is seen doing ghost investigations.

Ghosts Among Us. Crystal Home Video, 2007. DVD. In this
180-minute, two-disk DVD set, host Patrick McNee relates

ghostly goings-on across America. In the Hollywood section, he takes a close look at the murder of Elizabeth Short, the so-called Black Dahlia, and the hotel she is said to haunt.

Haunted History: Haunted Hollywood. A&E Television Networks, 2000. VHS. This show originally aired as a one-hour program on the History Channel on August 25, 2000. The tape describes ghosts sighted at the Roosevelt Hotel, the Knickerbocker Hotel, Hollywood Forever Cemetery, and Raleigh Studios in Hollywood as well as the Georgian Hotel in seaside Santa Monica. Expert commentary is provided by author Laurie Jacobson (*Hollywood Haunted*) and paranormal researchers Dr. Barry Taff and Dr. Larry Montz, among others.

Hollywood Ghosts and Gravesites. Delta Entertainment Corporation, 2003. DVD. This sixty-one-minute program surveys hauntings by including Marilyn Monroe, Rudolph Valentino, Harry Houdini, and Bugsy Siegel, amoung others. Also covered are the ghost phenomena on the former transatlantic liner, the *Queen Mary.*

Most Haunted. Castle Leslie episode. An Antix production for LIVINGtv, a Telewest Broadband Company, 2004. A British television series investigates the ghosts of Castle Leslie in the Republic of Ireland. Hostess Yvette Fielding, castle owner Sammy Leslie, historian Richard Felix, Spiritualist medium Derek Acorah, and parapsychologist Ciaran O'Keeffe appear on screen.

The Search for Haunted Hollywood. Tulsa, OK: Video Communications, 1992; originally released by Gold Key Entertainment,

1989. VHS. Ninety-two minutes. First aired as a TV special. John Davidson, host; starring Patrick Macnee. On-screen personalities Norm Crosby, Susan Ollson, and Jack Carter provide first-person ghost encounters. Mentalist Max Maven conducts an on-screen séance. Haunted legends that are investigated include those involving the famous HOLLYWOOD sign and spectral appearances by Marilyn Monroe and Montgomery Clift in the Roosevelt Hotel. Ghost investigators Hans Holzer, Nonie Fagatt, Daniel Hobbit, Richard Senate, and Barry Taff are also interviewed.

WEB SITES

www.bnbfinder.com/haunted.php
This site is designed to help vacationers plan, locate, and reserve appropriate bed-and-breakfasts for their travels. The particular page noted above lists more than two hundred inns that are purportedly haunted. Almost all of them are located in the United States. There is not a large international selection, just one or two in Canada, and another in India.

www.hauntedamericatours.com
This eclectic Web site has become one of my favorites. It's constantly updated with original feature articles on a wide variety of paranormal topics. There are details of upcoming paranormal conventions, a large store, lists of haunted places categorized by types of venues, and some of the best Top Ten collections I've ever seen. Readers are actively invited to contribute stories and photographs. And, as the site's name might suggest, Haunted America can assist you in booking local ghost tours throughout the United States.

www.haunted-places.com
Besides offering state-by-state and international listings, Haunted-Places.com provides information on books, TV, and radio programming devoted to the paranormal and the supernatural. It also offers a subscription to a newsletter, the *Haunted Places Report*.

www.theshadowlands.net
Founded by Dave Juliano in 1994
Dave Juliano and Tina Carlson, codirectors
The Shadowlands lists more than thirteen thousand haunted places located all over the world. There are brief descriptions—usually two to five sentences—of each venue, categorized by the country, state, and city in which the sightings occur. The Web site also offers links to information on UFOs and mysterious creatures such as Bigfoot and the Loch Ness monster.

Appendix B
Room Service

Ghosts can turn up anywhere. Because they usually return to (or never leave) places that had meaning to them when they were alive, it's only natural that a few of them may have become attached to some of the thousands of hotels, inns, and bed-and-breakfasts around the world.

The good news is that most of the hotels listed here are open for business and are happy to have you as overnight guests. But please note, they *are* businesses. Inquiring minds may want to know, but hotels are generally not comfortable having strangers casually meander throughout their premises. The merely curious certainly are not allowed to wander in their residential hallways. If you stick to the open public areas, a quick peek inside a hotel may pass unchallenged or unnoticed. If you want to spend any significant time in the building, however, take a room for the night or patronize one of their restaurants, bars, or gift shops.

Some places, such as the Menger Hotel in San Antonio, Texas, are quite proud of their spooks; a few tout them on their Web sites. Other inns are not so open; a few are downright evasive. Please respect the hotel's point of view. If your question about its resident spirit(s) is met with denial or hostility, it's best not to press the issue.

Some of the hotels you'll find here, such as the Knickerbocker, have been repurposed and no longer solicit or allow short-term guests. Please do not bother the owners or trespass on their properties. This appendix also lists a few homes and private venues whose exteriors can be viewed from the street. Other sites, like the Westwood cemetery where Marilyn Monroe is buried, have posted visiting hours.

Of special interest to amateur ghost hunters: Ghost tours are available in many of the cities where these hotels are located. I have tried to provide contact information for some of them in this appendix. Contents of the tours and operating hours are subject to change. Please check details or make reservations in advance.

Please note that the telephone numbers for Ireland, the United Kingdom, and Singapore are listed as they would be dialed from within the United States, although the international access code (011) has been omitted. Prefixes (such as country, area, and city codes) may vary or be unnecessary when phoning from outside the United States. Check locally for the correct format before dialing.

Neither the author nor the publisher is affiliated with any of the hotels, homes, businesses, landmarks, or services in *Haunted Hotels*. Their appearance in this listing should not be construed as an endorsement, recommendation, or advertisement for the companies.

CHAPTER 1: THE BRIDE WHO WAS NOT TO BE

Golden North Hotel

Third Street and Broadway
Skagway, AK 99840
(907) 983-2451

The Golden North Hotel closed to overnight guests in 2002. The ground floor now houses shops for tourists. When the hotel was open, its second story had sixteen rooms: Rooms 9, 13, and 14 were the ones most often mentioned as being haunted in local legend. The room in which Mary supposedly died, number 24, was also haunted. It was along the back side of the hotel and was one of fifteen guest rooms on the third floor.

Eagles Hall

Sixth Street and Broadway
Skagway, AK 99840
(907) 983-2234
The building is an active clubhouse for the Fraternal Order of Eagles, Aerie #25. Tourists are welcome during daytime visiting hours.

Red Onion Saloon

205 Broadway
Skagway, AK 99840
(907) 983-2414
(907) 983-2222 (bar)

Alaskan Hotel & Bar

167 S. Franklin St.
Juneau, AK 99801
(907) 586-1000 or (800) 327-9347
www.thealaskanhotel.com
The Alaskan Hotel is Juneau's oldest continuously operating hotel. In 1978, it was placed on the National Register of Historic Places.

CHAPTER 2: THE HEATHMAN HAUNTINGS

Heathman Hotel

1001 SW Broadway at Salmon Street
Portland, OR 97205
(503) 241-4100 or (800) 551-0011
www.heathmanportland.com

There are three ghost tours in Portland that might be of interest to visitors interested in the paranormal:

Portland Walking Tours

701 SW Sixth Svenue
Portland, OR 97204
(503) 774-4522
www.portlandwalkingtours.com
Tours operate March to November on Friday and Saturday nights. Advance ticket purchases are required. The walking tour lasts slightly less than two hours and covers a route that's less than a mile with no hills and limited stairs. Participants learn how to use a working electromagnetic field meter during the ghost hunt and are encouraged to bring their own cameras to capture apparitions and light orbs.

Portland Underground Tours

(also known as Shanghai Tunnel Tours)
(503) 622-4798
www.shanghaitunnels.info
The Portland Underground, also known as the Shanghai Tunnels, was a series of basements that were connected to each other through short, arched passageways. It was not their original purpose, but these linked subterranean thoroughfares allowed criminals to abduct (i.e., shanghai) unwilling individuals who would be pressed into service as sailors or prostitutes. The hour-and-a-half tours underneath Old Town are conducted by the Cascade Geographic Society. Most of the guided visits to the Underground are historical in nature, concentrating on the ethnic heritage of early Portland, but ghost tours (some in conjunction with the Trails End Paranormal Society) are offered on Friday and Saturday evenings as well as on the first Thursday of the month.

CHAPTER 3: THE MARILYN MIRROR

Hollywood Roosevelt Hotel
7000 Hollywood Boulevard
Hollywood, CA 90028
(323) 466-7000 or (800) 833-3333
www.hollywoodroosevelt.com
Now owned and operated by Thompson Hotels. For many years the Marilyn Monroe mirror was located in the rear of the building by the elevators on the lower level near the valet entrance to the hotel. Around 2000, it was moved near a gift shop on the mezzanine above the lobby. The mirror is currently in storage while the store undergoes renovation, and there is no word as to when, or if, it will be put back on public display. The other haunted areas of the hotel are open to guests and for special events only.

The former Marilyn Monroe residence
12305 Fifth Helena Drive
Brentwood, CA 90049

Pierce Brothers Westwood Village Memorial Park
1218 Glendon Avenue
Westwood, CA 90024
(310) 474-1579

Knickerbocker Hotel
(now the Hollywood Knickerbocker Apartments)
1714 Ivar Avenue
Hollywood, CA 90028
(323) 463-0096

Now a private housing complex for seniors. In the 1990s, when the building still operated as a hotel, Valentino's ghost was seen in the lobby nightclub, and Monroe's spirit turned up in the ladies' room adjacent to the bar.

Falcon Lair
1436 Bella Drive
Beverly Hills, CA 90210

The Falcon Lair stables
10051 Cielo Drive
Beverly Hills, CA 90210

Valentino's beach house
224 Cahuenga Street
Oxnard, CA 93030
Falcon Lair and the Oxnard beach house are now private residences.

Santa Maria Inn
801 S. Broadway
Santa Maria, CA 93454
(805) 928-7777
Valentino's presence is most often felt or heard in his favorite room at the hotel, Suite 210.

Hollywood Forever Cemetery
6000 Santa Monica Boulevard
Hollywood, CA 90028
(323) 469-1181
www.hollywoodforever.com

Valentino's presence is felt and his shadow is occasionally seen by his crypt, which is located in the Cathedral Mausoleum.

The former Oban Hotel
(now the Hotel Hollywood)
6364 Yucca Street
Hollywood, CA 90028
(323) 466-0524
www.thehotelhollywood.com

The Georgian Hotel
1415 Ocean Avenue
Santa Monica, CA 90401
(310) 395-9945 or (800) 538-8147
www.georgianhotel.com

Haunted Hollywood Tours
(818) 415-8269
www.hauntedhollywoodtours.com
Operated by Brian Sapir. The motorized tour, often conducted in a vintage automobile, lasts between ninety minutes and two hours. The itinerary passes by many haunted Tinseltown landmarks, famous murder sites, and houses that have been seen in classic horror films.

Tours depart around 7:30 p.m. nightly from the front of the Kodak Theatre, the site of the annual Academy Awards. The Kodak is located at 6801 Hollywood Boulevard, between Grauman's Chinese Theatre and the shopping complex Hollywood & Highland.

Private tours are available by special request.

CHAPTER 4: THE RIDDLE OF THE BLACK DAHLIA

Millennium Biltmore Hotel
506 S. Grand Avenue
Los Angeles, CA 90071
(213) 624-1011
www.millenniumhotels.com

The Alexandria
501 S. Spring Street
Los Angeles, CA 90013
(213) 626-7484
www.thealexandria.net

Esotouric
(323) 223-2767
www.esotouric.com
Esotouric, which visits Los Angeles locations associated with true crime, began its excursions in 2007. Among its various bus adventures into the provocative "secret heart" of the City of Angels is the Real Black Dahlia Tour. Sites visited on the four-hour coach tour include the Biltmore Hotel (where the expedition begins), the bus station, and the lot where Elizabeth Short's bisected body was discovered.

CHAPTER 5: THE GRAY GHOST

The Queen Mary
1126 Queen's Highway
Long Beach, CA 90802
(562) 435-3511 or (800) 437-2934
www.queenmary.com

Tourist attractions at the *Queen Mary*, separate from the hotel facilities, run from 10:00 a.m. to 6:00 p.m. daily. The box office closes at 5:00 p.m.

General admission includes an audio-visual show, intended to be theatrical in nature, entitled *Ghosts & Legends of the Queen Mary*. Most of the presentation takes place at the forward end of the ship, but the first-class inside swimming pool and engine room are also visited.

The Haunted Encounters Passport package includes the *Ghosts & Legends* show, but it also allows guests to see several actively haunted sites onboard, including the engine room, as part of a guided walk. Many of the locations are not otherwise accessible. Visitors receive a special orientation, view a *Haunted Encounters* film, take part in a ghost-sighting scavenger hunt, and take away a souvenir paranormal passport.

The ship also offers two-hour evening ghost tours. On Thursday, Friday, and Sunday, beginning at 8:00 p.m., guests can set out on a Paranormal Shipwalk Tour. A hands-on ghost hunt on the lower decks, usually led by Beyond Investigations founder Pat Wheelock, is available Friday at midnight.

CHAPTER 6: THE PHANTOM IN THE DEL

Hotel del Coronado
1500 Orange Avenue
Coronado, CA 92118
(619) 435-6611 or (800) 468-3533 (800-HOTEL-DEL)
www.hoteldel.com

The Hotel del Coronado is on Coronado Island, just a few minutes from downtown San Diego. The island is linked to the mainland by a 2.1-mile bridge from 1969 that towers two hundred feet over San Diego Bay.

The haunted rooms at the Del are all within the hotel's original section, now called the Victorian Building. Those who wish to stay in Room 3327 must specifically request it.

The shop known as Established in 1888 (or Est. 1888 for short) used to be located in the hotel's lower lobby shopping area. The store has recently been moved upstairs so that it now adjoins the main lobby. Reports vary as to whether it's still haunted. The activity stopped downstairs after the "Marilyn" items were moved to a less visible location.

Old Town San Diego Ghost Tours
(619) 972-3900
www.oldtownsmosthaunted.com

Ghostly Tours in History
(877) 220-4844
www.ghostlytoursinhistory.com

CHAPTER 7: THE MARINA MANIFESTATION

MGM Grand Hotel and Casino
3799 Las Vegas Boulevard S.
Las Vegas, NV 89109
(877) 880-0880
www.mgmgrand.com

The MGM Grand sits on property that once held the Tropicana Country Club and the Marina Hotel, which was located at 3805 Las Vegas Boulevard South. Only the guest room tower from the Marina still stands. It was completely renovated and incorporated into the MGM structure as its West Wing.

To see photographs of the Marina Hotel and how the residence tower was worked into the design on the MGM Grand, visit www.vegastodayandtomorrow.com/marina.htm.

Bally's Las Vegas Hotel and Casino
3645 Las Vegas Boulevard S.
Las Vegas, NV 89109
(800) 634-3434
www.ballyslasvegas.com
Bally's was the original MGM Grand Hotel. Built by Kirk Kerkorian in 1973 on the southeast corner of Las Vegas Boulevard and Flamingo Road, it was the site of the 1980 fire tragedy that killed eighty-five people. Bally's Corporation bought and renamed the property in 1986. The original residential tower, where most of the deaths occurred, remains in use.

The Flamingo Hotel and Casino
3555 Las Vegas Boulevard S.
Las Vegas, NV 89109
(702) 733-3111
www.flamingolasvegas.com
Two ghosts have materialized in the Presidential Suite and the rose garden. Many believe them to be the spirits of Bugsy Siegel and his lover Virginia Hill, even though the current Flamingo is not the same hotel built by the flamboyant mobster.

Las Vegas Hilton
3000 Paradise Road
Las Vegas, NV 89109
(702) 732-5111
www.lvhilton.com

Liberace Foundation & Museum
1775 E. Tropicana Avenue
Las Vegas, NV 89119
(702) 798-5595
www.liberace.org

Carluccio's Tivoli Gardens Restaurant
1775 E. Tropicana Avenue
Las Vegas, NV 89119
(702) 795-3236
www.carlucciosvegas.com

Haunted Vegas Tours
(702) 339-8744
www.hauntedvegastours.com
Operated by Robert Allen. This motorized tour visits many of Sin City's most spook-filled locations, including short stops for optional walks through the oasis area of the Tropicana Hotel and Green Valley Park in nearby Henderson. The tour runs daily at 9:30 p.m., except for the month of January. Restricted to age thirteen and older; those under eighteen must be accompanied by an adult. Ticket price includes entrance to the *Las Vegas Séance* show. Total time for the coach tour and séance is approximately three hours.

CHAPTER 8: THE BEN LOMOND BANSHEES

Ben Lomond Suites
2510 Washington Boulevard
Ogden, UT 84401
(801) 627-1900 or (877) 627-1900
www.benlomondsuites.com

Ogden Ghost Tour

www.storytours.com

Story Tours operates two different one-and-a-half- to two-hour tours of haunted venues in Ogden, Utah, year-round: the Ogden Ghost Tour and the Hysterical History Tour. A bus tour is also available during the month of October.

CHAPTER 9: "HERE'S JOHNNY . . ."

Stanley Hotel

333 E. Wonder View Avenue

Estes Park, CO 80517

(970) 586-3371 or (800) 976-1377 (reservations)

www.stanleyhotel.com

Owned by the Grand Heritage Hotel Group. The Stanley Hotel operates its own nightly Historic Ghost Tour, open to guests and the public alike. No children under five years of age. Reservations are recommended at least a week or two in advance. Ghost Haunts, led by resident paranormal expert Callea Sherrill, is a separate, five-hour, hands-on paranormal investigation in the concert hall erected on the Stanley property about two years after the main hotel building was completed. The ghost hunts take place in the auditorium, said to be home to two or three spirits, from 8:30 p.m. to 1:30 a.m. For more information, schedules, or reservations, contact Callea Sherrill at (907) 577-4110.

CHAPTER 10: SHADES OF THE OLD WEST

St. James Hotel

617 S. Collinson Ave.

Cimarron, NM 87714

(575) 376-2664

Collinson Avenue is NM 21. The hotel is located in the Cimarron Historical District, about a mile south of US 64 (the Kit Carson Highway).

New owners took over the St. James Hotel in 2009. Murder Mystery Weekends do continue, but only a few per year. Plan well ahead if you wish to attend the event or if you want to reserve a particular room at any time of the year. Room 18 is closed to guests.

CHAPTER 11: THE MENGER MYSTERIES

Menger Hotel
204 Alamo Plaza
San Antonio, TX 78205
(210) 223-4361
www.mengerhotel.com
The hotel is located directly across Crockett Road from the Alamo.

The Alamo
300 Alamo Plaza
San Antonio, TX 78205
(210) 225-1391
www.thealamo.org
The Alamo is owned and operated by the Daughters of the Republic of Texas (DRT). It is open Monday through Saturday 9:00 a.m. to 5:30 p.m. and Sunday 10:00 a.m. to 5:30 p.m. In June, July, and August it is open until 7:00 p.m. on Friday and Saturday. Closed Christmas Eve and Christmas Day. Admission is free.

Alamo City Ghost Tours
212 Losoya Street, Suite 8
San Antonio, TX 78205
(210) 336-7831
www.alamocityghosttours.com
In business since 1996, Alamo City Ghost Tours offers both daytime and nighttime tours of haunted sites in the River City. Some are motorized; others are walking tours.

Alamo Ghost Hunt
Hauntings History of San Antonio Ghost Hunt
(210) 348-6640
www.bestsanantonioghosttours.com
Founded by ghost hunter Martin Leal of Alamo City Paranormal in 1997. Walking tour departs every night at 8:30 p.m. from the Cenotaph in Alamo Plaza.

CHAPTER 12: THE BELLE OF NEW ORLEANS

Is there a hotel, inn, or bed-and-breakfast in the New Orleans French Quarter that isn't haunted? Here's the contact information for the eleven that are profiled in this chapter:

Le Pavillon Hotel
833 Poydras Street
New Orleans, LA 70112
(504) 581-3111 or (800) 535-9095
www.lepavillon.com

Dauphine Orleans Hotel
415 Dauphine Street
New Orleans, LA 70131
(504) 586-1800 or (800) 521-7111
www.dauphineorleans.com

Chateau Bourbon Hotel
(formerly the Chateau Sonesta Hotel)
800 Iberville Street
New Orleans, LA 70112
(504) 586-0800
www.wyndhamchateaubourbon.com

Hotel Monteleone
214 Royal Street
New Orleans, LA 70140
(504) 523-3341
www.hotelmonteleone.com

Omni Royal Orleans Hotel
621 St. Louis Street
New Orleans, LA 70140
(504) 529-5333
www.omnihotels.com

Hotel Maison de Ville
727 Toulouse Street
New Orleans, LA 70130
(504) 561-5858
www.hotelmaisondeville.com

Place D'Armes Hotel
625 St. Ann Street
New Orleans, LA 70116
(504) 524-4531 or (800) 366-2743
www.placedarmes.com

Andrew Jackson Hotel
919 Royal Street
New Orleans, LA 70116
(504) 561-5881 or (800) 654-0224
www.frenchquarterinns.com

Lafitte Guest House
1003 Bourbon Street
New Orleans, LA 70116
(504) 581-2678
www.lafitteguesthouse.com

Hotel Provincial
1024 Chartres Street
New Orleans, LA 70116
(504) 581-4995 or (800) 535-7922
www.hotelprovincial.com

The tale about the country-music-loving soldier who haunts the Provincial is particularly interesting because there's a similar legend attached to Cottage 4 at the Hotel Maison de Ville. Is it possible that, sometime in the past, storytellers got the two venues mixed up and the mistake has been perpetuated ever since? Stranger things have happened.

The specific radio station that the soldier enjoys also raises some questions. At the time of this writing, WTIX-FM 94.3 plays oldies rather than country-and-western music, but perhaps the old wives' tale that identifies the station is a holdover from a time when WTIX had a different format and playlist.

Le Richelieu Hotel
1234 Chartres Street
New Orleans, LA 70116
(504) 529-2492 or (800) 535-9653
www.lerichelieuhotel.com
While you're out and about calling on the haunted Crescent City hotels, you might want to peek in on the tomb of Marie Laveau, the Voodoo Queen. After passing through the Basin Street entrance to the cemetery where she's buried, you can find the mausoleum that's generally accepted as being hers about twenty-five to fifty feet to your left.

St. Louis Cemetery No. 1
400 Basin Street
New Orleans, LA 70116
(504) 596-3050 (administrative office)

The former Marie Laveau House
1020 St. Ann Street
New Orleans, LA 70116
The home is a private residence and cannot be visited by the public.

It's almost impossible to visit the French Quarter without running into advertisements for the many companies that offer ghost tours. There are both daytime and evening walking expeditions. Even if the tours don't visit specific haunted hotels, fans of the paranormal might still find them fun. Here are eleven tour operators to choose from:

Haunted History Tours
723 St. Peter Street
New Orleans, LA 70016
(504) 861-2727, (504) 628-1722, or (888) 6-GHOSTS
www.hauntedhistorytours.com
www.neworleansghosttour.com
Haunted History Tours offers a New Orleans Ghost Tour, a Garden District Ghost Tour, a New Orleans Cemetery Tour, a New Orleans Voodoo Tour, and a New Orleans Vampire Tour. Walks begin at different times throughout the day and night, setting out from various locations.

French Quarter Phantoms
625 St. Philip Street
New Orleans, LA 70116
(504) 666-8300 or (888) 90-GHOST
www.frenchquarterphantoms.com
The ghost tour's box office is located inside Flanagan's Pub, between Royal and Charles Streets. Walks depart at 8:00 p.m. nightly.

New Orleans Spirit Tours
621 Royal Street
New Orleans, LA 70130
(504) 314-0806 or (866) 369-1224
www.neworleanstours.net
Cemetery, voodoo, ghost, and vampire tours are available.

Bloody Mary's New Orleans Tour
144 S. Hennessey Street
New Orleans, LA 70119
(504) 915-7774
www.bloodymarystours.com

Historic New Orleans Walking Tours, Inc.

P.O. Box 19381

New Orleans, LA 70179

(504) 947-2120

www.tourneworleans.com

Nine different New Orleans–based excursions are offered, including a ghost and a cemetery tour. They also have motorized excursions to bayous, plantations, and hurricane-struck areas of the Big Easy.

New Orleans Tours

#1 Poydras

New Orleans, LA 70130 (ticket booth)

(504) 529-4567 or (800) 445-4109

www.bigeasytours.com

Two different ghost walks are available (one in the French Quarter, one in the Garden District), as well as a vampire tour, a voodoo tour, and a separate voodoo/cemetery tour. The office is located in the Riverwalk Marketplace in Spanish Plaza.

Big Easy Tours

4220 Howard Avenue

New Orleans, LA 70125

(504) 592-0560 or (800) 301-3184

www.bigeasytours.us

Big Easy offers sixteen walking and motorized expeditions. The two tours for aficionados of the supernatural are the New Orleans Cemetery & Gris-Gris Tour and the Ghost & Spirit Tour.

Le Monde Creole
1000 Bourbon Street, Suite 332
New Orleans, LA 70016 (mailing address)
(504) 568-1801
www.mondecreole.com
A unique two-hour tour of Creole New Orleans as the town would have been experienced by the Laura Locoul family. The walk also visits the tomb of Marie Laveau, the Voodoo Queen, in St. Louis Cemetery No. 1. Tours depart from 624 Royal Street. Reservations required.

Gray Line of New Orleans, Inc.
400 N. Peters Street, Suite 203
New Orleans, LA 70130
(504) 569-1401 or (800) 535-7786
www.graylineneworleans.com
This well-established company operates two haunted expeditions among its many New Orleans tour packages. One is a daytime cemetery visit, and the other is an evening ghost tour. Both are guided walking tours.

CHAPTER 13: PUZZLE AT THE PLANTATION

The Myrtles Plantation
7747 US Highway 61
P.O. Box 1100
St. Francisville, LA 70775
(225) 635-6277 or (800) 809-0565
www.myrtlesplantation.com
John and Teeta Moss, proprietors. St. Francisville is about thirty miles north of Baton Rogue. The mansion, which is on the National Register of Historic Places, operates as

a bed-and-breakfast. Overnight guests under the age of twenty-one must be accompanied by a responsible person aged twenty-one or older. The Carriage House Restaurant on the property serves lunch and dinner Monday and Wednesday through Saturday as well as Sunday brunch.

There are daily historic tours on the hour and half hour from 9:00 a.m. to 5:00 p.m. Also, evening "mystery tours" are conducted on Friday and Saturday nights.

CHAPTER 14: TAKING THE CURE

1886 Crescent Hotel & Spa
75 Prospect Avenue
Eureka Springs, AR 72632
(479) 253-9766 or (877) 342-9766
www.crescent-hotel.com
The five-story hotel (with additional penthouses) sits on fifteen acres in the Ozark Mountains. There are seventy-two rooms and suites in the original main building, plus thirty-eight new two-bedroom cottages on the grounds. The 1886 Crescent Hotel & Spa is listed as a Historic Hotel of America by the National Trust for Historic Preservation.

Crescent Hotel Ghost Tours
P.O. Box 189
Eureka Springs, AR 72632
(479) 253-6800
www.eureka-springs-ghost.com
Offered every night beginning at 8:00 p.m. by Ken Fugate and Carroll Heath. Tours last approximately one and a half to two hours. The tour office is located in Room 212 in the 1886 Crescent Hotel. Children under sixteen must be accompanied by an adult. No guest rooms are entered on the tour.

CHAPTER 15: THE WHISTLER

Blackhawk Hotel

200 E. Third St.

Davenport, IA 52801

The Blackhawk Hotel was severely damaged by fire in February 2006 after a purported meth lab exploded in one of the rooms on the eighth floor. After three years of finalizing arrangements, repairs were begun in January 2009. (The official ribbon-cutting ceremony took place the following April.) The $33 million renovation will restore the property to its original early-twentieth-century charm and, in the process, transform it into a boutique hotel with more than a hundred rooms, a few upscale apartments, and a refurbished ballroom. The restoration is set to be complete by December 2010.

CHAPTER 16: PFISTER RETURNS

The Pfister Hotel

424 E. Wisconsin Avenue

Milwaukee, WI 53202

(414) 273-8222 or (800) 558-8222

www.thepfisterhotel.com

The Pfister, now operated by the Marcus Corporation, acknowledges the many claims that it's haunted by the ghost of its founder, Charles Pfister. In fact, a three-minute clip from a tongue-in-cheek investigation of the hotel by NBC's *Today* program in 2009 has been embedded on its Web site.

Milwaukee Ghosts
(414) 807-7862
www.milwaukeeghosts.com
Founded by Allison Jornlin. The hour-and-a-half-long guided walking tour of the city's Third Ward (once known as the Bloody Third) leaves from the front of the Milwaukee Market at Water Street and St. Paul Avenue on most Friday and Saturday nights at 7:00 p.m. from May through November. Additional tours arranged by appointment. Points along the tour include Commission Row, the RiverWalk, and the Broadway Theatre. The Pfister Hotel is not visited—it's about a half mile from the Third Ward—but its hauntings are discussed on the tour.

CHAPTER 17: APPARITIONS IN THE ADIRONDACKS

The Sagamore
110 Sagamore Road
Bolton Landing, NY 12814
(518) 644-9400 or (800) 358-3585
www.thesagamore.com
The Sagamore closes for the season from late November through the end of April.

CHAPTER 18: THE BOHEMIAN SPIRIT

Hotel Chelsea
222 W. Twenty-third Street
New York, NY 10011
(212) 243-3700
www.hotelchelsea.com
The hotel is located in lower Manhattan between Seventh and Eighth Avenues.

Ghosts of New York
P.O. Box 656780
Flushing, NY 11365
(718) 591-4741 or (888) 377-4455
www.ghostsofny.com
Ghosts of New York, founded by Dr. Phil Schoenberg, offers five different ninety-minute walking tours in Manhattan, each of which covers about a mile. Though none pass by the Hotel Chelsea, the walks visit a wide variety of other haunted sites.

CHAPTER 19: ENTITIES AT THE INN

The Inn at Jim Thorpe
24 Broadway
Jim Thorpe, PA 18229
(570) 325-2599 or (800) 329-2599
www.innjt.com

The Emporium of Curious Goods
15 Broadway
Jim Thorpe, PA 18229
(570) 325-4038
Barrett Ravenhurst and Rick Brong, proprietors. The Emporium is open daily 11:00 a.m. to 5:00 p.m. Closed on major holidays.

The Old Jail Museum
128 W. Broadway
Jim Thorpe, PA 18229
(570) 325-5259
www.theoldjailmuseum.com
The ghostly handprint of Molly Maguire inmate Alexander

Campbell is found in Cell 17. Guided tours of the jail are available daily from noon until 4:30 p.m., Memorial Day through Labor Day, and weekends only in September and October. Special ghost tours are conducted in October.

GhostWalks in Old Mauch Chunk
(570) 325-2346
www.jimthorperotary.org/ghostwalks.cfm
This one-hour guided walk departs from the lobby of the Inn at Jim Thorpe and points out various buildings and sites said to be haunted in downtown Jim Thorpe (formerly known as Mauch Chunk). The tours, sponsored by the Rotary Club, are seasonal, usually taking place on Friday and Saturday evenings from September through mid-December. Reservations are suggested. Not recommended for children under seven years old.

CHAPTER 20: THE FELLOW ON THE THIRTEENTH FLOOR

Biltmore Hotel
1200 Anastasia Avenue
Coral Gables, FL 33134
(305) 913-1926 or (800) 727-1926
www.biltmorehotel.com
Three tours of the Biltmore, led by docents and lasting approximately fifty-five minutes, are available for the public on Sunday afternoon between 1:30 and 3:30 p.m.

CHAPTER 21: THE WEDDING WRAITH

Fairmont Banff Springs Hotel
405 Spray Ave.
Banff, Alberta T1L 1J4
Canada
(403) 762-2211 or (866) 540-4406
www.fairmont.com/banffsprings

Calgary Ghost Tours
(403) 472-1989
www.calgaryghosttours.com
Calgary Ghost Tours operates five different walking itineraries. Its Banff tour departs Wednesday and Friday evenings at 8:00 p.m. from the Visitor Information Center (the Parks Canada Building) in central Banff.

The Fairmont Hotel Vancouver
900 W. Georgia Street
Vancouver, British Columbia V6C 2W6
Canada
(604) 684-3131 or (866) 540-4452
www.fairmont.com/hotelvancouver

The Fairmont Royal York
100 Front Street W.
Toronto, Ontario M5J 1E3
Canada
(416) 368-2511 or (866) 540-4489
www.fairmont.com/royalyork

Muddy York Walking Tours

(416) 487-9017

www.muddyyorktours.com

Founded by Richard Fiennes-Clinton, who is also the principal tour guide. The company offers more than a dozen different itineraries, including the two-hour Haunted Streets of Downtown Toronto. Check their Web site for the current schedule.

Genova Tours

230 Rose Park Drive

Toronto, Ontario M4T 1R5

Canada

(416) 367-0380

www.genovatours.com

The two-and-a-half-hour ghost tour is conducted by storyteller Bill Genova and departs at 7:00 p.m. from the Royal Ontario Museum (ROM) at Bloor Street and Avenue Road.

Toronto After Dark Ghost Tour

(also known as Tour Guys)

(647) 230-7891

www.tourguys.ca

Founded by Jason Kucherawy (whose contact telephone number for reservations appears above) and Steve Woodall. The three-hour walking tour departs from outside the Hockey Hall of Fame at the corner of Yonge and Front Streets.

CHAPTER 22: THE LEGEND OF CASTLE LESLIE

Castle Leslie
Glaslough
County Monaghan
Republic of Ireland
(353)(0) 4788100
www.castleleslie.com

Brede Place
East Sussex
England
United Kingdom
The village of Brede is located in southern England about eight miles north of Hastings and four miles west of Rye. Brede Place is a private residence. It has occasionally been open to visitors in the past, but no current tour information is available.

CHAPTER 23: THE HELLFIRE HORROR

The George and Dragon
High Street
West Wycombe
Buckinghamshire HP14 3AB
England
United Kingdom
(44) 01494 464414
High Street, which passes through the center of West Wycombe, is the A40.

Hell-Fire Caves
West Wycombe Caves Ltd.
Church Lane
West Wycombe
Buckinghamshire HP14 3AH
England
United Kingdom
(44) 01494 533739
www.hellfirecaves.co.uk
It is approximately a third of a mile from the George and Dragon to the Hell-Fire Caves. The caves are open daily 11:00 a.m. to 4:30 p.m. from April through October and 11:00 a.m. to dusk from November to March. The last admission is thirty minutes before closing. In addition to regular operating hours, occasional guided ghost tours of the attraction are conducted by the local Ghostfinder Paranormal Society.

There are several other sites in West Wycombe associated with Sir Francis Dashwood. The Church of St. Lawrence, renovated by Dashwood, stands on a high hill overlooking the town on the grounds of a former Iron Age fortification. The church, open most Sundays in the summer months, is topped by a large, hollow golden ball that is large enough to seat several people inside.

The Dashwood Mausoleum is a hexagonal-shaped open-air monument located near the church. The Dashwood estate, now owned by the National Trust, lies within the five thousand acres of West Wycombe Park. The grounds are open year-round, Sunday through Thursday from 2:00 to 6:00 p.m. Tours of the house are available during the same hours from June through August.

CHAPTER 24: THE UNINVITED GUEST IN ROOM 333

The Langham
1c Portland Place
Regent Street
London W1B 1JA
England
United Kingdom
(40) (20) 7973 7626
www.london.langhamhotels.co.uk

London Walks
P.O. Box 1708
London, NW6 4LW
United Kingdom
(44) (20) 76249255 or (44) (20) 7624WALKS (information)
www.walks.com
London Walks offers four different guided ghost walks: Haunted London; Ghosts of the Old City; Ghosts, Gaslights & Guinness; and Apparitions, Alleyways & Ale. None passes the Langham, but they may be of great interest to ghost fans nevertheless.

CHAPTER 25: THE SINGAPORE SPECTRE

Raffles Hotel
1 Beach Road
Singapore 189673
Singapore
(65) 6337-1886 or (800) 768-0990 (from the United States and Canada only)
www.raffles.com

About the Author

Tom Ogden is one of America's most celebrated magicians. He has performed professionally since 1973, from the tinsel and sawdust of the circus ring to the glitter and sequins of Las Vegas, Atlantic City, and Lake Tahoe. He has opened for such acts as Robin Williams, Billy Crystal, and the Osmonds.

Ogden's television work has included appearances on NBC's *The World's Greatest Magic II* and FOX's *The Great Magic of Las Vegas,* as well as numerous commercials. He has twice been voted Parlour Magician of the Year at the world-famous Magic Castle in Hollywood and has received more than a dozen additional nominations in other categories.

Ogden's books include *200 Years of the American Circus* (which was named a Best Reference Work by both the American Library Association and the New York Public Library), *Wizards and Sorcerers,* three books in The Complete Idiot's Guide to . . . series (*Magic Tricks, Ghosts and Hauntings,* and *Street Magic*), as well as four titles in the Globe Pequot Haunted series (*Highways, Hollywood, Theaters,* and *Cemeteries*). Ogden has also been profiled in *Writer's Market.*

Ogden resides in Hollywood, California.